SPELLS
OF
BLOOD&
SORROW
BOOK FOUR

Spells of Blood and Sorrow
Tarot Academy, Book Four
Copyright © 2020 by Sarah Piper
SarahPiperBooks.com

Published by Two Gnomes Media

Cover design by Faera Lane

v5

E-book ISBN: 978-1-948455-49-7
Paperback ISBN: 978-1-948455-17-6
Audiobook ISBN: 978-1-494548-92-6

BOOK SERIES BY SARAH PIPER

Reverse Harem Romance Series

Claimed by Gargoyles

The Witch's Monsters

Tarot Academy

The Witch's Rebels

M/F Romance Series

Vampire Royals of New York

GET CONNECTED!

I love connecting with readers! There are a few different ways you can keep in touch:

Email: sarah@sarahpiperbooks.com

TikTok: @sarahpiperbooks

Facebook group: Sarah Piper's Sassy Witches

Twitter: @sarahpiperbooks

Newsletter: Never miss a new release or a sale! Sign up for the VIP Readers Club:
sarahpiperbooks.com/readers-club

ONE

CASS

Death has been hunting me for decades.

I know intimately the all-encompassing weight of its shadow, the icy scrape of its talons against my spine.

How many nights have I awoken in a cold sweat, certain it lingered at the foot of my bed, waiting for me to take that final breath? How many times have I gazed into its dark, empty eyes at the bottom of a bottle?

How many times have I secretly wished for its promise of peace? Of nothingness?

More than I can recount. Yet for all the nightmares and close-calls, *this*—this might be the thing that finally kills me.

"Tell me he's going to be all right, Doc," Stevie says. It's not a request, but a command, as if by sheer will alone she can save his life.

I remain silent. Ashamed. Petrified.

We move swiftly through the coal-black night. I can't

even look at Stevie; her fear is so palpable, I can practically feel it crawling on my skin.

Ani is as pale as a wraith, his body hanging limp in my arms. Blood leaks from his nose and mouth, drying in a sticky black smear down the side of his face.

I don't even know if he's still breathing. I don't dare stop to check.

It wasn't supposed to be like this. Not for Ani. Not for any of them.

Once again, Death is close on my heels, its fetid breath brushing the back of my neck. The ground is falling out from beneath my feet, and all I can do is keep running, hoping to stay at least one step ahead—for all our sakes.

"In here. Let's go." I push through the entrance to Time Out of Mind, heading right for the old grandfather clock at the back of the store. Behind it lies the off-grid portal that will ferry us to the safe house in Red Sands Canyon. All my hopes are on Professor Broome—that Kate can find some antidote, some magick brew to bring him back to us.

Kirin and Carly stayed behind to pack up some necessities from Stevie's suite and try to locate Baz, still missing since he took off from Harvest Eve dinner. Now, crammed into the dark space of the portal, it's down to three of us. All I care about—all I've got room to even think about—is getting them to safety. Protecting Stevie. Bringing Ani back to us, whole and undamaged.

I meant what I said to Anna Trello. If I have to leave with them—turn our backs on this Academy and this magickal fight, drive off into some dusty desert hideaway where nothing can ever touch them—I won't hesitate.

But I can't do that if he's not breathing.

"Ready?" Stevie asks, and I nod, tightening my hold on Ani as the magick cloaks us in its gossamer threads.

Through the haze of her worry and grief, Stevie manages to find the Six of Swords card for the portal spell. She holds it between us, ducking my gaze as swiftly as I'm ducking hers, and together we recite the spell.

We travel together through time and space
In my mind's eye, I hold the next place
Steer us safe and guide us true
The Six of Swords will see us through

Spell complete, Stevie wraps a shaky hand around my arm.

"Almost there," I whisper, pulling Ani close. Goddess, if I could carve my own beating heart out of my chest and give it to him, I'd do it. "Just hold on, Ani. Hold on."

One more breath, then the magick takes hold.

The portal deposits us unceremoniously in the coat closet just inside the home's front door. We bang our way through it, crashing into the house like a tempest.

"Professors!" I call out. "We need help!"

"Oh, thank *goddess*." Kate Broome rushes toward us, her forehead creased with worry. Her face pales as she takes in the sight of the broken body in my arms. "Kirin called— we've been expecting you. What happened?"

"Potion overdose," I say. "We think he's trapped in the dream realm."

She reaches for Ani's wrist and checks his pulse. A faint curse emanates from her lips, the lines in her forehead deepening. "Come on—let's get him into the back bedroom. We're all set up."

We follow her to the small guest room at the back of the house. The decorative bedding has been stripped, leaving only a set of stark white sheets tucked tightly around the mattress. A long, low table is set up beside the bed, scattered with magickal tools, herbs, crystals, and potions.

I lay Ani on the bed, the faint smell of bleach wafting up from the sheets. It reminds me of a hospital bed. The barriers in my memory rattle, an army of old ghosts threatening to break through.

Fuck every last one of you…

"Let me take a closer look, Cass." With a kind but firm touch, Kate nudges me aside, leaning down to examine Ani. She presses a hand to his forehead, then lifts his eyelids, checking his eyes. "What did he ingest, exactly?"

"Dream potion." Stevie hands over the remains of the broken vial we found clutched in his hand. "Silversword root, witch's cauldron, and moonstone elixir. Spelled for Dark Arcana communications."

Kate sniffs the vial, her eyes widening. "Did he take *all* of this?"

Our silence is confirmation.

"How long has he been using it?" she asks, right as

Kelly Maddox enters the room with a tray full of clean, wet towels.

"At least one other time that I know of." Stevie steps aside to let Kelly pass. "I didn't realize it then, but I'm pretty sure he used it Sunday night. We ended up in the dream realm together—it all happened really fast. I pulled him out, and he was kind of pissed about it. He kept talking about finding the Wand..." Her voice breaks, and she closes her eyes and shakes her head. "He must've taken the rest tonight."

"Good thinking to keep the broken glass," Kate says. "We may be able to use it for a banishing spell to counteract the potion in his bloodstream. Was he conscious when you found him?"

"Not exactly." Stevie opens her eyes, our gazes meeting for the briefest instant before she lowers hers again. Shame colors her cheeks as she describes the scene in her bedroom —Ani slumped in the chair. The black blood. Eyes half-open. Trembling. The vial. Her screams...

"I should've known something was wrong," she whispers, a tear sliding down her cheek. "He wanted to talk to me. I put him off so I could meet Carly. It's my fault."

My heart recoils at her words. If anyone is to blame for this tragedy, it's me. Everything in me wants to tell her as much, to go to her, to comfort her. But my feet are rooted to the floor, my muscles ignoring my every command.

Don't touch her, an old voice echoes inside, cruel and bright, precise in its mockery. *You are* poison, *Cassius Devane...*

"It's not the time for blame," Kelly says, gently cleaning the blood from Ani's face. "The best thing you can do for Ani right now is send him warm, healing energy. Love. Light."

While Kelly works to wash away the grime, Kate starts on his clothing, cutting through his T-shirt with a pair of shears.

"What in goddess's name..." Kate runs a hand down Ani's pale chest. "Was he in a fight before this happened? An accident?"

"Not that I'm aware of." I step closer to see what's got her so worried, and my stomach churns. Ani's flesh is covered in wounds—dark bruises, slashes, burns. I'm about to ask Stevie if she knows what happened when a blaze of orange sears his right palm, splitting the skin. The gaping wound glows like a hot coal, then fades, the skin turning black.

"No!" Stevie drops to her knees beside the bed, grabbing Ani's left hand, still unmarred. "Fight him, Ani. Please fight."

She presses her mouth to his palm, whispering against his skin, begging him to resist the invisible enemy.

I know the monster's identity at once.

"Judgment." I curl my fingers against my palm, wishing I could break something. "He must've found Ani in the dream realm, and now he's tormenting him, just as he tormented the others."

"None of us had such vicious wounds," Stevie says, looking across the scarred planes of Ani's chest. "I don't

6

know what's happening. Why is he tormenting Ani like this? Why isn't Ani fighting?"

The professors exchange a horrified glance, then they spring into action, new urgency lighting a fire under their feet.

"We need hematite, black tourmaline, and obsidian to ground him," Kate says, rummaging through the selection on the bedside table. She finds what she's looking for, then places a series of black and silver crystals in a line down Ani's sternum. At the foot of the bed, Kelly places three Tarot cards between Ani's feet—the Empress, Judgment, and Queen of Cups.

"We may be able to use the creation energy of the Empress and the compassionate, healing energy of the Queen to counteract the destruction of Judgment reversed," she explains. "Our first priority is preventing further injury. Once his physical body is stabilized, we can try to call his soul back."

Crystals and cards in place, Kelly begins a soft chant, and Kate lights a bowl of dried herbs, walking it around the room until the smoke touches all four corners.

"For years, I've used this blend to eliminate nightmares and encourage peaceful sleep," she says. "Combined with Kelly's Tarot spell and the grounding crystals, my hope is that it'll break Judgment's hold long enough for Ani to heal and find his way back to us."

Bedroom sufficiently smoked, Kate sets the bowl back on the table and touches Stevie's shoulder, gently urging her back to her feet.

Stevie looks like a zombie, her eyes glazed, her body sagging with the effort of standing up.

"Stevie, I need you to make some tea," Kate says softly. "Can you do that for me?"

Stevie blinks at her as if "tea" is a foreign language.

"Come on, sweetness. Let's go." Kate guides her toward the kitchen. "I know you're worried, but Ani needs us to focus right now. Go make your special tea—something he likes. I'm sure he'll be wanting a nice, hot cup when he wakes up."

At this, Stevie finally shows signs of life.

"Sex with a Caramel," she says resolutely, wiping away the last of her tears. "That's his favorite. Is the pantry well-stocked?"

"A tea maven's dream," Kate says.

Stevie offers a weak smile, but it's a smile nevertheless, one that leaves the tiniest spark of hope in its wake as she heads into the kitchen.

The moment Stevie's out of earshot, Kate looks at me and shakes her head, her eyes full of doubt.

"It's not like before," she tells me. "Kirin, Stevie, and Baz—they delved into the dream realm together. Ani's all alone out there, and he's under the influence of a potion designed to bind him to the very darkness that's now torturing him to within an inch of his life."

As if to underscore the point, a fresh bruise blackens Ani's cheek, blood trickling from his nose.

A tremor of anger rolls through me. "Make another

dream potion. Send me in there right now, and I'll hunt down that monster myself."

And if you think Ani looks bad, wait until you see what I've got in store for Judgment...

"You know I can't do that," she says. "You could end up in the same situation, and where would that leave Stevie and the others?"

"So there's no hope. That's what you're telling me."

"In my book, as long as there's magick, there's always hope." Kate rolls up her sleeves and reaches for a bottle from the bedside table, purple-blue liquid pulsating inside the opalescent glass. "I'm just saying it's going to take a while, and Kelly and I need to be left to our work. You've done all you can for him now. Let us take it from here."

She shakes the bottle, turning the liquid a deep red, then hands it over. "It's ready."

"What's this?" I ask, swirling it before the light. It looks like blood shot through with golden threads.

"Think of it as a time-release sedative."

"You won't send me to the realm, but you're trying to tranquilize me?"

"It's for Janelle and Casey. They'll be coming out of the binding spell soon, and when they do, we'll need to guide them back to consciousness slowly, through a careful meditation. If they come back too quickly, it could further damage their psyches and leave them even more susceptible to future possession. Phaines severed the connection, but I'm not convinced he's done with them."

"Phaines is dead." Saying the words out loud makes me realize for the first time how quickly this night unraveled, how much has imploded in the last couple of hours. Phaines's murder by Anna Trello, the discovery of the siphoned magick stolen from students on campus, Baz's vanishing act, Ani...

It's almost too much to bear.

Kate's eyebrows shoot up, but before I can tell her anything else about the murder, the headboard rattles against the wall and Kelly unleashes a string of curses.

"He's fighting the spell!" she cries. "Kate, we need to do the injection. Now."

"Injection?" I ask. Alarm shoots through my limbs, but Kate is already shoving me out the door.

"Go," she orders. "Keep Stevie out." She shuts and bolts the door, leaving me alone in the dark hallway with a bottle of potion and a hole in my chest the size of Arizona.

I press my palm to the door and close my eyes. On the other side, chaos erupts, the women shouting orders at each other, Ani thrashing against his dark tormentor, the world falling down.

It's been a long time since I've felt so desperately helpless.

"Just bring him back to us," I whisper. "Whatever it takes."

TWO

CASS

I find Stevie in the kitchen, furiously grating cinnamon sticks while the kettle bubbles on the stove. The kitchen counter is a riot of herbs and flowers, powders and teas, sweeteners, some of them in bottles, most of them spilled.

The kitchen is a disaster, but Stevie stands strong.

Her back is to me, and I lean against the wall and take a moment to admire her—her grace, her strength, her determination, all of it shining through loud and clear, even in the face of this nightmare.

Still, I don't miss the flinch of her shoulders every time one of the professors shouts another command.

Hold him down...

Goddess, he's fighting me every step...

Give him the full dosage. Do it now...

I'm falling apart inside, yet still, Stevie focuses on the task at hand. Silently, gracefully, she reaches for another bundle of cinnamon sticks.

The whole kitchen smells of it. Of a home I've dreamed of my entire life. And for the span of ten seconds, I close my eyes and inhale the sweet scent that mingles with her own, allowing myself the small comfort of a temporary fantasy.

I tell myself that Ani is alive, lighting up the room with his infectious smile.

That my brothers are here too—Kirin in the study with his nose in a book, Baz working on some project in the backyard.

That I've been tasked with nothing more arduous than selecting the best wine for tonight's meal.

That Stevie is making us another one of her infamous brews.

That all of us are happy and whole.

That we're a family in the truest sense—chosen. Bonded. Loved.

That this is our home.

I open my eyes. Take in the sight of her, that wild hair spiraling down her back, her shoulders set as she dumps the grated cinnamon into a pot and selects the next batch of herbs for a tea Ani will never drink.

Emotion tightens my throat.

She is our beacon. Our light. And I know that if I asked her to, she would come to me now. Come with me anywhere.

The pull I feel toward her is impossibly strong, a force I won't be able to ignore much longer. But when I try to imagine opening my heart to her, the fear rushes in, blocking out all else.

Back in the guest bedroom, something crashes to the floor, and Stevie jumps, tossing the entire pot into the sink with a clatter.

"The cinnamon is all wrong," she says. "I need True Ceylon, Doc. How can they expect me to make Sex with a Caramel without True Ceylon?"

She turns to face me, her blue eyes burning with rage.

Of course she knows I'm here. She's known it from the moment I stepped into the kitchen. She always does.

"I… I'm sorry," I say, hating myself for it. So insubstantial, so pointless.

Stevie folds her arms over her chest and shakes her head, once again lowering her gaze. Avoiding mine. Wishing, perhaps, for Kirin or Baz instead.

"Most people think it's the same thing," she says. "But it isn't. The medicinal properties of True Ceylon are far superior. The flavor profile is much more subtle, yet it's—" Her voice breaks, and her shoulders begin to tremble.

I want to run to her. To take her into my arms and promise her that soon the sun will rise, the brightest sun that's ever graced this painted desert, chasing away the horrid night.

But how can I make that promise when I'm not sure the sun will ever rise for us again?

"Stevie," I whisper, but I still can't move. Lead, guilt… My heart and feet are weighted with both. My arms ache to hold her, but all I can do is reach across the space between us and mutter another inane phrase. "Please don't cry."

She doesn't. She looks at me looking at her, looks at my

pathetic attempt at comfort, and then my sweet, beautiful, fiery Star fists her hair and lets out a scream so raw, so full of anguish it shatters what's left of my heart.

The sound of it breaks through the weights holding me in place, and I take a step toward her, still reaching, still aching to touch her.

But she's already turning back to the sink, retrieving her discarded pot of herbs. Carefully, silently, she places it on the stove and reaches for another cinnamon stick.

Forcing myself through the discomfort, I touch her shoulder.

She flinches away. "Don't."

"I'm sorry," I say again, still hating myself for it.

"It's fine," she says, shaking her head. "I'll make it work. It's just cinnamon, right? It's not like he'll know the difference."

My hand hovers behind her head, the faintest brush of her wild hair tickling my palm.

But Stevie has returned to her task.

As I must return to mine.

She drags the stick across the grater, the rich spice hitting my nose again.

But the fantasy of home and contentment has shattered.

I turn away from her and head toward the basement.

"Stay out of the bedroom," I call over my shoulder. "They don't want us interrupting their magick."

Stevie says nothing.

Gripping Kate's potion, I step onto the basement

landing and pull the door shut behind me, welcoming the cold, dark embrace. Grateful for it.

Here, in the absence of light, no one can see the tears.

THREE

CASS

By memory more than sight, I make my way down the stairs and across the cold chamber to the cots where we've kept our guests. The only light comes from the moon shining through the small, high windows around the perimeter, most of which are covered from the outside with tumbleweeds. It takes a long moment for my eyes to adjust, to pick out the shapes from the shadows.

Janelle lies on her side, facing away from me, her breathing deep and even. She's either asleep or unconscious —or possibly full of shit, just waiting for an opportunity to pounce.

But the cot adjacent to hers is empty, the sheets kicked to the ground.

I make my way around the room, but other than the cots, chairs, and tables we set up this week, there's little else here. No place to hide.

Casey is gone.

I press my hand to the mattress—still indented with the shape of her body, still slightly warm. She must've snuck away while we were all in the bedroom with Ani. Apparently, she came through the post-possession effects of the binding spell on her own, no sedative or guided meditation needed.

On her pillow, I find a hastily scrawled note, barely legible in the darkness.

"Fuck."

"Baz?" Janelle says, her voice weak and watery as she rolls over and peers up at me, attempting to identify me through heavily lidded eyes. "Is that you, sweetness?"

My stomach churns at the saccharine dripping from her voice. I can only imagine why she's calling for Baz at a time like this.

I shove Casey's note into my pocket.

"Guess again," I whisper, looking for a reason to make her suffer. A reason to make *anyone* suffer for what's happening to Ani. To Stevie. To all of us.

Janelle played a part in this. She's *still* playing a part, throwing her cards in with the Dark Arcana who'd just as soon snuff us out. And while my esteemed colleagues upstairs might have a hard limit against torturing this parasite, I've got no such scruples.

And the kind, compassionate professors who might've stopped me from pushing this too far are nowhere in sight.

Nowhere in screaming distance.

They're too busy trying to bring our beautiful, ginger-haired brother back from the brink of insanity.

Deep in my chest, a new feeling unfurls. Dark. Hungry. Filling up the empty spaces inside me like a slow, creeping fog.

You know what to do, Cassius, the old voice echoes. *Just like before.*

I glance at Kate's sedative potion in my hand, but no, this red-gold brew isn't going to do the trick tonight. I set it on the worktable and glance over the tools and ingredients still on display from our first few nights here.

Kate may be the Academy's unparalleled expert at crafting healing potions.

But me? I'm quite adept at the other kind.

And sometimes, the other kind is the best remedy. The true remedy.

The cost.

"How are we feeling tonight, Janelle?" I ask, unbuttoning my cuffs and rolling up my sleeves. My voice is so cold and detached, I hardly recognize it.

"Better now that you're here." She tries to sit up on the cot, but the last vestiges of the binding spell hang heavy, and she falls right back again. "So... tired."

"Yes, I can imagine. I understand you've had quite an adventure with Professor Phaines."

"I did it for you, Baz," she says, not an ounce of regret in her watery voice. "So we could be together."

Bile rises in my throat. What kind of sick, twisted things are playing out in her mind?

No matter. It's only going to get worse for her tonight.

I turn back to the worktable and make my selections,

carefully measuring ingredients into an empty glass bottle. It's been decades since I made this particular potion, but I'll never forget the recipe: a precise blend of Demon's Blood resin, Witch's Cauldron, Black Moonstone elixir, Essence of Poppy, rattlesnake venom, and Fairy's Breath. That last ingredient is the same magickal powder that allowed Phaines to take possession of her mind and body in the first place, but it's not Phaines seeking to control her thoughts tonight. It's someone much more determined, much more skilled in the fine art of mental manipulation, and much more dangerous to someone like Janelle Kirkpatrick.

Ingredients in place, I stopper the bottle and give it a gentle shake, drawing on the deceptive energy of the reversed Moon card as I recite my spell.

Black rider, void of light
I call upon the Mare of Night
Unleash the darkness in her mind
For evil sown is reaped in kind

Outside, dark clouds float across the moon, bathing us in all-encompassing darkness. The bottle warms in my hand.

"What... what are you doing?" Janelle mumbles.

"I've made something for you." I hold the bottle up before my eyes, barely visible in the shadows.

Nightmare's Lullaby. A vicious, hallucinogenic potion that's as black as Death itself, yet sheer as mist, swirling inside the bottle as it senses the call of my magick.

I turn back to Janelle and lean in close, so close I can smell her sour breath.

"Oh, Baz..." She tries to lift her hand to my face, but she's too weak. Her eyes are half-closed, her mouth slack. "I knew you'd come for me."

"I'm coming for you, all right." I uncork the bottle with my teeth, then grab her jaw in a cruel grip, digging my fingers into her flesh and forcing her mouth open. "Bottoms up, you psychotic bitch."

Her eyes go wide, but she has no strength, no fight. Nightmare's Lullaby knows *exactly* where the evil lurks, and it finds its path instantly, filling her mouth and seeping into her lungs, into her bloodstream, into her thoughts.

I watch as the whites of her eyes turn black.

I watch as the poison takes hold inside her mind.

I watch as her body trembles, then goes rigid with abject fear.

And then I close my eyes, call on the power of the dark moon, and conjure up a personal hell so bleak, so vile, it will haunt the rest of her days.

FOUR

STEVIE

Professors -

Sorry for sneaking out, but I have urgent business on campus and knew you wouldn't let me leave on my own.

ALL OF YOU ARE IN GRAVE DANGER.

I'll be back as soon as I can, but in the meantime, keep everyone inside the house until further notice. I'll set a cloaking spell on my way out, but you may want to add something stronger. You need all the protection you can get right now.

Do NOT contact anyone at APOA or the Academy.

Do NOT leave the property.

Do NOT let anyone else enter the house aside from your closest allies, Agent Quintana, or myself.

Do NOT let Janelle out of your sight. Re-bind her if necessary, and keep her under lock and key.

I'll return as soon as I can and will explain everything at that time. For now, I'm asking for your trust—it might just save your lives.

- Casey

I re-read the note, then hand it back to Doc, grateful for something to focus on besides the gulf opening up between us.

We're sitting at the table in the massive tile-and-steel kitchen, my faux Sex with a Caramel brew long since abandoned on the stove.

Down in the basement, Janelle screams again—a terror drawn from the darkest depths of her psyche, reverberating beneath our feet. Doc assures me this is all to be expected; that coming out of a ritual binding is a slow and painful process. That her screams will eventually stop.

I don't care. Not after what she did to us.

Besides, I'll take *her* screams over Ani's any day of the week.

His, at least, have subsided. But Professors Maddox and Broome are still hard at work in the bedroom, the door bolted tight.

"Way to be evasive," I say about the note. "Do you trust her?"

Doc, who hasn't looked me in the eye for more than ten seconds since this whole nightmare began, shrugs. "I don't believe she was in league with Phaines. But I also don't believe she's been entirely forthcoming about APOA's involvement with Anna Trello or the Academy, either."

"So what do we do?"

"I suppose we wait. Besides, I agree with her on one key

point—no one should leave this house. Not until we know where Trello is."

"Kirin and Baz are still on campus," I say. "Carly too. I haven't been able to reach any of them. And what about Nat and Isla? I don't like the idea of them being stuck out there with our psycho headmistress on the loose."

"I've already texted Nat and Isla. They've been staying at Isla's place together lately, but I convinced them to pack up and join us here."

"You texted them? Really?"

"They'll be heading through Kelly's portal first thing in the morning."

"Thank you," I whisper, swallowing past the tightness in my throat. Tears of gratitude threaten to spill, and I force myself to meet his eyes. After avoiding each other most of the night, looking into those dark gray depths feels like coming home.

This time, Doc doesn't look away either.

He smiles at me across the table, though his energy is sad and heavy, weighted with all the things he hasn't been able to say.

Not since we found Ani.

I want to tell him it's not his fault, but how can I? He'd only parrot the same words back to me. Neither of us would believe them.

So instead I just sit here, totally transfixed, caught in the storm brewing in his beautiful eyes, the briny scent of the sea carrying me off to some other time, some other place.

"I don't know how to make this right," he whispers, his

stormy eyes darkening. It feels like a confession—some old, secret shame surfacing from the depths of his memories.

"It's not your job to make it right," I say, but he's already shaking his head. Already breaking the connection. Already retreating back inside himself, shoring up his old walls, locking me outside.

But then, just before I've fully lost him, he curses under his breath, then rises and comes to my side of the table, kneeling before me and grabbing my hands in a fierce grip. His energy surges, barreling into me with a ferocity that nearly steals my breath.

Courage and fear in equal measure. Loyalty. Love. Determination. And a deep, all-encompassing regret, the origins of which I can only guess at.

"I can't lose him, Stevie," he says. "I can't lose any of you. It would destroy me. The thought of waking up to a world in which you don't exist... A world in which *any* of you are no longer part of my life... I couldn't bear it."

He looks up and meets my gaze again, his grip tightening, crushing my fingers.

"You won't," I say, not because I'm foolish enough to make such promises, not because I have my mother's gift of prophecy to back it up. I say it because right now, I just need him to believe it. To stay with me. To keep the faith that somehow, this is all going to turn out okay.

Because that's the only way *I'll* believe it.

"Stevie, there's... I need to tell you something." Doc's grip finally loosens, but he doesn't release my hands. Not even when his shoulders sag. Not even when his energy grows so dark, so intense, it threatens to drown us both. "About before I came to the Academy. About someone I—"

But before he can make his next confession, the bedroom door creaks open down the hall, and the house itself seems to let out a great sigh of relief.

Doc and I both take in a sharp breath, rising together and turning toward the hallway.

From its dark depths, exhausted and covered in something that looks a lot like blood, Professor Maddox finally emerges.

"I've got good news, bad news, and worse news," she says. "Which would you like to hear first?"

FIVE

STEVIE

"Ani's physical condition is stable," Professor Maddox says, heading to the sink to wash her hands, which I now realize aren't covered in Ani's blood, but her own Dragon's Blood resin.

I blow out a breath and fall back into my chair, my entire body going boneless with relief. Doc stands behind me, hands firm on my shoulders like he's trying to keep me from floating away.

"His body seems to be healing," she continues, "and there haven't been any new injuries in the last hour. We've neutralized the remaining dream potion in his system with a counteracting spell that should also weaken his connection to Judgment. *That's* the good news. As for the bad..."

She shuts off the water and dries her hands, then takes a seat across from me, casting a grim look our way.

I can't help but remember a similar situation five years ago—me sitting at a kitchen table, wrung out and numb,

2222.

Jessa a pillar of strength behind me as a kind but serious social worker tried to tell me how my parents died.

Do you understand what I'm saying, Miss Milan? Are you okay? Can I get you some water or...

"Ani took an extremely high dosage of the dream potion in a short period of time," Professor Maddox says, bringing me back to the present. "The human body wasn't made to process that kind of magick so quickly—there are bound to be side effects."

"What kind of side effects?" I ask.

"We won't know the extent of the damage until he regains consciousness, but I would anticipate muscle weakness and a lack of coordination, difficulty concentrating, migraines, possibly hallucinations. He'll likely have difficulty sleeping, or the opposite extreme—narcolepsy. It could be weeks or even months before he's back to himself on that front."

A shudder rolls through my body, and Doc's hands tighten on my shoulders.

"You said that was the bad news," he says. "What's the worse?"

Professor Maddox stares down into her lap and lets out a long sigh. It's like a cold wind, and my skin prickles with goosebumps.

"Ani's soul is still in the dream realm," she says softly. "His return is something we can't force—not with spells or magick, not with grounding stones, not with a shock to the system. Interfering with his soul's journey could have disastrous consequences."

I know all too well the consequences she's talking about. Baz is still dealing with them, and comparatively speaking, he wasn't in the dream realm all that long.

He wasn't on his own out there, either. Not for most of it.

Professor Maddox glances up at us again, her eyes rimmed in red. "Ani went to the realm intentionally, by himself, despite knowing the dangers you all faced on your own journey there. Whatever his reasons, he was so desperate to get there, he overdosed on your potion."

Guilt knifes through my insides, so tangible and real I have to hold my midsection to keep from doubling over.

"Make me another potion," I say. "Send me back there. I know my way around that hellscape better than anyone. I can find Ani and bring him home. I know I can."

Doc crouches down before me again, his grief and anguish palpable. "We don't know where he is, Stevie. We don't even know if he'd recognize us in his current state. He might just see us as the enemy."

"We have to try."

He tucks a lock of hair behind my ear, then cups my chin, his touch as gentle as his voice. "You nearly died on your last visit. We won't be taking that chance again."

"But we *will*. We already decided to go back for the Chalice of Blood and Sorrow. Ani's way more important than that."

"Without question," Doc says. "But given the turn of events... Ani's present state... No, I'm not comfortable with *anyone* going back there now. We'll have to find another way—for Ani *and* for the Chalice."

"Cass is right," Professor Maddox says. "Stevie, I know how much Ani means to you. But trust me when I say this —he needs to find his own way back from this darkness."

I rise from the chair and head to the kitchen counter, busying myself by cleaning up the mess of herbs and spices I left there. My hands shake, my whole body wound tight with the effort of holding back another scream.

It's Ani. *Ani*! Our gingersnap. Our sunshine. The man who lights up the room as much as he lights up my heart. How can we just leave him out there with those monsters?

"So what the hell are we supposed to do?" I snap. "Just stay here and play house together while the world burns down around us? Hope that if we cast enough spells and pray to the right goddesses, he'll eventually just... wake up?"

Professor Maddox joins me at the counter, reaching for the bundle of dried lavender in my hands, saving it from getting pulverized. When I meet her eyes, she smiles, her compassionate energy washing over me in a soothing wave.

Again I'm reminded of one of the verses she shared with me about the four queens of the Tarot, another of Mom's cryptic prophecies. This one is about Queen of Cups, which also happens to be Professor Maddox's affinity:

> *The Queen of Water extends a gift*
> *Love and compassion to mend the rift*
> *Keep watch by your mind, but open your heart*

For that is when her friendship starts

Now more than ever, I'm certain my mother meant this verse about the professor. They were best friends, and perhaps Mom meant for me to share in that friendship too, all these years later.

Whatever kindness she's sending me, it's working. I return her smile and reach for a bottle of star anise, gently replacing it in the cupboard as some of my anxiety finally dissipates.

"We're not powerless here, Stevie," she says. "When I say Ani needs to find his own way back, that doesn't mean the rest of us should do nothing. Quite the contrary. We'll take care of him. We'll feed and bathe him. We'll encourage him with love and support—not just through spells and prayers, but by reminding him of everything and everyone waiting for him back home. But in the end, Ani's soul will return by the strength of his own will and determination, or..." She trails off and squeezes my hand, her eyes shining with emotion.

She doesn't say the rest of her sentence out loud. She doesn't have to.

Ani's soul will return by the strength of his own will and determination...

Or it won't return at all.

"Can I see him?" I ask.

"Professor Broome is staying with him tonight—she wants to make sure he doesn't have an adverse reaction to the spells. But tomorrow, yes. Go to him. Tell him how

33

much he means to you. Talk to him. Tell him stories, share memories, let him hear your laughter. The stronger the connection we can create for him here, the more likely he'll be able to anchor into that feeling and use it to guide his spirit home when he's ready."

When, she said. Not *if*. A small sliver of hope, perhaps unintentional on her part, but I'll take it.

I'm about to ask if anyone would like some tea when a commotion at the front of the house draws our attention. Seconds later, three women stumble out of the closet, hauling enough luggage for a month-long vacation overseas.

"Goddess, you two are even more annoying than Stevie. Remind me never to portal with you again." Carly flicks her raven-black hair and waltzes into the foyer, Nat and Isla following behind. "We brought all your stuff, Twink. You can thank me later."

Relief floods my chest, but it's not about my stuff. Without warning or precedent, I run into the foyer and launch myself into the arms of frenemy number one.

"Goddess, I was so worried about you." I crush her in a hug, inhaling the scent of her overpriced hair products as she squirms against my hold.

"Whoa! Pump the brakes, girl. I did *not* consent to this level of personal space invasion." She finally breaks free, but her energy says it all—she needed that hug as much as I did.

"Are you okay?" I ask, looking her over. The last time I saw her—*really* saw her—we were back at Jumpin' Jack's

Java after our gruesome discovery at the library, waiting for Doc and Kirin to meet us. I barely remember the trip to my suite, and after that, there's only Ani.

"You mean, aside from the fact that we witnessed a murder and Ani's trapped in some kind of dream realm battling Dark Arcana forces and my mother is an evil minion who pimped herself out to a dark mage and now she's chained up in the basement and I had to pack up your entire ridiculous wardrobe and all your tea shit and basically everything is *terrible*?" She shoots me her usual eye-roll. "I'm awesome. Truly stellar."

"I take it Kirin filled you in."

"That he did." She walks past me, taking in the sight of the huge, open-plan house as if she's deciding whether to move in permanently. "He's still out looking for Baz, but he asked me to round up the Wonder Twins here and head back to Red Sands. How's Ani, anyway?"

"He's... stable," I say, leaving it at that for now, despite the sincerity in her energy. "Carly, I'm really sorry about your mother. I wanted to tell you earlier, but everything happened so fast..."

Carly waves a hand. "It's fine. I probably wouldn't have believed you anyway. You *do* have a tendency toward the dramatic."

Ignoring the dig, I say, "Do you want to see her? She's—"

"That's *really* not a good idea," Doc says, shooting me a warning glare.

Shit. I forgot about Janelle's "transition" out of the bind-

35

ing. She stopped screaming a while ago, but who knows how long that little respite will last? Doc says she's still in and out of consciousness, and chances are he's going to have to bind her again anyway—assuming we can trust Casey's dire warnings.

Ugh, *Casey*. We haven't even had time to tell the other professors about her disappearing act yet, let alone the ominous note.

"Maybe Doc's right," I say, but Carly's already shaking her head.

"Let her rot for all I care." She blinks back tears, dark clouds sweeping through her energy. "What the hell was she thinking? How long has she been working with him? Goddess, what did she even want out of the deal? I mean, of *course* she wouldn't come to the Academy without an agenda—*that's* obvious. I just never thought her vileness ran so deep. But... you know. Whatever."

Carly tries to shrug it off, but her energy doesn't lie. Deep down, some part of her hoped her mother took the Academy job in order to be closer to her. To protect her, as a mother should, from whatever evil had befallen us.

Unfortunately, Janelle is incapable of being a mother. Carly and Baz are both a testament to that. Not only did she fail to protect her daughter from the evil—she perpetuated it. She's *still* perpetuating it.

"We believe she was after the Arcana artifacts, at the very least," Doc says. "Do you know anything about that?"

"Sure, Mom and every other magickal Lara Croft wannabe. She's been babbling about those legends my whole life. That's how she knew Baz's parents—they were all after the same prize. And look where it got them. Look where it got *us*."

"We don't know the extent of her plans," Doc says, though I can feel the doubt in his voice. He may be trying to soften the blow for Carly, but I won't forget the flashes of triumph that sparked through his energy every time the woman in the basement screamed. "Perhaps she was just taking advantage of an opportunity."

"Or she was trying to strip a bunch of innocents of their magick and murder a few more in the process." Carly shrugs. "Either way, she picked her side the moment she buddied up with the sick asshole who tortured Stevie. As far as I'm concerned, she deserves to suffer, and I've got nothing more to say about that."

I look up just in time to catch Nat and Isla's wide-eyed expressions across the room.

Did Carly just stick up for me?

"What about Blue and Emory?" I ask, shifting gears before my brain explodes. "Have you been in touch with them tonight?"

"No," Carly says. "I don't think they're in immediate danger. They weren't really on Trello's radar. None of us were—not since Phaines lost interest in our psychic abilities and pulled his disappearing act."

"If that changes," Doc says, "we'll bring them here. But for now, I think it's best we keep the group as small as possible. To borrow a phrase from our *former* headmistress, we don't want to cause mass panic. Right now, the fewer people who know about any of this—Phaines, Trello's involvement, what happened with Casey and Janelle, the Dark Arcana, Ani's situation—the better."

All of us agree to that.

And, since no world-ending, crisis-management session is complete without a plethora of snacks, alcohol, caffeine, or some combination thereof, the whole group shuffles back into the kitchen like cattle.

We've just finished setting out bowls of tortilla chips, salsa, sour cream, and melted cheese when Doc clears his throat, his energy shifting back into dark mode.

"Carly, Stevie," he says, and I brace myself for what I know is coming next. "Now that Ani's stable, I was hoping you could tell us more about what you witnessed tonight in the library."

Carly and I exchange a glance, my stomach bubbling as images from Phaines's chamber of horrors flash through my mind.

I give her hand a quick squeeze, then let out a sigh. "Guess I'd better put the kettle back on."

SIX

STEVIE

It's not every night we discover a secret lair and unmask an evil minion posing as headmistress, so to commemorate the occasion, I invent a new brew—Mocha Minty Mwah-Ha-Ha. It's a rich, deceptively dark blend of spearmint and peppermint leaves, dark chocolate, melted butter, espresso beans, and a dash of amethyst elixir to boost our intuition, all topped with a dollop of whipped cream that's perfect for frothing up your villain 'stache.

Isla's my taste-tester, and her first sip unleashes a near-orgasmic moan. "Girl, *what*? If I could drink this every day, I'd never need to have sex again."

"Careful what you wish for," Nat teases, already reaching for a mug of her own.

I hand one over, trying not to get a big head about it, but my tea game is on *fire* lately. If I keep banging out custom blends of this caliber—during a rapidly approaching apocalypse, no less—I'll be famous in no time.

Assuming the world doesn't implode first.

Satisfied with the new blend, I prepare a frothy, steaming mug for everyone while Doc shares the news about our disappearing APOA agent. We all agree that lying low in Red Sands is a good idea—at least until we've got a better handle on what Casey's up to, where Trello might be hiding, and Ani's prognosis.

Oh, Ani...

Worry tightens my chest, but I breathe through it. With Professor Broome camped out at his bedside tonight, I know he's in good hands. Tomorrow will be here soon enough; I'll finally get to hold him in my arms, to run my fingers through his hair, to tell him how much he means to me.

Yes, tomorrow will definitely be better. And for now, that's as far into the future as I'm willing to go.

"Do you think Casey knows about Phaines's death?" Professor Maddox asks.

"It's possible," I say, gathering up the rest of the full mugs and distributing them around the table. "She would've felt it the moment his hold broke, so she might've drawn the conclusion about his death. It's also possible she got in touch with her APOA team as soon as she came out of the binding, and they told her what was going on."

"But she said we shouldn't contact APOA," Doc says. "Or anyone at the Academy, for that matter."

"Yeah, I don't get that part." I take a seat between Isla and Carly, directly across from Doc. "She also said Agent

Quintana was allowed in the house here, so obviously not *all* the APOA guys are off-limits."

"Eastman's not on the guest list, though." Carly picks up Casey's note for another look. "And he's their boss."

"Actually, I wonder if *anyone* from APOA knows about Phaines," I say. "At this point, we have no idea if Trello went back for the body after we left, or if she reported it anonymously, or even at all. Maybe he's still down there."

A shiver rattles my bones as I picture him lying there, his body rigid, the whole place full of glowing, pulsating jars of stolen magick.

"Yes, on that note," Doc says, and Carly and I let out a joint sigh, knowing we can't put it off any longer.

Time to relive the glory days of witnessing a magickal murder in the Academy library basement.

We take another steadying gulp of tea, then do our best to get the story out, one horrifying piece at a time:

Carly's premonition at the café, followed by Trello's sudden appearance on the path outside.

Tracking our disgraced headmistress to the library.

Discovering the broken security cameras above the basement door.

Finding the secret sub-basement beneath the storage area, full of the magickal essences stolen from our fellow witches and mages, along with their missing chunks of hair, bagged and neatly tacked to the bulletin board.

And finally, the grim discovery of Professor Phaines himself, the Dark Hierophant, hooked up to his magickal

IVs, siphoning stolen magick until his killer came and put a stop to it.

"I shouldn't have been surprised," I say. "The Hierophant card was stalking me all day. Even Carly had a premonition about it when we met up at the coffee shop. We kept assuming he fled campus, but the cards were trying to tell me the truth—he was right there all along."

"Show them the pictures," Carly says.

I'd nearly forgotten about those, but now I take out my phone and pass it around, showcasing the photos I snapped on our little torture tour.

Beneath the table, Isla reaches for my hand. "Goddess, Stevie. What if you'd been caught?"

"Trello was on a mission," Carly says. "She only had eyes for Phaines."

"And you're certain she killed him?" Doc asks.

"Totally," Carly says. "She had these big-ass syringes filled with some kind of glowing red potion. She went in, said her piece, and then it was done. She was gone in a blink after that."

"We checked the body," I say. "No pulse, no signs of life, and all the machines and IVs went dead."

"If I'm doing the math right," Professor Maddox says, "the approximate time of death coincides with the time his connection to Casey and Janelle broke. What did the headmistress say to him, exactly?"

"Something about how Phaines was drawing too much attention, and they'd reached the end of their agreement." I lift my mug to my face, inhaling the calming scent of the mint. For all Trello's bullshit, I still can't believe she was in league with Phaines.

"Obviously Trello knew he was there," Carly says. "Probably the whole time. They were working together— she said as much. They had an agreement."

"But to what end?" Doc asks. "And who else knew about it, other than Janelle?"

I set down my mug and reach for a tortilla chip, smothering it in sour cream. "Honestly, we still don't know Janelle was totally in on it."

"Stevie, she'd been ingesting Fairy's Breath since her first day on campus," Doc says. "You said so yourself."

"Right, but it's possible she was drugged. Most people can't smell it."

"She wasn't drugged, guys," Carly says. "My mother came here with an agenda, like I said. She literally showed up the day after Phaines's disappearance. That can't be a coincidence."

"Okay," I say, "but are you saying that because you truly believe it, or because you're pissed at her for being such a shitty mother?"

Doc holds up a hand, attempting to head off a confrontation. "I'm fairly certain Janelle was a willing participant. When I checked on her tonight, she made a comment in her half-conscious state to that effect."

"What did she say?" Carly asks.

He lowers his eyes, his energy pulsing with something that makes my skin crawl. "That she did it for... for Baz."

"That *bitch*." Carly's energy spikes with the same kind

of creeped-out vibe as Doc's, but before I can press her on it, Professor Maddox pipes in.

"The good news is, if the essence you found is still viable, there's a chance—small, but a chance—we might be able to return it to its rightful owners."

"Seriously?" I ask. "I thought the damage was permanent."

"It won't be easy, and I'm certainly not the expert—Professor Broome would know more about such things. But if we could somehow match the magickal signature to each individual student and come up with a powerful enough spell, we might be able to reverse the process."

"That's if we can even get to the magick again," I say. "Trello may have already notified APOA, or gone back herself to take care of the evidence."

Carly nods. "Yeah, I can't imagine she'd leave all that stuff for someone else to find. I got the sense she'd either go back later tonight, or she'd report it and make it look like she just discovered everything herself."

"What a fucking mess." Doc's energy shifts again, a wave of anger and frustration so powerful it's got him jumping to his feet, nearly knocking his chair backward. "What is Trello's angle here? She all but ordered us to bring Stevie to the Academy and put her to work translating her mother's prophecies. She called in APOA to investigate the crimes against students. I thought she was on our side, for fuck's sake. But then the attacks started on campus, and she completely lost her spine. She fought me on putting additional security measures in place—I had to threaten her just to get access to this house. Now we're learning she's involved with the Dark Arcana and the student attacks, not to mention Janelle Kirkpatrick... What the hell is her end game?"

"Maybe she wants the artifacts too," Nat says. "Maybe she and Phaines have been planning this for years. Decades, even."

I catch Doc's eye, and know at once our minds just jumped to the same place: What if Trello is one of the Dark Arcana?

But something about that idea doesn't hit the mark, either. All along, we've been operating under the assumption that there are four Dark Arcana energies at work right now—the Magician, the Hierophant, the Chariot, and Judgment. One, five, seven, twenty—that's what my visions revealed. There's a chance others could be turned, but that would mean Trello started out as a Light Arcana, and that doesn't feel quite true either.

I see Doc making the same calculations, drawing the same conclusion. Blowing out a breath, he shakes his head, then heads to the dishwasher, loading up some of the now-empty mugs.

"If Nat's suggestion is true," Professor Maddox says, "perhaps that's why Trello booted the Milans out of the Academy. Melissa must've figured out Trello had turned to the dark side—or she at least became suspicious. Perhaps there was a confrontation."

"Maybe." I swirl the remaining tea inside my mug,

considering all of this. Professor Maddox's hypothesis is a good one, but still. I don't buy it.

Something about the whole mess just isn't adding up. Sure, Trello's been cold and distant with me, and a completely inadequate leader when it comes to keeping students safe during what's quickly becoming a worldwide crisis for witches and mages. She's been evasive and aloof, and her inaction on the security stuff might end up costing lives—and there's no excuse for that kind of epic failure.

I could even buy that she's after the artifacts, and that her quest for riches and glory is blinding her to all else.

But *evil*? Truly evil? The kind of witch who attacks young students and robs them of their magick in some twisted Dark Arcana plot? A witch who allows a dark mage to torture a student and possess a new staff member and an APOA agent?

"There's a *but* in that maybe," Isla says.

"A big one." I set down my mug and look at everyone seated around me. "If Trello went dark all those years ago, why did she wait until now to start stealing magick—especially with APOA agents on the scene, like Doc said? She's had access to student witches and mages for decades. And if Mom was the one who figured out Trello's evil machinations, then why in goddess's name would Trello push so hard to enroll me, of all people? To make me crack the code on Mom's prophecies? Surely she knows I would've found something on her by now—whatever stuff Mom uncovered in the first place. There would've been traces of those suspicions in her work.

After all the shit we've seen, we're saying the creepy, ice-queen headmistress was the bad guy all along? No way. We're missing something."

I shake my head, eyes brimming with tears of frustration. Goddess, I wish Mom were here. I wish she could tell me what to do, or at least point me on the right path. We're spinning in circles, no closer to figuring any of this out than we were when Phaines tied me to a tree in the Forest of Iron and Bone.

I drain the last of my tea, more than ready to call it a night, but movement at the bottom of the mug catches my eye. At first it's just the dregs of the leaves, but then they take shape into something else, blooming from the tea residue like bright, otherworldly flowers.

Tarot cards.

I pluck them out of the mug and set them on the table, wet with tea leaves and melted chocolate.

"Hi, Mom," I say with a laugh, not caring how crazy it sounds.

"Your mother is communicating from the great beyond with magickally appearing Tarot cards?" Carly huffs. "Are you *serious* right now?"

"It's kind of a thing with them," Nat says.

"And the messages are never wrong," Isla says. "Because Melissa Milan is as badass as her daughter."

Professor Maddox reaches out and touches the cards, her eyes misting. "Hello, my dear friend." Then, to me, "What is she saying tonight, Stevie?"

Three of Pentacles reversed comes first, showing a man

chiseling pentacles and other Celtic symbols into a massive stone while three onlookers scrutinize his work.

Next up is Two of Cups. The card depicts a young couple standing in a flowering meadow beside a lake, sharing chalices of wine as they gaze lovingly into each other's eyes.

Finally, The Moon reversed appears, moonlight gleaming over a dark ocean, a wolf and a dog howling before a stone gateway.

I touch each card, gazing into the brightly colored images and listening for their messages.

"It's about agreements or partnerships," I say. "Not friendships exactly, but a kind of working relationship. Some of those bonds have been strained or broken, while others have emerged from unexpected places. Nothing is what it seems on the surface." Tapping the Moon card, I look up at Professor Maddox. "We're right to keep questioning this. To keep digging, no matter how clear the evidence looks."

"All that, and Mommy Dearest is *still* talking." Carly smirks, plucking two new cards from the mug and handing them over. "Guess we know where you get it from, Twink."

She rolls her eyes again, but she's smiling now, her energy warm and engaged as I look over the new cards— Queen of Swords and Queen of Pentacles. The first shows a queen with long gray locks, dressed in a deep purple dress, her cape tattered from years of wear. Her eyes are closed, but she holds her sword proudly, as if to remind us that she still knows how to use that thing.

"Wow," Carly says. "Now there's a woman who does *not* have time for your bullshit."

I crack up at that; the card gives me the exact same vibe.

The Queen of Pentacles is a bit warmer, featuring a woman seated on a throne in a bright red dress and green cape, an ancient Celtic drum in her lap, as if she's waiting to serenade us all before getting back to the practical tasks of managing her household.

I know at once these cards are talking about actual people rather than personality traits or situations, and again I'm reminded of the verse Professor Maddox shared with me about the Queens.

First, the swords, which correspond with the air element:

> *Fear not the evasive Queen of Air*
> *Though her manner is coarse, her outcome is fair*
> *By thought or by deed, by word or by blade*
> *Her sacrifice can't be unmade*

And then the Pentacles—the earth element:

> *By the Queen of Earth, you may be vexed*
> *But trust you must her diligence*
> *Sisterhood too, you'll find within*
> *But only when it's welcomed in*

"So who are the Queens supposed to be?" Carly asks.

"I'm not sure yet," I say, "but something tells me whoever they are, they're on our side."

Carly sighs. "Great. More new friends. Can't wait."

"Would you rather have more new enemies?" Isla gives her a shove, but it's playful and good-natured, and Carly shoves her right back. Nat chucks a tortilla chip at Carly, and with that, the Tarot cards disappear.

"Wait, that's it?" Carly asks. "She goes through all the effort of reaching out from the great beyond, and that's all we get? Why didn't she just leave a note or something?"

"It doesn't work that way," I say, and the room falls into silence once again.

"Okay, team. We're not going to crack this mystery tonight," Professor Maddox finally says. "We need more information from Casey, first and foremost. She's the missing link."

"Yes, but can we even trust her?" Doc asks.

"I don't appreciate her sneaking out on us tonight, but my gut says her intentions are pure and her instincts are good. For now, I'm willing to extend my trust a little longer, but not by much."

"One day," Doc says firmly. "If she doesn't check in by tomorrow night, she's on the enemy list, and I'm breaking her cloaking spell and replacing it with one that keeps *her* out too."

"Fair enough." Professor Maddox yawns, then slowly rises from the chair, her knees creaking. "I'm going to check on Kate and Ani, then I'm turning in. I'll see you all… well, perhaps morning is a bit too optimistic. Let's plan on brunch."

With a soft pat on my shoulder and a quick nod to Doc, Professor Maddox heads out.

"What should we do in the meantime?" Carly asks, looking to Doc as if our mental magicks professor has all the answers my mother's cards couldn't deliver.

"Find a bedroom," he says. "Goddess knows the house is big enough for an army."

"And then what?"

"I don't know what tomorrow holds, but I do know this —things are likely to get a lot worse before they get better. So if I were you, Miss Kirkpatrick, I'd probably get some rest."

He glances my way for no more than a heartbeat, then turns his back, dropping the last mug in the dishwasher and heading upstairs without another word.

SEVEN

STEVIE

There's no rest tonight.

An hour after our meeting, the house has fallen silent, but sleep eludes us all. I can feel it; the uncomfortable heaviness of our collective energy permeates the very walls.

Janelle's is the strongest, furious and frightened even in her half-unconscious state, her anger simmering up through the floorboards. Her screams stopped hours ago, but whatever caused them still torments her. Does she sense the presence of her daughter, I wonder? Does she even care that Carly's here?

For all the jokes and snarky comments, Carly herself is broken and confused, her energy a tangle of sharp edges and the deep longing of a child who was never truly loved. From the adjacent bedroom, her soft sobs echo through the wall, despite her best efforts at muffling them.

Isla and Nat are sharing one of the larger rooms at the other end of the hall, soft candles still burning as they whisper into the night. I feel their relief and gratitude at being here with us, but they're worried too, unsure how to prepare for whatever fight we've got coming.

Though Professor Maddox said her goodnights, she decided to keep Professor Broome company instead, sitting with her as they watch over Ani like fierce magickal mama bears.

Ani's energy is faint, but still present, a tiny spot of warmth emanating from the back corner of the house. It gives me hope, and I guard it fiercely, refusing to let it fade.

And lastly, I reach out for the energy of my stern, commanding Dr. Devane, pacing alone in his bedroom, stewing in a cocktail of self-loathing, fear, and blame. I wish I could tell him to let it all go, but that would make me a hypocrite; his agony is a mirror image of my own emotional torment.

I lean against the wall of my new bedroom, my heart aching with every beat. Since we found Ani in my suite, Doc and I have been like the tides on the shore—racing toward each other in a breathless rush, only to recede again, growing further apart with each passing wave.

Despite all the confusion and mixed signals, despite the uncertainty of Ani's situation and the mystery of what lies ahead, it's my tortured, enigmatic professor I seek out now, when I've run out of floors to pace and worries to ponder.

It's him I seek out now, when I need the firm challenge of his rules and regulations on a night when I'm in danger of becoming completely unmoored.

It's him I seek out now, hoping—despite everything—he

might bend those rules for me even once, giving himself over to the passion burning behind his every distant, measured word.

I miss him. I need him. Whatever we are to each other, whatever our future holds, I know it isn't this—two Arcana blessed souls passing like ships in the night, refusing to acknowledge our feelings.

Or act on them.

"This is bullshit," I mutter. "And it ends tonight."

Dressed in a long button-down flannel and the hoodie Baz gave me the night he saved me from the river, I pad down the hallway to Doc's room, determined to lay it all out, once and for all.

His door is ajar, and I push it open another crack, peering into the darkness. The lights are off and the room is dead silent, but the antique iron bed is unoccupied, the pillows and comforter undisturbed.

"Doc?" I whisper. "You in here?"

I feel him before I see him, the warm rush of his energy caressing my skin—happiness that I'm here. Affection. Desire. Concern.

"Has there been a change?" he asks. "Is he awake?"

I follow the sound of his voice to the big window that overlooks the sprawling backyard, my eyes finally picking out the dark shape of him before the glass. He's still wearing his usual dress pants, but now he's shirtless, his muscular arms and shoulders limned in moonlight.

"No change," I say, following the lines down to his hips, where the pants hang low and inviting. "Professor Broome said the sedative she made will keep him unconscious a few more days. She's hoping it will give his body more time to heal while his soul tries to come back."

Doc turns from the window to face me, his features lost in shadow. He pauses a beat, then finally sighs. "Come in, Stevie."

I do as he asks, closing the door behind me. Alone in the dark once again, I'm reminded of his other bedroom back on campus, the closeness we shared before Harvest Eve dinner. How is it possible it was only several hours ago? Goddess, it seems like another lifetime.

I wait a moment for my eyes to fully adjust, then join him by the window, looking out across the backyard. The house is part of a larger neighborhood owned by Arcana Academy, but this one is set further back, tucked into the shadows away from the other homes. Outside, the desert scrub stretches on forever, the saguaros turned deep blue in the moonlight. For a moment, I allow myself to think of home.

Talk about another lifetime…

"Are you okay?" he asks softly, the scent of whiskey lingering on his breath.

I press my finger to the windowpane, tracing an outline of the tallest saguaro. Goddess, I told myself I'd be strong. That I'd keep my shit together, at least until we got Ani back from the realm. But Doc's soft voice, his concerned energy, the constant push-and-pull between us…

"I'm barely holding on, Doc," I admit.

The tide surges, and he's close again, reaching out for

me, drawing me into his impossibly strong embrace, pressing his lips to the top of my head. Warmth floods my limbs, and I let myself go soft as I lean into him, trusting the smooth, strong planes of his chest. Trusting that he won't let me fall.

"Tell me how to make this better for you," he says, rubbing my back. "I see your pain—I can *feel* it. All I want to do is take it away from you."

A thousand answers come to mind—*then tell me how you really feel, let me in, kiss me, invite me into your bed tonight*—but I don't dare voice them. Not even when he tightens his hold and the heat surges between us, unleashing a tsunami of images—moonlight glinting off the ocean, the salty air caressing my skin, a hot mouth dragged along my inner thigh...

It's all too much—too big to put into words, too needy, too selfish, especially on a night when one of the men I love is downstairs fighting for his life and two others are somewhere on campus, yet to check in.

Forcing the sultry, moonlit images out of my mind, I pull away from Doc's hold and take a seat on the edge of the bed, willing my pulse to slow. "Don't suppose you've got any more of that whiskey?"

Doc's back to speaking in sighs, but after a few more of those, he finally reaches behind him, grabbing the bottle off the dresser and joining me on the bed.

"It's practically morning," he says. "I suppose that makes us day drinkers."

"Well, you know what they say. It's five o'clock *somewhere* in the world."

"Cheers, then." He uncaps the bottle and tips it back for a good long gulp, then holds it up high, just out of my reach.

"Seriously? I come to you in the predawn hours, my casual alcoholism on full display, and you're going for the tease?"

"Not a tease. A trade."

"*I'm* here for the whiskey. What do *you* want?"

"The truth."

"Which one?"

"Ladies' choice." Doc offers the bottle with a wide grin, but the alcohol hasn't done anything to lighten his mood. Beneath the charming smile, his guilt still simmers, hot and fresh.

"Fine, here's your truth." I snatch the bottle and toss back a healthy swig, wincing at the burn. "It's my fault, Doc. I brought them into my nightmare world, and this is what happened. Ani's trapped. Baz is… I don't even have a word for it. And Kirin? He seems okay so far, but after everything else? No way. We're crazy to think *anyone's* getting out this unscathed."

"Baz and Kirin *chose* to walk into that world with you. Any of us would have done the same and would do the same again, no question. And Ani…" He takes the bottle back for another go. "That's on me. I should've seen the signs. I should've been there for him. Been stronger for him. For *all* of you."

"Ani thought he needed to prove something to me. *That's* on me." I reach for the bottle, but Doc shakes his head, grabbing my hand and lacing our fingers together instead. His touch is warm and firm, insistent, and I hold my breath, terrified that even the slightest movement will shatter this moment.

"Everything about you sets me on fire," he whispers, pressing a soft kiss to my fingers.

My heart stutters, and I gasp at the warmth of his lips, but before I can utter another word, he stops.

It's like someone flipped the master switch and cut off the power. Doc drops my hand and pulls away, rising from the bed and heading back to gaze out the window, seeking solace from the bottle rather than from my touch.

Again, I feel the tide of his conflicting emotions, an endless war he'll never win. *Resist, give in. Resist, give in. Resist, give in...*

"Don't push me away," I say, not bothering to hide the disappointment in my voice. "I'm here because I want to be. I'm here because *you* want it too."

"Stevie..." He lowers his head, then shakes it, still refusing to face me. "I'm sorry. I... I just can't."

"You just *won't*. There's a difference."

"I have my reasons."

"So you keep saying. Or *not* saying, to be more accurate." I fold my arms across my chest and dig in for the fight. He can rehash his rules and regulations all he wants, but we both know that if Isla hadn't interrupted us at his place before Harvest Eve dinner, we would've followed that kiss to the blazing end.

If we'd slept together, would he still be pushing me away like this? Would I be letting him get away with it?

"I've wanted to tell you so many times," he says, his voice pained. "But it just never... The timing is always... Goddess, I'm doing it again. Fumbling. Hurting you. Hating myself for all of it."

I close my eyes, forcing myself to take a deep breath. To be fair, he did say he wanted to tell me something earlier, but that was before Professor Maddox came in with the update about Ani, and our ongoing little tug-of-war was all but forgotten.

Doc leans his forehead against the glass and sighs, his breath misting on the windowpane. I take a step toward him and reach for his shoulder, but the moment my fingers brush his skin, a fresh wave of sadness hits me, full of old regrets and a deep, all-consuming shame.

"It was about someone from your past, right?" I try to remember exactly what he said in the kitchen earlier. "From before you became a professor?"

Another sigh. Another wave of darkness and regret.

I stand behind him, trying to give him space, trying to let him come to me in his own time. But the silence drags on endlessly, and eventually, I break.

"I'm not here to convince you to be with me," I say. "I'm pretty sure you know how I feel. But whatever your reasons, whatever happened in the past... This has to end, Doc. I can't keep chasing you on this rollercoaster. It's—"

"No," he says suddenly.

"No?"

"It's not from before I became a professor," he says. "Just before I came to this Academy."

I blink, my mind trying to catch up with his words. "I thought you'd always taught here."

"I began my teaching career in Copenhagen."

I try to picture Doc on another campus, in a foreign city with different students, different landscapes. A younger version of him comes to my mind, his hair jet black without the touches of gray, the lines around his eyes smoother. Maybe he was less troubled then.

But that man is a stranger to me. I can barely hold the image.

"It's not something I usually talk about," he says, abandoning the whiskey bottle back on the dresser. "There's... history there."

"What sort of history?"

"Elizabeth Voorhees history," he says. "She was a student of mine. A first-year. Brightest in the class, full of life and magick. Potential. Stubborn too, like someone else I know." A soft chuckle escapes, but then it fades, replaced once again by the darkness. "She dreamed of working for the APOA, but she never got the chance."

I don't know what to say. Clearly, this woman meant something to him. And clearly, something terrible happened to her. Were they close? *Together* close? Did she pass away?

Why am I so scared to ask about this?

I wait for him to continue, but again, the silence drags on. He's pulling away from me, retreating, but I can't let him go. Not tonight. Not now.

Steadying myself, I reach out for his energy again, feeling very much like a trespasser chasing him through the coldest, most shadowy places of his heart.

And then I find it. The black core of it all—a guilt so heavy and all-consuming, he's drowning in it.

I don't know what happened in Copenhagen, and maybe that story was never meant for me. Maybe forcing him to justify his hot-and-cold reactions to me by digging through his past makes me a selfish, terrible person.

But selfish or not, I'm in this now. Deep. And every instinct inside me is screaming the same dire warning.

If I don't find a way to pull him back from this tonight, I'm going to lose him forever.

EIGHT

STEVIE

"Elizabeth Voorhees," I say gently. "It sounds like you cared a great deal for her."

"Not in the way you're thinking, no. But in her mind…" At this, he finally turns to face me, and I can't help the gasp that escapes my lips. Moments ago, he was my Doc—rigid, difficult, definitely hiding things. But still my Doc. Still the man I'm falling in love with.

Now, I'm staring at a wraith. I've never seen him so haunted, and it takes everything in me not to run to him, to silence the rest of this awful tale with kisses before he reaches the inevitable ending.

But he needs to get there. More than he needs comfort, more than he needs healing, he needs to let this go.

"She was infatuated with me," he says. "There's no other way to say it. I knew it. My colleagues knew it. And though I didn't return or even encourage her feelings, I didn't *discourage* them, either. She put me on a pedestal from the very first, and there I allowed myself to remain, even basking in the attention a bit. Inappropriate? Perhaps. Though the age difference was minimal then, she was still my student. And in a thousand other lifetimes, under a thousand other circumstances, maybe it wouldn't have mattered. Maybe one day she would've confessed her feelings directly, and my rejection—no matter how gentle—would've broken her heart, but she would've moved on. She would've found someone who returned her affections. She would've built a life for herself, and eventually, forgotten all about the young, cocky professor she once held in such high regard. Alas..."

He turns back to the window and reaches for the bottle, but doesn't open it. Just grips it tight, his knuckles whitening.

"During our first winter break, Elizabeth was manipulated by a dark mage. From what I could piece together from her journals later, he got into her mind and convinced her that he was actually me. And from there?" Doc releases a long breath, fogging the windowpane. With his free hand, he draws a spiral in the mist. "Understand, Stevie. The most dangerous thing about true mental manipulation is that it requires very little upkeep. All he had to do was plant a few tiny lies, like scattering seeds in a freshly tilled field. With little encouragement, those seeds eventually rooted, and from there, they bloomed into a tangled garden of deep, dark deceptions."

My skin erupts in goosebumps, and I wrap my arms around myself, trying to keep the chill at bay.

"Elizabeth had very quickly invented an alternate reality, one in which she and I were married and in love, hiding our relationship to avoid accusations of favoritism. But after several weeks of this, she decided my lack of affection was due not to my standards of professionalism, but to an affair. She convinced herself I was sneaking around behind her back, mocking her ignorance, undermining her credibility as a woman as well as a witch. She never discussed this with me, of course—it was all unfolding in her mind. It only came to light through her journals. During this time, my colleagues and I knew she wasn't well—her grades had dropped, she'd shut out her friends and fellow students, she was exhausted and delirious on the best of days—but no one could get through to her. Not even the headmaster or the academy healers."

"What about her family?"

"She was twenty years old, no guardians or next of kin listed in her records. For months, we were at a total loss. All we could do was try to encourage her studies and keep an eye on her to the limited extent we were able."

"Goddess, that's awful."

"It's a *horrible* thing to watch someone's mind unravel before your eyes, with no idea how to stop it. How to help. She was clearly angry with me, but I couldn't for the life of me figure out why. She'd never expressed her feelings to me directly or acted inappropriately, so it's not like there was a rejection to contend with. From what we could tell, there were no substance or alcohol issues, no missing magickal ingredients from the potions classes. We'd reached the point where we considered bringing in magickal specialists from London to work with her privately, but then things got a bit better. She was participating in class again, her health had improved, some of the spark had returned to her eyes. But one day, she walked into my classroom while I was alone with another student—a third-year witch who needed help with visualizations. Elizabeth saw us practicing the role-playing exercises and assumed the worst. She tore into the room, crying and shouting, ripping up papers and tossing books on the floor... I'd never seen such a tantrum.

"We contacted one of the healers, who gave her a mild sedative and took her back to the healing center to rest. Later that night, Elizabeth attacked the healer, snuck out of the center, and broke into the other student's suite. She..." Doc shakes his head, then finally cracks open the bottle again, taking another swig before continuing. "She beat that poor girl into a coma, Stevie. Broke her ribs, carved her face up with an athame, left her blind in one eye... She told the authorities that I implored her to do it. That I thought the student was plotting to kill us... Goddess, it was such a twisted fantasy, such an impossible tale. But in her mind, all of it made perfect sense. *We* were the crazy ones for doubting her."

Doc lifts the bottle to his lips again, but changes his mind, setting it back on the dresser and taking a seat on the bed. I sit down next to him, leaving a little space between us, not wanting to crowd him.

"After the attack, one of her former friends was finally able to track down next of kin—an aunt in Munich—and the authorities agreed to release Elizabeth into the woman's care. They'd found her journals by this point, and after a thorough review, turned them over to me. That's when I learned about the man she'd encountered over winter break. The way she described their encounters, I knew immediately what had happened. Likely, he'd been watching us both for many months. He knew exactly how to prey on her vulnerabilities—on her feelings for me."

"Was he ever caught?"

Doc shifts uncomfortably, the muscle in his jaw ticking. "To quote the authorities, the rambling diaries of a mentally unstable witch obsessed with her professor were not compelling enough evidence to justify an investigation. But no matter." He lowers his head, shame flooding his energy again. "The mage may have planted those seeds, but I tilled the field. By my action or my inaction, I destroyed that girl's life."

I reach for him, fingers skimming his knee. "Doc, no. You—"

"I could've stopped it. If I'd set clear boundaries, if I'd maintained a proper distance from the onset, her feelings for me would never have progressed. She would've understood that I'd never return her affections. She would've focused more on her studies and less on her professor. Her mind wouldn't have been so open to the power of the dark mage's suggestions—she wouldn't have *wanted* to believe he was me. She wouldn't have been trying to please me. Goddess, sometimes I still can't believe he bested her like that. Of all my students, she was

67

the strongest. The most clever. I never would've thought..."

He trails off, rising from the bed and crossing back to the dresser, staring at his reflection in the mirror.

"I couldn't bear to be there," he says. "I had to leave. The headmaster got in touch with Anna Trello, and after some favors promised and exchanged, I was released from my contract in Copenhagen and transferred. And here, I regained control. I dedicated myself to teaching students *not* how to manipulate through magickal means, but how to defend against it."

He grips the edges of the dresser and drops his head, the muscles of his back and shoulders rippling as he struggles to contain the darkness inside.

The confession leaves me reeling. It explains so much— why he has so many rules and boundaries, why he's so afraid to get close, why he blames himself for Ani.

There's still so much pain inside him, so much bleakness. Sharing this with me hasn't unburdened him at all; if anything, it's made him feel worse, shame and loathing burning hot through his energy.

But no matter how deep his wounds, running beneath the waves of self-loathing is an energy of pure, golden love. Hope. Desire. He wants to be near me, wants me to help him through this.

He wants to allow himself to love me.

Yet still, he fights. He fears.

Slowly, I get to my feet and go to him, standing behind him, waiting for him to meet my eyes in the mirror.

"I'm not Elizabeth," I begin, but fear chokes off the rest. I can't find the right words, the right way back to him. Logically, he *knows* I'm not Elizabeth. He knows our circumstances are completely different. He knows Ani's condition isn't his fault.

He's just punishing himself.

"Doc," I say. "*Cassius*, please."

At the sound of his full name, he finally meets my gaze in the mirror, storms raging in those slate-gray eyes, shadows haunting every plane of his beautiful face, heartache bleeding through his energy, threatening to drown out the rest.

"The day I left Copenhagen," he says, "I told myself—I *swore* it on my own magick—I would never, ever let the lines between professor and student blur again. And for nearly fifteen *years*, I've had no problem keeping that oath."

Until you came along, he means, but he doesn't say that part out loud.

"Doc, I—"

"Just... just go." He lowers his eyes, breaking our connection. "I'm sorry I've been so unclear about this— that's on me. But it ends now, Miss Milan."

"Don't call me that. Not here."

"Go," he says again. "I want to be alone."

"But—"

"*Go!*" The dresser rattles with the force of his rage, but it doesn't scare me.

It fucking *ignites* me.

In a flash, the sadness and sympathy I felt seconds ago

burn away, leaving only a white-hot flame crackling in my chest.

"You know something, *Dr. Devane*?" I snap. "You're a goddess-damned liar."

He meets my eyes in the mirror again, jaw ticking, fresh anger simmering. "Excuse me?"

"You heard me. A goddess-damned liar. I'll let you get away with it tonight, but that's all you get. One more night. One more night to be pissed off at the world, to push away all the people who care about you, to punish yourself over a past you didn't cause and damn well can't change. Because after tonight? This game between us is over. It's time to face the truth—you don't *want* to be alone. Not tonight. Not ever."

"You don't know what you're talking about," he grinds out. "And I suggest you take that righteous attitude and leave before you say something you—"

"Something I what—regret?" I let out a bitter laugh, the tension between us seconds from sparking into a full-on inferno. "Not a chance, Doc. You know why? Because saying things—even harsh, ugly things—isn't the problem. It's the *not* saying things that keeps fucking us all up. So I'm saying all of it tonight. Laying it right out there."

"Save your breath," he says, squeezing his eyes shut as if he can make me disappear. "I told you—I want to be alone."

"Bullshit. Look—I'm not trying to minimize what happened to Elizabeth, or tell you how you should feel about it. I'm just saying we've *all* done things we're not proud of, we've all fucked up, we've all destroyed lives and broken hearts and caused immeasurable pain. But that doesn't mean we don't get to love. To *be* loved."

I reach for his arm, and though he turns to face me, he doesn't open his eyes. He crosses his arms over his chest, his jaw set tight, brows drawn low. Everything about him screams *back off*.

But I don't. I can't.

"Your past," I say, "your oaths, all the things you've broken, all the things that've broken you... None of them matter to me. And none of them change how *you* feel about *me*, either."

He finally opens his eyes again, fury and frustration colliding in his gaze, his body practically vibrating with it. "You presume to know how I feel about you?"

My heart stutters at the quiet menace in his voice, but I refuse to back down.

"I can *feel* it," I say, pressing a hand to my chest. "Right here. Every time you look at me. Every time you say my name. All the rest—the darkness, the fear, the boundaries? It's all some story you keep telling yourself so you don't have to face the fact that you're falling in love with me. That I'm falling in love with you. And you keep pushing me away because deep down, you don't believe you deserve *any* of it. So yeah, I'll leave you tonight. Fine. But I'm still calling you a liar, *Dr. Devane*. A scared, angry, control-freak of a liar."

I turn on my heel, stalk across the room, and reach for the door. I've barely opened it a sliver when it slams shut again, Doc's hands flat against the wood, his arms a cage around my head. Behind me, the solid wall of his chest leaves no escape.

He leans in closer and crowds me against the door, breath hot on my neck, his steel-hard cock digging into my lower back.

"You're right, Miss Milan," he says in that eerily quiet voice. "I *am* a liar. The worst kind. Because this isn't just about the oaths I made after Copenhagen. I've been making oaths from the very moment I found you in that prison. Promises to keep you safe—not just from the guards, not just from the dark mages that attacked your friend Luke, not just from the unknown dangers awaiting you at the Academy. No. I promised to protect you from *me*—the poisonous viper lurking in the shadows, waiting for a chance to strike."

I turn around inside the cage of his arms, ready to fight to the death over that particular bit of bullshit, but Doc presses a finger to my lips, immediately cutting me off. His eyes are full of new dangers now, promises and threats and everything in between, and my pulse skyrockets, my blood superheated, my body suddenly desperate for more of his commanding touch.

"From the moment I first laid eyes on you," he says, one hand still braced against the door, "strong and defiant even in your worst moments, I felt it. The tide of you, pulling me close. You seduced me in ways I couldn't explain, couldn't define. But I swore to keep my distance, no matter how difficult. I swore I wouldn't—under *any* circumstances—touch you. Not even if you *begged* me for it."

He trails his fingertip down my chin, my throat, swirling over the triangle of bare skin visible above my zipper.

"I've held fast to that promise," he says, dipping his head low and dragging the tip of his nose down the same path, "despite coming close to shattering it so many times I've lost count. I've fought my feelings at every turn, even when I knew damn well you could read them like a book, line by line, word by fucking word. There's *never* hiding anything from you—not then, and not now. Yet I tried. I'm *still* trying." His tongue darts out to lick the hollow of my throat, then he lifts his head, mouth brushing across mine with a soft moan that makes me instantly wet. There he hovers, the taste of whiskey sharp and seductive on his breath, my pulse jumping beneath the press of his thumb, my core throbbing.

I don't say a word. Don't move. Don't even breathe.

"Congratulations, Miss Milan. You've finally done it. Utterly ruined me, as I always knew you would. You're here in this house, in this room, and I can't take a damn *breath* without tasting your scent, without imagining my mouth on your skin. Without imagining..." He drags his mouth to my ear, hot breath making me shiver. "...the sound of your moans as you come for me."

A gasp of pleasure escapes my lips, and slowly, torturously, he unzips Baz's hoodie and pushes it off my shoulders, then goes for the buttons on my flannel.

"So please," he says, popping open the first one. "Call my bluff. Make a damn liar out of me. Obliterate the last vestiges of my control." Hard knuckles brush over my nipple, then he turns his hand, cupping my breast through the fabric and teasing the aching flesh with his thumb. "Because tonight?"

I lean back against the door and close my eyes, my knees weakening, my body melting, desire weaving a spell through every last nerve ending...

"Tonight, I'm going to break *every*..."

Fingers tighten around my collar, and he hauls me close, his energy cresting in a wave of rage and frustration and pure, uncut lust.

"*Last...*"

He tears open the flannel, the remaining buttons scattering across the hardwood floor.

"*Vow.*"

He yanks the shirt from my arms and tosses it to the floor, exposing my bare flesh to the cool air. Wild, feral, he devours me with his eyes as I stand before him in nothing but a pair of purple underwear, my nipples hard and tight, long hair tickling my shoulders.

"Goddess," he breathes, reaching between my thighs, his fingers tracing the shape of that lacy triangle.

Close enough I can feel the heat radiating from his skin.

Far enough to make me *ache*.

"Is this what you want?" he demands in that bone-chilling voice, eyes blazing a warning I feel deep in my core. He presses a hot kiss to my neck as his fingers slide inside the waistband, brushing my flesh with teasing strokes, moving lower and lower but still just out of reach.

My stomach is trembling, my breath ragged, my nerves burning for more, but I bite my lip to keep from crying out. From letting him know how quickly he's unraveling me.

"Is this why you came to me tonight," he says, teeth grazing my earlobe, "hot and wet, half-naked, knowing it would drive me out of my mind?"

"I didn't... I thought..." I swallow hard, words tangling in my throat as he finally reaches my clit. I arch my hips, hungry for more. Desperate for it. *Dying* for it.

"Sorry, I didn't quite catch that," he teases. "And here I thought it was the *not* saying things that kept fucking us all up. Isn't that what you said?"

I nod, damn near losing my mind.

"What is it, then? Now's your chance to tell me all those things you've been holding back. All those hot, reckless things you want me to do to you."

A tremor rolls down my spine, my heart banging wildly, stars swimming before my eyes. I can't hold out another moment. "Are you... are you going to touch me?"

"Touch you? Like this?" He moves past my clit, fingers tracing my outer lips, then dipping inside, slow and deep. I gasp and reach for his shoulders, fingernails digging into his flesh as he pulls out, then slides back in, unleashing a rush of pure pleasure between my thighs.

But just before I lose myself completely, he pulls back out, dragging his fingers up to my neck, wrapping his hand around my throat and pinning me against the door. With his free hand, he fumbles with his pants—the clank of the metal belt buckle, a quick zip, the heat of his cock pressing urgently against my abdomen.

"No, my beautiful Star. I'm not going to touch you." His mouth ghosts over my lips again, teeth glinting in the moonlight with a smile that portends my doom. "Tonight, I'm going to *own* you."

NINE

BAZ

The stars are spinning. Or maybe *I'm* spinning. Either way, I'm flat on my back in the Iron and Bone common room, and something is seriously out of whack right now. Especially since I'm seeing stars and I'm not even outside.

Wait—am I?

More importantly, do I actually give a shit?

Survey says…

Fuck it.

I lift the bottle to my face and squint at the label. I don't even know what's in this shit—some homemade brew one of the first-years left, abandoning their Dungeons-and-Dragons game the moment I came tearing through here. All I know is I introduced myself to it two hours ago with that first blissful sip, and now we're old friends.

"And oh, what a good friend you are." I kiss the bottle, then lift my head just enough to take another swig. It burns all the way to my fucking bones, but that burn is a hell of a lot better than the other one. The one that claws at my chest and tears at my soul, making me forget I ever gave a shit about anything.

About anyone.

"Fuck you," I say. To the monsters from the past. To my broken, murderous brother. To the druid in the blood-stained robe. To anyone who thinks they can fuck with me now. I found the fucking cure, assholes.

I take another swig.

Deep inside, some shit-sucking little voice tries to convince me I'm going to regret this later, but you know what? Fuck him too. Another swig, another problem solved. Bam.

"That's how it's done, boys," I say. And I'm feeling pretty damn clever about the whole thing too—until some douchebag in hipster glasses and a Star Wars T-shirt bobs into view, glaring down at me like some kind of self-appointed god on the mountain.

"Kirin Weber!" I slur, pointing up at his face. "Anyone ever tell you how cute you are when you're scowling?"

"Seriously?" He's disgusted—doesn't even try to hide it. "We've been calling and texting you for hours, you dick."

My face splits into a grin. "Dude. I never realized how fucking massive your head is. It's like the Goodyear blimp. And now it's spinning!"

"Get up, Baz. We've got some serious shit to deal with, and this drunk-and-disorderly act isn't helping."

"Who said I wanted to help? Was there a sign-up sheet? 'Cause I don't remember signing—"

He gives my boot a good kick, then swipes the bottle from my hand, taking a whiff. "This shit smells like it could strip the paint off walls. No wonder you don't remember."

"Gets the job done."

Kirin helps himself to a nice gulp, then winces. "What job is that? Hollow out your organs and make you piss fire?"

"That, and it keeps the fucking nightmares out of my head."

A flash of compassion flickers in his eyes, which is just about the last thing I want to see right now. He offers me a hand up, but I ignore it, stealing the booze back instead.

I've got all the compassion I need in this sweet little bottle.

I roll over on my hip and face the fireplace, content to stare into the flames and ignore him, but the stubborn bastard can't take a hint. He's on me like a first-year at the Smash cheese fountain.

"On your feet, asshole." He grabs me under the arms and yanks me into a standing position. "There. Was that so hard?"

The whole room tips sideways, and I sway, latching onto his shoulder for stability. "What do you think?"

"I think it's time for you to run upstairs, mainline some coffee, and pack your shit. We need to get off-campus, back to Stevie and—"

"*Don't.*" I'm in his face in a heartbeat, rage boiling up from nowhere. Logically, some part of me knows I'm off my rocker tonight, but when has logic ever stopped a drunken asshole from being a drunken asshole? "Don't you say her *fucking* name."

"Oh, I'll say it. I'll scream it if that's what it takes to get you to pull your head out of your ass." Kirin shoves me, and I rock back on my heels. "What are you *doing*? She needs you, Baz. We all need you."

"You don't need me."

Kirin glances at his phone. "Is this the part of the show where you start feeling sorry for yourself? Because trust me on this one, brother. We do *not* have time."

"I'm no good for her." I can barely stand on my own two feet, but I'm not too blitzed to remember that. "I'm no good for *you*. So take your phone and your cute glasses and your Judgy McJudgerson ass and go—*fuck*!"

Like a world-class dildo, I trip over my own feet, nearly face-planting into the fireplace. The only thing that saves my head from becoming a shish kebob is Kirin—he catches me just in time, hauling me against his chest.

I should maybe thank him for that. Maybe not. Either way, now the four-eyed fucker won't let me go.

"Nice save," I say, smacking him on the back, but he's still got me in a lock, arms tight around me, refusing to budge.

"Kirin, seriously. I'm good."

No response.

"Look. I'm sorry if I sent mixed signals, but I'm *really* not in the mood for a cuddle tonight, so if you don't mind..." I try to wrench free again, but he only holds on tighter, like some kind of boa constrictor about to crush the life out of me.

"It's okay, brother," he says softly.

"Fuck off."

"I got you."

"You're gonna get my fist in your face if you don't let go."

"I got you, Baz. I got you."

He keeps on saying it, over and over, refusing to release me from his death grip. And I keep on fighting. Trying to push him away. Trying to push *all* of this away, as if we could ever go back to a time where it didn't hurt so fucking much.

But we can't. And eventually, I just… break.

All the fight drains out of me, and I collapse in Kirin's arms like a rag doll, two minutes from giving up completely and chucking my own ass into the fire.

Kirin won't let that happen, though. Instead, he pours me into one of the leather chairs and takes a seat across from me, his eyes glassy, his face pinched with worry. "Talk to me, Baz."

Talk. Right. Where the hell do I even begin? I drop my head and stare down at my hands, pale and useless in my lap, wishing instead they were covered in blood.

Janelle Kirkpatrick's blood. Dark and warm and glistening…

The thought seizes me in an instant, chasing away the drunken haze with a flood of adrenaline. Purpose. Passion.

Kill her. Slay your demons in this realm, just as you did in the land of dreams. She's weak. No one would blame you. It would be so easy…

"Baz?" Kirin's hand on my knee snaps me back to reality. I try to suck in a deep breath, but a shudder rolls through my body, leaving a blistering pain in its wake.

"*Fuck.*" I grind my teeth and clutch my chest. Kirin's on his feet in a flash, reaching for me, trying to help me sit up again, but all I can do is ride it out and hope to goddess I'm still in my right mind when it's over.

It's never been this bad before—a brutally searing agony, like my flesh is melting down to the bone. In a fit of desperation, I tear off my shirt and pitch it into the fireplace, then snatch the bottle back—the only thing guaranteed to numb the pain.

Kirin watches helplessly as I chug. And slowly, the pain recedes.

"Goddess, that's… Wow." Kirin shakes his head, his eyes wide, fixated on the mark on my chest. It's starting to fade now, but he saw it. I know he did.

XX. The mark of Judgment.

"He's still with me," I finally confess, because what the fuck else can I do? This shit is either going to kill me, or turn me into an empty, drooling husk. I can't keep outrunning it. Can't keep hurting the people I love by keeping them in the dark. "Don't ask me how, but he is. The minute I'm sober, or lying awake at night, or hell—jerking off in the damn shower, that motherfucker's waiting to pounce. Half the time I can't even tell the difference between my own thoughts and his crazy-ass rantings."

Like the one where he's trying to get me to kill that bitch...

I take another sip of the booze, but it's quickly losing its luster.

"And this is why you've been ghosting us?" he asks.

"What choice do I have? I'm not in my right mind when it happens—I could hurt someone. What you saw tonight? That shit would've been a hell of a lot worse without mage's little helper here." I shake the bottle in front of his face.

Kirin sighs and reaches for it. After a long pull, he meets my gaze again, his own eyes haunted. "I've... I've felt his presence too."

"Since we've been back?"

"Yeah. Not as bad as you, though," he says, nodding at my chest. The mark has almost completely faded now, but I still feel the echo of that burn. "For me, it's mostly confined to dreams."

"Nightmares, more like."

"It's like he's trying to goad me. Remind me of all the terrible shit from the past—things I fucked up with my family. Back in the realm, he burned me too. Same place." Kirin rubs his chest, the memories making him grimace. "But he hasn't touched me on the material plane. All that stuff with my family... I don't know. My theory is he feeds on it."

"Awesome. So I'm basically a walking buffet." I force a grin, but it doesn't last.

Turning away, I stare into the fireplace, watching the flames flicker and sway, wondering what kind of fucked-up shit makes someone turn so completely dark. As Arcana mages, our power is pure and infinite, our potential unlimited. We're supposed to use that power to *protect* magick, not destroy it. Not *possess* it.

"Baz," Kirin says softly, "when we found you in that house…"

Fuck. I close my eyes, willing this conversation to go in another direction. *Any* direction. But of course it won't. It can't.

"What were you fighting in there?" he asks.

A shock of guilt races down my spine, pooling in my gut like hot stew spiked with glass. My face goes red—I can feel it happening, not a damn thing I can change about that.

But I'm not interested in inviting my demons out for drinks—no thanks. Especially not so soon after Judgment paid me his little fireside visit tonight.

"Doesn't matter," I say. "Point is, Judgment may be fucking with us from the great beyond, but Stevie's the one he's really after. She's the key to *all* this—her mother knew it too. It's probably right there in one of her damn prophecies. Tell me you can't feel it."

"I agree with you, but we still don't know exactly how the prophecies tie into the—"

"Fuck the prophecies, man. They want her dead!" Goddess, just saying the words out loud puts my heart through the shredder.

"If you're so worried about our girl," Kirin says, getting to his feet, "why are you here, jerking off with a bottle of moonshine instead of helping us figure out how to defeat these monsters?"

"Because I love her, dickhead."

"We all love her. That's exactly why we need to get back to Red Sands Canyon and figure out our next move."

"I'll tell you what our next move *isn't* going to be— marching back into the dream realm with a hunting party, looking for more trouble. I know that was the plan, but that's off the table now."

"I'm not saying we—"

"The Dark Arcana can go fuck themselves."

"Baz, listen to me. After Cass's party tonight, things—"

"Artifacts? Grimoires? Magick? Let 'em have it. All of it."

"We need to get back to—"

"Let 'em burn the whole world down for it."

"You don't understand. Ani—"

"Far as I'm concerned, *none* of us is going back to that fucking realm. Got it?"

Rant over, I finally meet his gaze again, hoping he's ready to go fuck off somewhere else and leave me to close out this miserable Harvest Eve alone.

But Kirin just sighs and shakes his head, his eyes full of that special kind of pity that can only come from someone who knows he's about to upend your entire world.

"Yeah, about that whole not-going-back-to-the-realm thing..." He holds out his hand, offering me one last chance. "I've got some bad news for you, brother."

TEN

STEVIE

A hurricane.

Strong, powerful, impossible to outrun. A tempestuous force of nature that steals my breath and rivals the storm in his eyes.

That's how it feels when Doc kisses me.

His mouth is hot and fierce and *everywhere*—my lips, my neck, my breasts, a sharp bite and a soothing lick as he teases my nipple. I lean back against the door again, barely able to hold myself upright as he strips off my underwear, kissing his way down.

I slide my fingers into his hair and breathe his name, and his lips buzz between my thighs, tongue flicking against my clit, a red-hot preview of what's to come. He waits for the telltale tremble in my legs, the heat unfurling low in my belly, a fire licking its way across every nerve ending…

And then he's pulling back, unleashing a whimper of protest from my lips before he's back to my mouth again, silencing me with another kiss.

He grabs my ass and lifts me up, fingers digging into my flesh as I wrap my legs around his hips. The smooth, hard planes of his chest and abs radiate heat against my bare skin, and in that moment, I *hate* that he's holding me so close. All I want is to run my tongue along those firm ridges, to taste the salt of his skin, to feel him.

I try to touch him, but I can't reach.

"Not yet, beautiful," he whispers as his cock throbs between us, his body as hot and eager as mine. I writhe in his arms, desperate for the hot slide of him inside me, but Doc is clearly calling the shots, unwilling to cede even an *inch* of control.

Tightening his hold, he carries me back to the bed and throws me down, wild and merciless and so fucking sexy. With a grip so firm it's almost scary, he pins my wrists down and collapses on top of me, crushing my mouth in another devastating kiss.

His cock digs into my belly, his belt buckle cool and sharp against my hip, but I don't care. I can't even move.

I don't *want* to move.

I want him to fucking *own* me, just like he promised.

His kiss is out to destroy me, and I'm more than ready to let it happen. But before I can get my fill, he's rising up on his knees to stare down at my nakedness, eyes glinting with a primal spark.

"Let me touch you," I breathe, reaching for him.

"No touching until I say so."

"You're fucking killing me!"

"This mouth." Doc drags a thumb across my lips, his eyes dark with desire. "Goddess, you make me lose control, Miss Milan—a state that agitates me greatly. So I'm going to take it back. One touch, one kiss, one orgasm at a time."

He fists his cock, stroking himself slowly, deliberately, torturously, his gaze locked fiercely on mine, daring me to defy him.

But this isn't mental magicks class. To defy him right now—to do *anything* that might delay the sensual promises hidden in his teasing threats—would only be punishing myself.

"Please," I whisper, my hips arching, my body ready to unravel. "I need to touch you. To feel you inside me."

Begging. He's reduced me to begging, and he's loving every red-hot minute of it.

So am I.

Goddess, I'm so wet for him, the ache between my thighs so deep, so endless... If he doesn't do something about it soon, I'm going to combust.

Ignoring his warnings, I reach for his cock again, out of my mind with lust. But clearly I'm no match for Doc's control issues tonight.

With a cruel, delicious smile, he pushes me down again, then grabs the end of his belt.

"I should've known you'd disobey." He whips the belt

free from his pants—a soft swish of leather against fabric, a bright snap in the air that makes my nerve endings stand at attention. "Put your hands up over your head."

"Why?" I stare at him with wide, curious eyes, my breathing shallow, my mind racing with possibilities. Low in my belly, butterflies spin a frantic ballet, but I raise my arms anyway, eager to follow his every command. "What... what are you doing?"

"I'm your professor, Miss Milan." He leans forward again, buzzing his lips along the shell of my ear. "I'm teaching you a lesson about the consequences of insubordination."

Quickly, efficiently, he loops the belt around my wrists, then secures it to the iron bars behind me, pulling tight.

Cool leather bites into my skin. I tug hard, but there's no breaking free.

I'm completely at his mercy.

The realization unleashes a new rush of desire, dark and forbidden and utterly intoxicating.

Doc runs his hands down my bare arms, his stern gaze gentling when he meets my eyes. Cupping my face, he whispers earnestly, "Do you trust me?"

Like an untamed river finally bursting through a dam, his energy washes over me in a rush, full of love and wanting, full of consideration and care, full of an intense desire to bring me as much pleasure as he feels. For this brief moment, all pretense of domination and control has vanished, and the purity of his true feelings shines through.

Not even when he confessed the darkness of his past did he allow so much honesty. So much vulnerability. And in this fragile moment, we both know he's not just asking me to trust him with my body.

Cassius Devane is a master of mental magicks; his feelings, no matter how clearly I sense them, could very well be a ruse.

He's asking me to trust that they aren't. To believe it. To *know* it, deep down in my soul.

Emotion surges within me, the force of it making me stutter. "I've never... I mean, I..."

"You've never what, my beautiful Star?" Doc smiles softly, tracing a feather-light path along my jaw, content to ignore his throbbing erection as he waits patiently for my consent.

"I've never..." I swallow hard. I know what I want to say, but I can't quite form the words.

I've never let anyone tie me up before.

I've never relinquished all control.

I've never given myself over so completely.

I've never wanted anything so deeply.

I've never needed anything to be so true, so real as I need this to be...

The last thought sends the butterflies swirling again, my whole body buzzing with the sheer terror of what it truly means to want this. To want *him*. Not just right now, not just in his bed.

But in my heart.

That wanting, that need, that ache... It means my commanding, naughty, complicated Dr. Devane doesn't just have the power to tie me to his bed and dominate me tonight.

It means he has the power to break my heart.

How many times has he pushed me away already? How many times has he buried his own feelings and shut me out?

Yes, I want this night of bliss—my body is already melting for him. And deep down, I know he's not manipulating my mind.

But this night, this moment... What if this is *it* for us? One night of pure, reckless passion before the walls go up again, and we're back to pretending our feelings are just some side-effect of the Arcana bond?

Doc trails his fingers down my throat, my chest, his palms grazing my nipples, the heat of his touch radiating right through me.

"It's okay," he whispers, as if he can sense the direction of my thoughts. My fears. "I'm right here with you. I'm not going anywhere."

"I know," I whisper back.

"Do you trust me?" he asks again, his voice thick with emotion, his energy warming with the promise that yes, this is real. That he wants is as much as I do. That the dam around his heart has finally broken, the river unleashed, and there's no changing its course now.

A smile breaks across my face, the warmth of his energy flooding my heart.

Suddenly, those butterflies don't feel so scary.

I'm *not* afraid.

I'm simply… in love.

I open my eyes, the right words finally emerging. "I've never trusted anyone the way I trust you, Doc. Tonight, tomorrow, always."

He steals another kiss, lingering there for a deep, delicious minute.

"Cassius," he finally says, pulling back with a smile. "In my bed, you call me Cassius."

After the seriousness of the last few minutes, his latest command makes me laugh. "More rules for me, *Cassius*? Good to know some things never change."

"Yes, and while we're on the subject…" Doc—rather, *Cassius*—traces the shape of a heart over my chest, intensity building between us once again. "I've never known anyone with such an infinite heart—one I'm honored to share with my brothers. However…" He trails his hand down between my thighs, and a fierce wave of possessiveness rolls over me. "I will *not* share you here. When you come to me at night, when you're lying naked and bound in *my* bed, you are *mine*, Starla Milan. Understand?"

"I'm yours," I say, my own possessive energy rising just as fiercely. "But if you're claiming me, I'm claiming you too."

He brushes a finger over my clit, eyes sparkling with amusement. "And what does that entail, I wonder?"

"It's simple. No more mixed signals and near-kisses. No more games, no more pushing me away, no more denying your feelings. I understand the need for discretion, but I will *not* compete with the ghosts of your past. You are *mine*, Cassius Devane. Understand?"

"I suppose I can live with that." He offers one last smile, and then he's inching his way down again, replacing his teasing fingers with his—

Oh, goddess. That mouth…

I strain against the leather belt, spreading my thighs as he licks a hot path between them. He swirls his tongue over my clit, then sucks it between his lips, gripping my thighs and spreading me wider, deepening his kiss.

After all the touching and teasing tonight, it doesn't take much to push me to the very edge, and soon my thighs are trembling again, the heat in my core building furiously as he devours me, the deft strokes of his tongue growing more urgent as I arch closer, my muscles clenching, my breath turning shallow and desperate…

"Cassius!" I cry out as I finally shatter beneath his mouth, and he moans in response, the deep, gravelly sound of it vibrating across my clit as another wave of pleasure pulses through my core. Heat spreads down my thighs, wrapping my body in an electric buzz as the orgasm ever so slowly recedes.

But *he* isn't ready to recede.

He presses his lips to my flesh again, sliding his tongue inside me, his grip on my thighs tightening as he continues to take back every last inch of control.

It's almost too intense, almost too much, but I'm powerless to resist the seductive demands of his touch.

He pushes me past the blissful orgasm, past the after-shocks, right to the edge of total overwhelm. Soon I'm squirming, my skin on fire, my thighs clenching beneath his firm grip, my body desperate to escape his relentless kiss. But no matter how hard I try, he's always *right* there —tasting me. Claiming me. *Owning* me, just like he promised.

Then, just before I'm certain my body's going to revolt, certain I'm going to pass out from the overwhelming inten-sity, I feel it building again, a slow but steady climb, each stroke of his tongue unlocking new levels of desire that demand even *more* of his touch, more of his hot, perfect mouth.

He moans again, teeth grazing my clit, and that's all it takes. I come with an intensity that borders on chaos, a pleasure so pure and otherworldly I'm not even sure I'm in my body anymore. I wonder if I've been struck by light-ning, my skin vibrating, my nerves sizzling, my bones melting inside me. By the time he pulls back, I can't even scream his name; all I've got left is a gasp.

I'm still reeling as he drags his mouth along my inner thigh, kissing a fresh path up my stomach.

I'm still reeling as he slides out of his pants and boxers, then settles his weight between my thighs, his cock hard and eager.

I'm still reeling when he positions himself at my entrance, looking at me with a deep, desperate hunger, his mouth glistening, his hair as wild as his eyes.

"Okay?" he asks.

There's only one word that matters now, only one word I remember, and I offer it up like a gift. "*Yes.*"

He plunges inside me, my body gripping him tight, still pulsing with the final waves of the ecstasy he just delivered.

He breathes my name and buries his face against my neck, inhaling the scent of my skin.

And then, naked and stripped of all pretense, Dr. Cassius Devane—a man who once pretended to shoot me in order to save my life, a man who's protected and cared for me every day since, a man who would lay down his life for me and my Arcana brothers without question —*fucks* me.

It's the only word for it, and not because it's shallow or vulgar or casual. No—it's deep and dark and possessive, an act of pure, primal instinct that leaves no more room for doubts and denials, no more room for fear.

Only love. Only perfect trust.

He fucks me hard, then soft. Teasing strokes, then deep, all-consuming lunges.

He fucks me with his eyes open, as if he doesn't want to miss a single expression, a single smile.

He fucks me in a way that marks me forever, in a way that claims me, just as I've claimed him.

Only when I'm crying out his name again, only when I'm writhing beneath him, only when my body trembles in the grip of a final, epic orgasm…

Only then does he close his eyes and surrender, once and for all.

He comes with a shudder that rolls through his every

muscle, vibrating against me as we both fall headlong into bliss, letting that wild, untamed river carry us away.

* * *

We emerge slowly, one breath at a time, neither of us wanting the moment to end. But my hands are numb from being restrained for so long, and we're both in desperate need of a hot shower and some sleep.

Doc releases me from the binds, gently massaging my arms and pressing light kisses to each wrist. Blood rushes back into my fingers, making my hands tingle, but I like the feeling. It reminds me of everything we gave each other tonight.

Promises. Honesty. Vulnerability. Trust.

"Are you feeling all right?" he asks.

"Just sleepy and a little sore." I smile, barely stifling a yawn. "The good kind, I mean."

"Yes, well… There's one other thing we should probably get out in the open, just so there's no misunderstanding." He slides his hands into my hair, drawing me close. "I'm in love with you, my beautiful Star. I'll never make you doubt it again."

* * *

After a quick shower and a change of bedding, we fall into a deep sleep together. I don't know how many hours pass, but when I open my eyes again, I'm still wrapped up in his strong embrace, my back against his chest, his face buried in my hair, my arms and thighs aching with a delicious burn.

But I'm no longer lying in the antique iron bed.

I'm underwater, cold and swift and full of blood.

And I can't breathe.

ELEVEN

KIRIN

Nothing sobers up a drunken fool like a healthy dose of bad news, and by the time I finish filling Baz in on the details—including a new text from Cass about my sister's disappearing act and everything Stevie and Carly discovered beneath the library—he's cleaned up, coffeed up, and packed up, ready to follow me to the ends of the earth.

But for the moment, we're only going as far as the library—a quick detour en route to the portal at Time Out of Mind. I need to get the laptops from my office and—as much as I hate the idea of breaking my own security protocols—Stevie's research notebooks from the archives. Something tells me we're going to be stuck in Red Sands Canyon for the long haul, and unfortunately, our work on the prophecies can't wait.

"Fifteen minutes," I tell Baz as we creep around the side of the massive building, doing our best to stick to the shadows. Given the ominous warnings in Casey's note, we have to assume the library isn't safe—especially if Phaines's body is still in the basement. "If I'm not out by then, call the calvary."

"I *am* the calvary, asshole. If you're not out by then, I'm coming in after you." Baz hikes his duffel bag up on his shoulder, shaking his head. "On second thought, fuck off. I'm not letting you go in there alone. Lead the way."

"You need to stay out here and be my lookout."

"What good will a lookout do if the bad guys are in *there* instead of out *here*?" He grabs the back of my head and gives me a shake. "Come on, genius. Think about it. Phaines's body could still be inside. Which means Trello could be lurking around, or any of the other—how many is it now? A hundred?—enemies we've amassed this week. So stop trying to be a hero. We're a team, brother."

I let out a frustrated sigh, but he's right. As much as I hate putting us both at risk, splitting up is a bad idea.

"Stay behind me," I say. "And keep your mouth shut."

Without another word, he follows me in through the door that leads into my office.

Even before my eyes adjust to the darkness, I know something's wrong. Baz must sense it too; behind me, he tenses up for a fight.

Someone's in here, crouching behind my desk. The faint sound of breathing is a dead giveaway.

I call on my air magick, toppling a few books from the shelves behind them, hoping for a direct hit.

Bingo.

The criminal lets out a yelp, followed by a string of curses in a voice I'd recognized anywhere.

"*Casey*?" I flick on the lights just as she emerges from beneath the desk, rubbing her head. I barely have time to process the sight of her when the rest of the scene hits me—chairs tipped over, desk drawers dumped and tossed on the floor, papers scattered everywhere. The monitors are still on my desk, but my main computer tower and the two laptops are gone.

Anger burns through my gut, racing up my spine with a profound sense of betrayal. It fills me completely, hot and prickly, nearly choking off my air supply.

My own fucking sister. Even after everything we've been through, even after watching her wave a gun at my friends, even after Cass's warning about her vanishing from Red Sands... I never thought she'd stoop this low.

The bookshelves rattle as the anger inside me spikes, sending a few more tomes toppling to the ground.

"Turn the lights off!" Casey shout-whispers, gesturing wildly with her hands.

Rage and confusion cement me in place, but she's already moving past me, reaching for the wall switch. She hits the lights hard, bathing us in near-darkness once again.

"What the hell are you doing here?" she demands, keeping her voice low. For the first time since she climbed out from behind the desk, I notice the gun in her hand.

The words finally break free from the knot in my throat. "You're going to shoot me for walking into my own office?"

"You shouldn't be here." Casey sighs, then holsters her

weapon, her voice laced with defeat and exhaustion. "Neither of you. Go back to Red Sands and wait for me there."

"I'm not going anywhere until you tell me why you broke into my office." I try to hold on to my anger, but it's already dissipating. In its place, concern for my sister seeps in.

"Dickhead move on your part, Case." Baz drops his duffel and steps in front of me, crowding into her space, forcing her to look up to meet his eyes. He's got several inches on her, and right now he's just pissed off enough to be scary. "Trashing your own brother's office? Seriously? Have you heard of family therapy?"

Never one to be intimidated, Casey simply wrinkles her nose. "Are you *drunk*?"

"It's a long story," I say.

"Yeah, it goes a little something like this," Baz says, still looming over her. "Once upon a time, some crazy-ass bitches took me and my friends hostage at gunpoint, demanding we retrieve a magickal sword from the dream realm for them... Wait, stop me if you've heard this one before."

Casey doesn't back down. "We were possessed by Professor Phaines. I never would've—"

"We know." I hold up my hand, sparing us all another recap. "But that doesn't explain why you bolted from Red Sands with nothing but a cryptic note, and now you're breaking-and-entering, destroying Academy property, and stealing my shit. Where are my laptops?"

"I have no idea, Kirin. Goddess, I just got my body back

from a psychotic mage—not to mention one hell of a binding spell. And don't even get me started on Dr. Devane's bedside manner. Do they seriously allow that man around students? And now you're accusing me of stealing?"

"Correct me if I'm wrong," Baz says, glancing around at the disaster zone formerly known as my office, "but I believe this is what you agent-types call a smoking gun."

"It was like this when I got here." Casey finally steps away from Baz and heads back to the desk, her feet crunching over broken glass. Coffee mug? Picture frame? No idea, but I'm pretty sure none of my personal effects survived the ransacking.

She picks up the fallen books and places them back on the shelf, a futile gesture that nevertheless makes my heart hurt with longing. For her, for our family, for all the things I've missed.

"Why are you here at all?" I ask. "Why did you leave Red Sands before we even got there? Phaines is dead—he was murdered tonight by Trello."

If this last part surprises her, she doesn't show it. In fact, she has no reaction to this news at all.

"You knew," I say.

She turns back to the shelves, busying herself with arranging the books. "I needed to see your research, but apparently someone beat me to it—a scenario I was hoping to avoid."

"Why are you suddenly interested in my work? What about Eastman and Quintana? Are they in on this too?"

Anger simmers inside me again, threatening to erupt. "You could've been honest with me, Case. You could've—"

"There was no time. Goddess, there's still so much you don't know."

"So tell us!" Baz says, just as exasperated as I am.

"Not now. I need you both to leave. Get back to—"

"I'm not going anywhere," I say. "Ever since you got here, you've been sneaking around, asking all your prying questions while never sharing a single thing of relevance, despite the fact that all our lives are in danger. We could've come together on this. Compared notes, figured out—"

"Come *together*?" She lets out a bitter laugh, apparently no longer concerned about the noise. "For fuck's sake, Kirin. You ignored me for a decade. You put me in cold storage and never once looked back. Now you're mad because I didn't show up with a six-pack and a big smile, hoping we could pal around and sing a few campfire songs?"

I turn my back on her, unable to meet her eyes. I hate that she's right. I hate that I cut her out so completely, and instead of doing the same to me, she spent the last ten years walking around with a hole in her heart, wondering what the fuck happened. I hate myself for what I did, for what I'm still doing.

Every time I look at her, I see flashes of that little girl in the dream realm, the shiny blonde pigtails, the little bumblebee dress.

My dead parents.

Casey's tears dampening my shoulder.

But you didn't even say goodbye... Now they're dead, and you never even said goodbye...

My gut twists.

Deep down, I still love my sister. I will always love my sister.

But I don't trust her. Not fully.

I reach for a book from the top shelf—a doorstopper on symbols of wealth and prosperity in the Tarot—and flip it open, revealing a cutaway with four USB drives tucked inside.

I turn to her and offer it up.

"What's all this?" she asks, fingering the drives. "Backups?"

"You could've just asked me," I say, some old, leftover bullshit need to get the last word on the matter. "The good news is, whoever stole the computers is out of luck. There's no way they can crack my passwords—they won't even be able to boot up the systems. Everything's encrypted and coded to my personal magickal signature. Everything but these."

Casey narrows her eyes. "You keep sensitive research backups hidden in a book on your shelf, just sitting there for anyone to grab?"

"No one ever thinks to look there."

It's true. The entire office is trashed. Even part of the carpet is torn up from the floorboards; likely someone was looking for a floor safe or secret cache. But the drives remained secure, tucked into a dusty tome alongside a hundred other dusty tomes, completely unremarkable in the office of a research librarian.

My sister holds my gaze, fingers hovering over the drives, neither of us speaking for a long moment.

"I'm sorry," she finally whispers.

"So am I."

With a heavy sigh, she pulls her hand back, relinquishing her prize.

I set the book on the desk, blowing out a breath.

I still don't trust her—she's keeping secrets, and she's definitely up to something tonight.

But she didn't take the bait. Maybe she's not one of the bad guys after all.

"I'll explain *everything* later," she says. "I promise. But please listen to me on this. You and Baz need to leave campus right now. Take your research back to Red Sands and put it somewhere safe. Keep watch over Ani. And don't let anyone into the house that you don't completely trust."

"So that's it?" Baz asks.

"That's it for now."

"Right." He leans back against the wall, folding his arms over his chest. "We're gonna need a *little* more to go on here, Case."

Casey looks to me to put Baz in his place, but as far as I'm concerned, she hasn't earned full membership in the circle of trust.

"Where are you going?" I ask.

"To meet Agent Quintana and discuss our plan of

action."

"Here's your plan," Baz says. "Arrest Anna Trello. Lock that bitch up and throw away the key. Then light Phaines's dead ass on fire while you're at it."

"Despite what you may believe," she says, "Trello is on our side. So is Agent Quintana. Beyond that, I can't vouch for anyone."

A flicker of unease pings my chest. "Eastman?"

Casey's eyes blaze with raw anger, her jaw clenching. Wordlessly, she shakes her head.

"Are you kidding me?" I ask. "Not three weeks ago, you stood in this very room, singing the man's praises. Said he was a good man. Dedicated. Smart." I glare at her, needing her to push back, just this once. To tell me he *is* a good, dedicated man.

Because if Casey no longer has faith in her boss—a man she openly admired, a man who's worked for the APOA for decades, a man who swore to uphold the laws of our magickal society at all costs...

"I was wrong," she says. "That ends now."

Wrong. The word burns through my chest, twisting inside me.

"Kirin." She puts her hand on my forearm and meets my eyes, her own soft and pleading. "We'll talk more at Red Sands. I'll be there as soon as I can."

My instinct is to fight her on this, but I'm way out of my depth. My head is spinning, I'm fucking exhausted, and we need to get back to the others and regroup.

"Let me just grab a few things from the archives," I say. "Then we'll head out."

"Archives? What could you possibly need tonight?"

"The primary sources for the prophecies. Melissa Milan's journals, Stevie's translations, some of the other magickal books we've been working with."

"But... but what about your backups?" Casey asks. Alarm tinges her voice, filling me with new dread.

"We really need the source material."

Casey shakes her head, eyes glazing with something that looks a lot like sympathy.

My heart jackhammers in my chest, my mouth going dry. "What happened?"

"I'm sorry, Kirin. Whoever stole your computers... They hit the archives too."

"When you say hit the archives..."

"There's nothing left but the furniture. Everything else was completely stripped. I'm sorry."

Casey's phone buzzes in her pocket, and she finally looks away, pulling it out to check the text.

"Who is it?" Baz asks.

"Quintana. Time's up, guys. I have to go." Casey thumbs a quick reply, then puts the phone away and heads for the door, turning back to me with a final plea. "Promise me you'll go straight back to Red Sands?"

I nod mutely, watching her slip out of the office and into the dark library beyond, feeling like I've just lost a piece of my soul.

"That sister of yours is a real charmer." Baz grabs his

duffel bag, then clamps a hand over my shoulder. "We're not seriously going back to Red Sands, right?"

"Not on your fucking life." I scoop the backups out of the Tarot book, shove them into my pocket, and follow Agent Casey Appleton out into the lion's den.

TWELVE

STEVIE

Panic seizes my limbs as the rushing water sucks me under. Far above, a red light glows, soft and inviting, calling me home.

Lungs burning, desperate for a gulp of air, I fight against the current and reach for that light with everything I have, but I'm no match for the vicious churn. I try once more, only for my legs to cramp up and freeze. I'm utterly paralyzed, engulfed by icy red darkness.

Bright spots dance before my eyes, and my mouth opens in desperate confusion, the cold, dark water rushing in to steal the last of my air...

An arm snakes around my midsection and clamps down tight. Adrenaline spikes in a hot rush, and suddenly I'm rocketing upward, bursting through the surface. Air rushes into my lungs with a force so strong and fierce, my first full breath burns like fire.

"Don't fight me!" The man orders from behind, his voice

dark and urgent. I try to place it, but the sound of the rushing water is too loud, too disorienting.

"Damn it, Stevie!" He tightens his hold, nearly crushing me against his rock-solid chest. "Stop struggling! I'm not going to hurt you!"

A trick. It has to be.

Half-drowned, half-rabid with fear, I kick and fight, clawing at my attacker's arm. I dig my nails in, flailing like a beached fish, kicking his shins and thighs, gulping up as much air as I can before he drags me back down.

But the churning water renders my attacks useless, and my captor's grip is too strong. The harder I fight, the harder he holds on, draining my reserves.

The current thrashes me from all sides, filling my mouth with rust-red water that makes me sputter and cough. My whole body goes limp in his arms.

"Relax," the man says, his mouth close to my ear, his grip loosening just enough to let me breathe. "I've got you. You're safe. I promise I won't let you go."

His voice is less urgent now, the deep, resonant sound of it almost comforting as he navigates us through the water.

With little strength to do much else, I reach out for his energy. It's calming and warm. Protective, just like his touch.

My heart suddenly thaws, the numbness receding from my extremities.

I know that energy. That voice. The warmth of his touch...

"Doc!"

Recognition shatters the spell of irrational fear, and tears of relief sting my eyes. I squeeze his arm—gently this time—to let him know I understand.

Still holding me close, he raises a hand and recites a water spell. The churning abates, and the water—frothy and furious just moments ago—settles into a gentle flow.

He guides us to the shore, and together we climb out, dragging ourselves to the top of a muddy bank. I sit down hard and pull my knees to my chest, desperate to ease the chill.

"Goddess, Stevie." Doc wraps me in his arms, pressing a kiss to the top of my head. "I thought I was losing you."

"I'm sorry I attacked you." I snuggle into the embrace, inhaling his familiar scent—salt and moonlight and mystery, his own intoxicating mix. "I don't do well with water. Especially the rushing kind."

"You're safe now. That's all that matters." He rubs his hand up and down my back, chasing off the last of the chill.

Despite our unexpected soaking, the night air is actually warm and pleasant, the scent of mud and water and living things filling me with a sense of normality and relief. We're outdoors, away from all signs of civilization. Still breathing. Still alive.

Glancing down at the water that nearly ended me, I finally realize where we are.

"The River of Blood and Sorrow," I say, and Doc lets out a soft hum of agreement.

The last time I saw it up close was at that back-to-school party where Carly and her friends tried to drown me. If it wasn't for my owl bursting forth and scaring the hell out of everyone—and Baz pulling me out after I took a tumble—they might've succeeded.

But there's no owl tonight. No party. And as I finally take notice of the heavy, elaborate dress clinging to my body—red instead of its usual white—I know why.

We're not at the real River of Blood and Sorrow. We're in the dream realm.

A new shiver takes hold, rattling me to the core.

"He knows," I whisper. "Judgment knows we're here."

"We don't know that for certain," Doc says evenly, though he can't hide the concern flickering through his energy.

"Lala told me we leave a piece of ourselves behind every time we visit the dream realm. He obviously knows I'm afraid of rushing water—it's what killed my parents. He's using it to prey on my guilt. They died protecting me, and…"

No. I close my eyes, staving off the barrage of memories. I won't let him manipulate me again. I can't. Our very survival depends on it.

"How did we get here?" I ask. "Did you take a potion?"

Dream sharing isn't easy. Last time, the guys and I had to form a blood bond and drink Professor Broome's potion. Then Doc guided us through a dream meditation designed to keep us together in the realm—and even then, we didn't all arrive in the same place.

So how the hell did Doc and I end up falling into the realm—*together*—without even trying?

"I'm the Moon Arcana, Stevie," he says. "My magick is

deeply aligned with the realm of dreams and intuition. In that sense, I *am* the potion."

I pull out of his embrace and meet his steely gray gaze. "And the blood bond?"

"After what we shared tonight, emotionally as well as physically... I suppose nothing else was needed." He cups my face, his eyes holding the red-hot memories of our passionate night together.

My body holds the same memories, my skin still tingling everywhere his lips touched me, everywhere his commanding hands took control. Doc's right—tonight, we formed a bond as deep and powerful as two people can. Add his intense Moon energy into the mix...

Yeah. We *really* should've known better.

Yeah. I *really* wish he'd touch me like that again.

But as much as I'd love to lose myself in those deliciously overwhelming sensations, it's a different set of memories that wins out now, dark and malicious and ugly.

Judgment, torturing us with the Wand of Flame and Fury.

Judgment, devouring an innocent child, blood soaking his robes.

Judgment, incinerating the men I love, only to resurrect them and do it all over again.

Called to confess, called to atone. Beg for your flesh, your blood, and your bones...

Unworthy! Unworthy! Unworthy!

"We need to leave," I warn. "Now. The others don't even know we're gone. We could end up trapped here for

—" I gasp, a new realization slamming into me. "Doc, we're in the dream realm! We can find Ani!"

I move to get to my feet, but Doc stops me, his grip on my arm unyielding.

"You said it yourself, Stevie. We can't linger here. We need to find our way back—the sooner the better."

"Without even *trying*? Are you serious right now?" I stare at him, incredulous. We've been desperate to reach Ani all night, and nothing has worked. No spells, no potions, no prayers. Now we're in the same damn realm, and Doc's ready to throw in the towel?

"If Ani's after the Wand," he says, his calm demeanor ebbing into fresh anger, "he's nowhere near the river. And even if he were, the realm is constantly shifting, constantly reforming. We could no more pinpoint his location than that of a lone pebble beneath the Towers of Breath and Blade. In fact, we'd probably have better luck with the latter."

I yank my arm out of his grip and stand up. "That's no reason not to try."

"No?" Doc jumps to his feet, crowding right back into my space, towering over me. "Then here's another one. You could *die*. All indications are that a death in this realm results in a death in our own—I can't risk that."

"So you're willing to risk Ani's life, but not mine?"

"The best thing we can do for Ani is find our own way home so we can be there, alive and healthy, when he gets back."

"Nice deflection." I cross my arms over my chest, the

cold settling back into my bones. "We can't just leave him here—not when we're so close. We have to at least try, even if it means risking our lives. We took an oath, Doc. And more than that, I... I love him."

"As. Do. I." His eyes burn with fury, and he reaches for me again, grabbing my shoulders. "Damn it, Stevie. I would risk my own life without hesitation. For any one of you, over no more than a *shred* of a chance. But I'll *not* risk yours. Searching for him here... It's a fool's errand. Deep down, you *must* know that."

I glare at him, tears stinging my eyes even as the anger recedes from his.

"A fool's errand is still an errand!" I say. "Forward momentum. Action. *Something* other than standing around sprinkling fairy dust and hoping he makes it back on his own."

"Not action—distraction. One that would give us the illusion of forward momentum while we chased our tails through this nightmare realm, abandoning the people who need us most at a time when we're all holding on by a thread."

"But... I just... I can't..." Words fail me, and my head drops low, tears spilling as the fire fades from my blood.

He's right, of course. He always is.

Doc slides his arms around me, and I lean into him, burying my face against his chest.

"I hate everything about this," he says, stroking my back. "Not the least of which is telling you no when you've got your mind set on something."

"And I hate that you're always right."

"Well, not *always*." He pulls back, hooking a finger under my chin. Then, with a teasing smile, "Ninety-nine percent of the time, perhaps. But not always."

"Kirin says eighty-four percent of statistics are made up on the spot."

"Not this one." He dips his head, pressing a soft kiss to my mouth. "One *hundred* percent of the time, I will do what needs to be done to keep you safe. Even if it means you'll hate me for it."

It's always been that way, I realize now. Not just for me, but with all the guys.

Each of us has our strengths, our charms, and our skills —magickal as well as mundane. But Doc is the one making the hard decisions. The one doing all the dirty work behind the scenes, saying all the things no one else has the balls to say, risking his very soul so the rest of us don't have to.

His is a quiet and determined strength, fierce and unwavering, often unacknowledged.

And though he'll never admit it, bearing the weight of our collective burdens costs him a little more of himself every day.

My heart fills with deep love and admiration. I lay my hands against his chest and smile up at him, marveling at the fact that I can touch him so freely now, so openly.

Through a soft smile, I whisper, "I could *never* hate you, Cassius Devane."

He tries for another smile of his own, but it falters quickly, a familiar shame burning through his energy. Turning away from my touch, he shakes his head and says, "You don't know me well enough to make a proclamation like that."

"I may not know all your stories," I say, reaching for his hand and pulling him back toward me. "Or your history. But I know your heart, Doc. That's one thing you *can't* hide from me."

He lifts my hand to his mouth and kisses my palm, whispering against my skin. "And that, my Star, may be our downfall."

The sadness in his eyes makes me ache for him—for all the pain he's endured, for all the guilt he still carries. But just as I sense the shame and loss hiding within him, I also know it's not the time to push. He's still learning what it means to truly, deeply trust.

And he's got a long way to go.

So do we, if we have any hope of escaping this place.

"We'll see about that," I tease, sensing we both need a bit of levity. "So what's our next move, Mr. Ninety-Nine Percent Right?"

This gets a small laugh, some of the light returning to his eyes. "I suppose we just make our way back. Right?"

I nod, but we both know it won't be that simple—this isn't a regular dream that will fade away the moment we wake up in the morning. Though it wasn't our intention, we arrived here magickally, just like the guys and I did last time.

Getting back means our souls need to reconnect with

our bodies, hopefully without the interference of our enemies, and I have no idea how to make that happen.

So for now, we just walk.

We're about ten steps along the riverbank when the air shimmers like a sheer curtain before us, wrapping us in warm, tingling magick. It recedes as quickly as it arrived, leaving us both fully dry, styled, and runway-ready.

My blood-red gown shimmers beneath the moonlight, my hair woven into the same elaborate style as last time, complete with purple hyacinths. The requisite bouquet of black dahlias adds the finishing touch.

I let out a deep sigh and toss the flowers to the ground. "Great. More tricks."

Doc, who's now dressed in a sky-blue button-down shirt and black slacks with faint gray pinstripes, can only gape.

"Don't," I warn, sensing the compliment on his lips.

"I can't help it. Goddess, you're absolutely *stunning*, like some sort of vampire gothic princess of old. Only, not old. And really much more of a queen than a princess, if we're being honest."

"Aww. I bet you say that to all the human sacrifices."

"The... what?"

"Well, when it comes to Starla Milan's dream-realm fashion picks, it's less 'Goth Barbie's dream wedding' and more 'sacrificial gown worn by women deemed unfit to carry the magick within.'"

His eyes darken, lips curling in disgust.

"Apparently it was a whole *thing* back then," I explain.

"They'd doll you up in the dress and toss your sparkly ass into the fire, hoping it would prove to the elemental deities and the First Fool that magick was more important to them than a woman's life." A shudder rolls through me, but I shake it off. "Lala told me it's symbolic—I keep showing up here in some form of this dress because deep down, I don't believe I'm worthy of my magick. I'm—"

"Get rid of it. Now." His eyes go from dark storm to raging inferno in a heartbeat. Without waiting for a response, he hastily unbuttons his shirt, revealing the glorious muscles I had the distinct pleasure of being pinned beneath only hours ago.

I'm still staring at him, equally confused and turned on, when he fists the bodice of my dress in both hands and tears it right down the middle, shredding the delicate lace and casting sequins all along the riverbank. The skirt drops away, leaving me bare in his presence once again.

Despite its elaborate construction, the remnants of my dress look like tissue paper in Doc's strong hands.

Goddess, he's fucking crazy.

Goddess, I'm fucking wet.

"Cassius Devane, ladies and gentlemen," I tease. "Proving once again that no article of clothing is safe in the hands of a mental magicks professor with control issues."

Ignoring the jab, he strips out of his shirt and wraps it around my shoulders, gesturing for me to put my arms through the sleeves. I do as he asks, relishing in the warmth of his body that still lingers inside. Dream realm or not, it smells like him—a scent forever emblazoned on my senses, especially after tonight.

He takes great care to fasten each button, his fingers brushing softly against my skin as he works his way up to the top. When it's all done up, he places his hands on my shoulders and lowers his mouth to mine, gifting me with a sweet kiss.

"You are *more* than worthy to carry the magick within you, my Star," he whispers. "You were *born* worthy, and every day you walk this earth, in this realm or the next, you utterly shine."

He kisses me again, slow and deep, a promise that unlocks something inside me, finally setting it free. I feel my heart expanding in my chest, my blood singing with magick.

He's right. I *am* worthy of this. And though I'm still learning my way through it, stumbling over challenges and facing down what feels like impossible odds and yes, screwing up more than a few things along the way, I'm growing into it too. I'm making it my own. I'm embracing it.

My parents wanted to protect me from this life, to shield me from the perils and pitfalls of magick and the Academy. But somehow, I know—really, truly know—they'd be proud of me too.

They *are* proud of me.

"Stevie. Look." Doc pulls away from our kiss and glances at the ground between us, where several of the hyacinth buds have fallen from my hair. The red-brown earth swallows them whole, and in their place, yellow roses bloom, their sweetness mingling with the spicy scent of frankincense—a combination I've always associated with my mother.

"Mom," I whisper, tears of gratitude blurring my vision. I've no sooner said the word when I feel her otherworldly touch on my cheek, followed by a new weight settling into my shirt pocket.

Tarot cards.

Doc lets out a quick breath. "I'm not sure I'll ever get used to that."

Blinking away my tears, I retrieve the first card. It's the Six of Cups, depicting a man holding a chalice, gazing out his window at two children playing outside. Overhead, clouds gather, but the children are none the wiser.

I often associate this card with nostalgia; sometimes it's a message to look back on memories with fondness and gratitude. Other times, it's a warning about the dangers of living in the past.

Tonight, it's the latter.

My throat tightens, and immediately my mind's eye flashes to a photograph of two young boys, one dark-haired and one blond, arms slung over shoulders as if they're the best of friends. It's Doc and his brother Xavier—the photo he showed me before Harvest Eve dinner when he told me about his brother's passing.

I glance at the Tarot card again, this time at the man. There's love in his eyes, but a deep sadness lingers too. Regret. Unlike the cups outside, overflowing with the children's toys, his chalice holds something different. Something that speaks to me of Doc's whiskey bottles—the medicine he so often relies on to get through the night.

Reaching into my shirt pocket, I fish out the second card.

Judgment.

"What is it?" Doc asks, his energy turning tense. I almost don't want to show him, but this message was meant for both of us.

"Doc, being here... We're not just facing the physical dangers of losing our soul's connection to the body. I told you that Judgment already knows we're here—I'm sure he can sense our comings and goings at this point. But if he actually finds us... If our paths cross..." I shake my head, handing over the cards. "He gets into our minds. More than his wand, that's his greatest weapon. He digs through our memories and uncovers the worst, most terrifying ones, twisting them into even darker versions, forcing us to relive our greatest pains and regrets. And as Baz has proven all too well, when we wake up from this realm, we don't always leave the nightmares behind."

Doc's face pales, his hands trembling as he stares at the cards. He doesn't need me to translate.

After a beat, the cards vanish.

Doc wipes his hand on his pants as if he can remove the stain of the Tarot's ominous warning, then reaches for my hand again. "So let's be sure he *doesn't* cross our path."

Keeping me in a firm grip, he leads us along the muddy banks, following the direction of the river to what we hope is a way out—or at least a way to avoid Judgment long enough for us to wake up and return home.

After what feels like an hour, we reach a small sandstone cave, its wide mouth pulsing with the same ruby-red light I saw in the water.

We pause at the entrance, both of us trying to peer inside. But despite the glow, I can't see beyond the first couple of feet. Everything else is couched in shadow.

"Do you know what it is?" I ask. "If it leads somewhere?"

Doc shakes his head. "I've never explored this far north."

"Do you think it actually exists? In our realm, I mean?"

"It's possible, though I'm not sure about that red glow." He considers it another moment, then shrugs. "Should we check it out?"

Before I can answer, my skin erupts in goosebumps, and a deep sense of unease crawls down my spine. I cock an ear, but other than the river and a few chatty night birds, the land around us is silent.

"Something is off," I say.

Doc sighs, tightening his grip on my hand. "I feel it too. I just don't know whether it's better to follow the river's path, or head into the cave and get out of sight."

"I think he's close." I take a deep breath, then look up into his eyes, the sense of unease quickly turning to dread. It pools in my stomach, as cold and sticky as raw dough.

The back of my throat tastes of ash.

It's no longer a matter of *if*, but when.

"When we see him," I say urgently, "if he gets a hold of either one of us, just remember—whatever happens, whatever remnants of the past he tries to dredge up—none of it is real. *Nothing* in this place is real."

"*You're* real," he says, brushing his knuckles across my jaw. "As long as I hold on to that, I'll—"

His words cut off abruptly, his mouth going slack, eyes filling with pain.

"Doc?" I reach for his face, trying to get him to meet my gaze, but it's like he doesn't even know I'm here. "What's happening? Doc! *Cassius!*"

He drops to his knees and clutches at his heart, his whole body shuddering as he fights to catch his breath.

And there on his bare chest, right behind his desperately clawing fingers, a fiery red wound blazes to life.

XX. The mark of Dark Judgment.

THIRTEEN

KIRIN

Even at this late hour, a handful of diehard grad students occupy the library, tucked into research cubbies with ancient manuscripts and contraband coffee drinks, diligently checking their facts and compiling research, cramming their heads full of esoteric knowledge on everything from magickal correspondences to poisons to the myths and legends that form the backbone of our beliefs.

The soft glow of their lamps, the smell of old books, the muted click of laptop keyboards, the singular beauty of the architecture... All of it feels like home. The academy library has been my sanctuary for as long as I can remember. It literally saved my life.

But tonight, it fills me with uncertainty. A deep sense of foreboding snakes around my heart, squeezing tight.

I take a steadying breath, willing away the darkness, forcing my attention back to Casey.

Moving through the main level like a one-woman locust

swarm, she has no trouble dispersing the lingering students, likely employing some elaborate APOA scare tactics.

Run along, good little witches and mages! Go home and lock your doors! Don't leave your candles burning unattended! And most of all, don't let the bogeymen steal your magick!

Hovering in the shadows with Baz just inside the main entrance, I let out a deep sigh. *Scare tactics.* Right. As if we're not facing down the biggest *actual* threat against the magickal community in centuries. Maybe even millennia.

"You good, brother?" Baz asks, his voice low in the darkness.

"Not exactly. But lucky for you, we don't have time for another therapy session tonight."

"Dodged a bullet, then." He cracks a smile, but his firm grip on the back of my neck tells me he's not screwing around. We're in this together, wherever the night takes us.

Goddess, what a fucking shit show. As much as I want to fully trust my sister, my insides are still vibrating with a toxic mix of anger and fear and the hot, prickly paranoia that comes from being violated. The archives... I still can't believe it. Melissa's life's work, Stevie's legacy, her deepest connection to her deceased mother—not to mention most of the hand-written work Stevie herself amassed—it's all gone. And for what? To what ends? Who's to blame? Was it Eastman? Trello? Some other agent provocateur we can only guess at?

For all her talk of our safety, Casey left us with very little to go on.

Right now, the only thing keeping her from earning a permanent position on my shit list is the fact that she didn't take my backups. Whoever stole the primary research must believe they can benefit from Stevie's translations, or prevent us from doing so. Either way, if Casey was in on the sabotage, she would've swiped the drives out of that book in an instant.

That's what I keep telling myself, anyway. That Casey really is on our side.

"Here we go," Baz whispers, nodding toward the back of the library, where Agent Quintana has just stepped out of the shadows carrying a black duffel bag. "Looks like she's meeting Quintana, just like she said."

"Another point for Casey." I don't bother hiding the relief in my voice.

Their conversation is indecipherable at this distance, but judging from the urgent gestures, they're not exactly meeting up for APOA happy hour.

After a brief catch-up, they split up and do a quick sweep of the back area for any lingering witches or mages. Apparently satisfied they're in the clear, they head down the corridor behind the elevators, disappearing into the darkness.

Doesn't take a genius to figure out where they're going —Casey all but admitted she already knew Trello murdered Phaines, which means she knows where the body is. The question is—why are they going down there at all? If it were simply to tape off the crime scene, collect the evidence, and remove the body, why all the sneaking around? Shouldn't they be calling this in to the higher-ups at APOA?

Is it possible that Trello returned, and now she's down in the basement waiting for them so they can concoct their cover story?

And what's going on with Eastman? Casey intimated he was on the wrong side of this, but what does that mean, exactly?

How deep does this shit run?

We wait a few more minutes until we're sure Casey and Agent Quintana are out of range, then we follow the same path, keeping our eyes peeled for any surprises. Casey did a good job securing the area, though—there's not another witch or mage in sight.

After stashing Baz's duffel bag in a supply closet, we head straight for the big metal door at the end of the corridor. Overhead, the busted security cameras hang at odd angles, totally useless, just like Stevie said.

Slowly, I inch open the big metal door, pausing to listen. Only silence echoes back.

Fairly certain Casey and Agent Quintana have made it into the inner chamber, I gesture for Baz to follow me inside, letting the door sweep closed behind us. On soft footsteps, we creep down to the basement in near-total darkness, sticking to the walls as best we can, not wanting to risk even one second with a flashlight.

We pass by towering bookcases, each one crammed with piles of old manuscripts and discarded books. My heart breaks a little for all the lost knowledge, for the neglect, but

I press on. We need to find that hidden door. We need to see what my sister's up to. We need some damn answers, and for the first time in my life, I'm pretty sure we won't find them in the dusty pages of these forgotten tomes.

"There," Baz whispers, pointing at a metal desk across the room. "There's a glow around the wall, just behind it."

I peer over the top of my glasses, and sure enough, I spot it. A faint light illuminating the edge of a door no more than four feet high. On the right-hand side, there's a small keypad.

"Fuck," I say. "I don't have the code." I pull out my phone, debating whether to text Cass and Stevie, but Baz saves me the trouble.

"I've got this," he says, grin glinting in the darkness.

"When the hell did you get the code? You were pissing yourself drunk half the night."

"We don't need a code." He grabs my arm, then presses his other hand against the adjacent stone wall. "Me and rocks? We're tight as hell."

He whispers a quick spell, and a sparkling purple light illuminates the darkness, enveloping us both.

"Brace yourself," he warns, just as the portal magick takes hold. "I don't know what's waiting for us on the other side."

The magick tugs on my gut, and then we're hurtling through space-time, dumped at the base of a narrow staircase onto a packed dirt floor. Quickly and quietly, we scramble to our feet, then slip into the shadows against a side wall, taking in the scene.

The stench of death hangs heavy in the air, turning my stomach, but I force myself to stay focused.

We're in the chamber below the storage room, one more level down. The space here is brighter, illuminated by the glow of dozens upon dozens of magick jars and bottles. On one of the taller bookcases, every jar on every shelf swirls with white, opalescent magick, mesmerizing and beautiful.

Essence, just like Stevie and Carly described.

Behind the shelves, the telltale bulletin board hangs ominously, every square inch tacked with tiny baggies of hair that belongs to the owners of the magickal essence—students that were attacked on campus and stripped of their powers.

Rage roils inside me, and I close my eyes and take a deep breath, ignoring the rotten stench, forcing myself to calm down. I can't risk getting upset in here. According to Cass's text, Professor Maddox believes there's a chance we can save the students' magick. One ill-timed Hulk-out from me could shatter the jars, destroying the essences and permanently depriving the students of their most precious gifts.

Faint murmuring at the far end of the room catches our attention, and Baz and I scoot along the wall, trying to pinpoint exactly where it's coming from. I've just spotted the inner chamber—the one where Stevie and Carly discovered Phaines in the hospital bed—when Casey and Quintana step out of it, their voices growing louder.

Baz and I scurry back into the shadows, crouching down behind a utility shelf to watch the scene unfold.

"She finished it, just like she said she would." Casey peels off a pair of latex gloves and drops them into an evidence bag Quintana holds open. "He's dead."

"And you're sure it's not a spell?" he asks, sealing the bag and labeling it with a Sharpie. He kneels down to where his duffel bag sits on the dirt floor and tucks the evidence inside.

"All the magickal signatures are gone. He's definitely dead, James." Casey leans against the wall and closes her eyes, her shoulders slumping. I don't need Stevie's empathic abilities to know what she must be feeling—my sister and I have a lot of the same wiring. Exhaustion—that much is obvious. Anger and disgust over what Phaines did to her. Determination to do her job and do it well, despite her boss's apparent treachery. Conflict, confusion, uncertainty—all of it likely churning an endless spin-cycle in her head.

As eager as she might've been to take the Academy assignment, there's no way Casey was prepared for this. None of us were.

"You trust her?" Quintana asks, and Casey nods. I can only assume they're talking about Trello.

He gets to his feet. "Then I guess we need to call it in and start bagging him up. Make it official."

"James." Casey opens her eyes and meets his gaze, taking a step closer. "Last chance. Are you *sure* you're on board with this? What I'm asking of you—"

"Is no less than I'd ask of *you*, Agent—to have your partner's back. The fact that you *keep* asking me... Hell, Case. At this point, it's damn near insulting."

"Fair enough." Casey's tone is all business, but her smile shines with relief.

I have to admit, my respect for Quintana just leveled up a notch.

"Official story?" he asks.

"Anonymous tip. Reports of a disturbance in the library after hours." She glances at her phone. "We cleared out the last of the students about fifteen minutes ago, so let's wait another fifteen before we call it in. I don't want the times overlapping—we can't risk any of them contradicting the story."

"Good call. Gives us more time to do another sweep down here. Far as I can tell, Trello didn't leave a trace, but we should take another look to confirm."

"Let's pack up the essences and personal effects first. I don't want any of that mishandled or lost—not if there's a chance we can still heal those students."

"You believe it?"

"Trello seems to think so."

"Again, I have to ask—"

"Yes, I trust her, James. I may not agree with all her methods, and I was slow to warm up at first. But after this, I believe—and I'm talking gut-level here—she's got the students' best interests at heart. She cares about them. Cares about her faculty too."

"And your brother—"

"Is not on the list of approved conversational topics."

I try not to take it personally. It's not like I've been super eager to talk about her, either.

"Noted," he says. "You want photos?"

"No time. We need to get this stuff back to your house in Red Sands—I'm thinking that's the safest place right now. Once Trello makes contact again, we'll figure out our next steps."

"I'm on packing duty," Agent Quintana says, heading for a bookcase stacked with file boxes. He grabs one off the top and dumps out the paperwork, then carries the empty box to the shelves holding the essence. "You deal with the stiff."

Casey laughs. "You really need to work on your dead body issues."

"Hey now. We made a deal in training, remember? I carry the heavy shit. You handle the stiffs."

"For fuck's sake," Baz whispers next to me. "Get a room."

I elbow him in the ribs, then shift positions, trying to prevent my legs from going numb. Unless we want to out ourselves, sounds like we're going to be here a while. Might as well get comfortable.

I send a quick text to Cass with an update on the situation, then Baz and I settle in for the long haul. Fortunately, Agent Quintana and Casey work quickly and efficiently, and by the time she's cleared Phaines's room of anything incriminating, Quintana's got all the important jars and baggies of hair secured in a few of the file boxes, along with some relevant spellbooks he found.

"Let's take the boxes up to the main storage area first," she says. "Put them somewhere out of sight. Then I'll call it in and we'll start taping off the area. We'll need to seal off the entrances to the main building as well—I don't want anyone from the Academy nosing around in here."

"Sounds like a plan." He grabs two of the boxes and she takes another, following him up the narrow staircase to the next level.

Certain they're gone, we get to our feet.

"What's our move?" Baz asks. "Set Phaines's dead ass on fire?"

"And fuck up my sister's investigation? We'll never hear the end of it." I force out a quiet laugh, but the truth is, I don't want to even *look* at that traitor. Because that's all it would take—one look. One look, and I'd be losing my shit, bringing the whole damn place down on our heads.

"We need to get back to Red Sands," I say. "Sounds like Casey and Quintana are headed there too—we'll catch up with them later. Can you portal us?"

"Not all the way home—I'm running low on fuel."

"Just get us outside, then. We'll use the portal at Time Out of Mind."

He takes one last look around the place, barely suppressing a shudder. "Goddess, if I never see a creepy-ass basement again, it'll be too fucking soon."

He grabs my arm and calls on his earth energy. The first twinges of purple magick have just appeared before us when a commotion explodes near the top of the staircase.

Baz drops the spell. "What the fuck?"

"Casey!" Quintana shouts. "Behind you!"

We bolt for the stairs, but before we can figure out what's happening, a flash of blinding yellow light explodes on top of us.

And then all hell breaks loose.

FOURTEEN

CASS

I tear down the mud-soaked banks of the river, ignoring the burn in my calves, the wild thud in my chest as I charge through the darkness. Minutes? Hours? Time means nothing here, and I've lost all sense of direction too.

All I know is I *must* find her.

One minute, Stevie was holding my hands, imploring me to heed her warnings about the dream realm, and the next minute, she was gone, slipping away like water through my fingers.

My heart burned at the loss—I damn near forgot how to breathe. But just before the darkness took me, her face appeared in my mind again. Her voice, urging me to fight. I staggered to my feet, and something told me to run. That I'd find her, if only I didn't stop searching.

"Stevie!" I call out now, scaring off a few bats nestled beneath a rocky overhang. "Where *are* you? Stevie!"

I stop running only long enough to listen.

There's no response. There's never any response.

"Starla Milan, where are you?" I shout, the echo of my voice a mockery. Deep in my chest, my heart burns again, shooting fire through my veins with every beat. "Stevie!"

"She's probably not coming back," someone says, a small voice cutting through the darkness. "They never come back."

"Who's there?" I ask.

"It's true. They don't."

I follow the sound further down the river's path. Just around the next bend, I find a small boy seated on the riverbank, thin and pale, digging in the muck with an old porcelain bowl. Water seeps up through the rivets he's made in the mud, red and viscous between his fingers, and my stomach churns.

For a brief moment, he looks like a ghoul digging into a rotting corpse.

I close my eyes and take a deep breath, steadying myself. When I open my eyes again, the boy is no longer a monster. Just an abandoned child playing in the mud.

"What do you mean, they never come back?" I ask.

"He takes them. Well, not the little ones. The little ones he eats. But the big ones he takes."

He says this with such confidence, it's hard not to take him at his word, despite the fact that my mind rails against it.

Just a little boy afraid of the dark. Dreams and shadows, that's all...

"He hasn't eaten you, though, has he?" I crouch down

beside him, careful not to get too close. "Which means you must be either very strong or very clever. Perhaps both."

The boy doesn't respond, doesn't even look my way. His fixation on the porcelain bowl sends a frisson of dread through my chest. It's rough and chipped on the edges, stained black inside. I can only imagine what sort of dark rituals it was used for before he adopted it as his toy.

"He takes them," he says again, this time with a simple shrug of the shoulder, as though he couldn't care less whether I believe it or not.

"*Who* takes them? Someone you know?"

"The druid."

Instinct pushes me to my feet, and I take a step backward, Stevie's voice an ominous echo in my mind.

He knows. Judgment knows we're here...

He gets into our minds... digs through our memories and uncovers the worst, most terrifying ones, twisting them... forcing us to relive our greatest pains and regrets...

Whatever happens, whatever remnants of the past he tries to dredge up—none of it is real. Nothing *in this place is real...*

This child isn't real. His words, his ghoulish features, the blood on his hands... It can't be...

"You're going to take it, aren't you?" The boy's image flashes before my eyes, ghoulish for an instant, then back to a lost little child once again. "He said you'd take it from me."

I fight to keep the tremor from my voice. The weakness. "Take what?"

He hangs his head low and thrusts his hands upward, presenting the porcelain bowl like an offering.

Leave, a voice warns inside me, distant and vague. Fading.

I can't leave. Not until I find... What was it? I could've sworn I came here searching for someone. Something. Was it this?

I glance down at the bowl, the inside gleaming in the moonlight with a sheen of magick I hadn't noticed before. I take the offering, my hands warming, power tingling across my palms. On closer inspection, I see that it's not porcelain at all.

It's bone.

Filed smooth in places, the outside is carved with an intricate pattern of pentacles, elaborate Celtic spirals, and alchemical symbols, many of which I don't recognize. That it's old and powerful is obvious; its magick is so strong, it's nauseating, yet I can't deny its magnetism. It calls to something ancient and powerful within me. Something dangerous.

I close my eyes, opening myself up fully to the call of its intense magick. Inside, my blood sings in response, my heart beating wildly, my mind reverberating with the sound of waves crashing and the deep, bone-chilling cry of a lone wolf...

"But it's mine," the boy says softly. Desperately. "Please don't take it from me. It's all I have left."

The emptiness and hopelessness in his voice weighs heavy, instantly cooling the magick inside me.

I open my eyes, taking in the sight of him once again. He still hasn't met my gaze, but beneath a layer of mud and grime, he looks to be about eight, with blond hair and dimples. He wears the clothing of a much healthier boy, his shirt hanging loose off his frame.

Where are his parents? How did he end up here? How did this sacred vessel come to rest in his possession?

"Where did you find it?" I ask.

"I don't remember."

"I have no desire to take this from you, but this bowl... It's not a toy."

"It's not a bowl either."

I glance down at the object in my hands, my thumbs running over the rough, scalloped edges. The feeling is so foreign, yet familiar, almost like...

Teeth.

My eyes widen, and I take another look.

He's right—it's not a bowl. It's a human skull.

I'm holding the top half of a human skull. And it's as old as the river itself.

Realization grips me hard, stealing my breath.

"The Chalice of Blood and Sorrow," I whisper.

The boy finally looks up and meets my eyes, the sight of him stopping my heart cold.

Xavier.

Chalice forgotten, I drop it into the mud as my deceased brother rises to his feet. He transforms before my eyes, aging from a boy to a teenager in an instant. When he finally turns to face me full on, the sight of him is so horrible, so devastating, I stumble back, desperate to get away.

His skull is collapsed on one side, red-black blood spilling from the massive wound, gushing like the river itself. It leaks into his mouth, down his chin, staining his shirt. His eyes remain fixed on mine, glassy and dark and lifeless.

It's precisely how I found him, shot dead by his own hand.

Driven to it by mine.

Decades collapse in a heartbeat. The bones in my body are no longer capable of holding my weight. I fall to my knees, mud soaking through my pants, as thick and wet as the blood I kneeled in the night my baby brother took his final breath in my arms.

"Xavier..." The pain in my voice is so raw, so close, I barely recognize it.

"Why did you do it?" he asks plainly, blood bubbling out from between his lips.

"I'm sorry. I'm sorry. Oh, Goddess, I'm so sorry." I say it again and again, a dozen times, a hundred, but I can't alter this outcome now any more than I could twenty years ago, bargaining my own soul away on the bloody garage floor.

I'm sinking into the earth, letting it swallow me. Consume me. Mud, blood, guilt, memory—I can no longer tell the difference. My body shudders uncontrollably, the sharp bite of copper filling my senses and making me retch.

Xavier crouches before me, his blood soaking the earth between us. All around us, black dahlias bloom, a cruel reminder of my betrayal, my worst crime, my darkest shame.

With a trembling hand, I reach for his face, stopping just short of touching his cheek. "I'm—"

"Sorry, I know," he says with a sigh. "You're always sorry."

"I... I don't know what else to... If I could bring you back, I..."

"I don't want to come back."

Behind him, a massive white shape takes form, descending onto a rocky perch. I blink rapidly, trying to focus, trying to remember the word for such a magnificent creature...

Owl. It's a snowy owl.

"Stevie," I whisper, my eyes drifting closed. The sweet scent of honeysuckle floats on the night air, tugging at another memory, more recent, more real...

Doc, come back to me...

I hold my breath, trying to zero in on the sound. Is it the breeze? The soft rush of the river? My own pulse thudding in my ears?

Doc, listen to me... It isn't real... He's twisting your memories...

"It isn't real," I repeat, clinging to the idea like a life raft. "He's twisting them... twisting them..."

"But he isn't, that's the thing," Xavier whispers. "You should've told her the rest of it, Cass."

Shame burns through me, and I open my eyes, searching for Xavier's in the darkness. He frowns at me, and once again, I watch helplessly as the life drains from his eyes.

I reach for him, but just as my fingers brush his blood-soaked shirt, he slips away and falls into the river, the current carrying him faster and farther than I could ever hope to follow, taking my heart with him.

Just like before.

Kneeling in the cold, red mud, I stare at the space he vacated for a long time. Hours? Days? Again, time is lost to me. My gaze fixates on the Chalice, the bone a pale slash against the ruddy earth. I reach for it, but I don't dare touch it.

I can't. Not now. It's his. It should've been his. I shouldn't even be here.

We need to leave... We could end up trapped here...

The wind shifts, and a shadow falls over my face. A swath of bright red fabric caresses my hands, still hovering over the Chalice.

"Stevie," I gasp, memories slamming into me, chasing away the confusion.

Dream realm. Twisted memories. We need to leave.

I look up, eager to see her smile, to see those wild curls blowing around her face.

But when I tilt my face up toward the moonlight, I don't find the woman I love, standing in her red vampire princess gown.

It's our enemy, Dark Judgment, towering over me in his blood-stained robes, the Wand burning like a smoldering branch in his hand.

"Did you and Xavier enjoy your visit?" he asks. "I know you must miss him terribly after all these years."

My chest burns, the bare flesh over my heart glowing with his double-X brand. But this time, I don't even flinch. I'm numb. Broken. Empty.

"There is no pain you can inflict that I haven't already inflicted upon myself," I say. "So do your worst, Dark Druid. I'm well beyond aching at your cruel command."

He laughs, a sound as dark and bitter as a primordial wind. "Oh, Cassius. You make this too easy."

He steps aside, revealing a silent figure kneeling obediently behind him.

She's dressed in nothing but a sky-blue men's dress shirt, matted curls hanging loose around her shoulders, blood leaking from her eyes like tears. In her hands, the Chalice glows like the moon, the alchemical symbols blazing.

"The blood of the Unworthy is yours, child," he says. "Drink."

She lifts the vessel to her lips.

"Stevie, no!" I lunge for her, my hands wrapping around the edge of the bone, but it's too late. Her mouth is stained red, the dark liquid running down her chin. I try to pull her close, try to kiss the blood from her mouth, but it's too late. *I'm* too late.

She slides out of my arms and tips into the water.

Without a second thought, I dive in after her, following the shape of her into the blood-red light.

FIFTEEN

KIRIN

My head is a ringing bell, the sound so all-encompassing it makes the room tilt sideways. Sparks of light dance before my eyes. I can't catch my breath. Can't see through the blinding flashes of magick igniting the air.

Out of the haze, rough hands grab my shirt, hauling me to my feet and shoving me behind a bookcase just as another blast descends.

All around us, glass shatters, books topple, magick explodes. The chaos finally breaks through my shock, snapping me to attention. Another blast rockets down the staircase, and Baz grabs my arm, portaling us out of there just before the whole room collapses.

We land hard in the middle of the main storage area above, just in time to see a half-dozen black-cloaked mages closing in on Casey at the other end of the room. Quintana is on his back beside her, blood leaking from his temple. My sister's got her gun drawn, but she doesn't know where to aim—the mages are too quick and elusive, like ants scurrying over spilled sugar.

"Casey!" I shout.

From across the room, her gaze locks on mine, her eyes widening with new fear.

"Get out of here!" she shouts.

"Not happening." I'm back on my feet in an instant, raising my arms and calling on my Tower magick with everything I've got. Standing beside me, Baz chants his own spell, dropping half a stone wall on two of the mages.

All around us, bookshelves fall like dominoes. Another mage goes down, buried beneath a pile of ancient tomes, the confusion buying Casey just enough time to take aim.

She hits a fourth mage square in the chest.

But just as quickly as they fall, the mages reform, gathering like smoke that thickens and solidifies before our eyes, once again ready for battle.

"What the *hell*?" I grind out.

"Black-mirror magick!" Baz shouts, and my gut clenches.

I've never seen it in action, but I've read about it—a kind of projection spell that makes it impossible to know where the actual casters are standing, or how many of them are even surrounding us.

"How the fuck do we fight them?" I shout.

"No clue, but if we don't figure it out, your parents are picking out two headstones tomorrow!"

Wasting no more time, I push myself to my energetic limits, reaching out for every ounce of black magick I can sense, pulling the darkness from the mage spells into my own. The Tower card is crystal clear in my mind—a dark stone spire rising from the sea, a powerful bolt of lightning striking the top. Thick, red-black smoke roils in the sky, and two beings jump from the tallest tower window to escape the flames inside, likely to their deaths.

I hold the terrifying image in my mind, calling on its transformative energy. The spell comes to me easily:

> *Tower of fury, tower of rage*
> *Siphon the power that fuels the dark mage*
> *Collapse and destroy, remake and reform*
> *I call on their chaos, for I am the storm*

I repeat it seven times, my voice getting louder with each recitation, my skin electrified, blood simmering in my veins, my entire body on fire with magick. Soon I can no longer separate the feeling of my physical form from the force of the magick storm swirling around me. Smoke rises from my skin, lightning arcing through it, power gathering inside and out.

The mages flicker before us like an old TV picture, then finally solidify for good, no longer able to call on their dark magick.

My dark magick, I realize. All of it, held fast in the palms of my hands, crackling and hot, ready to do my bidding.

And it feels…

Holy shit, it feels fucking *amazing*.

Drunk with power, I let out a laugh I barely recognize, everything inside me humming with intense pleasure. Soon I can no longer recall a time when I *ever* feared this darkness.

I was *born* to claim it.

I can't even remember where I am, what I'm doing, why it matters.

There is only chaos. Only destruction. Only this endless, seductive power…

"Kirin, now!" Baz shouts from behind me. "Do it now or she's dead!"

The urgency in his voice breaks through my giddy haze, snapping me back to reality.

Library.

Dark mage attack.

My sister.

"Casey! *Move!*"

Without another thought, I shove my hands forward, throwing all that power straight toward the mages rushing at my sister. Two of them take a direct hit, their bodies incinerating on contact. The rest of the magick hits the stone wall behind them with a blast so intense, it sends a shock wave rippling back across the floor like an ocean tide, knocking us all on our asses.

The last of the magick evaporates from my hands, leaving me totally drained. I don't even have the strength to sit up.

"You okay?" Baz asks, crawling to my side.

I nod and gesture for him to go help Casey. He gets to

his feet in a blink, leaping over the obstacle course of toppled bookcases just as two mages join forces for another spell, aiming right for my sister.

But Casey's a step ahead of them.

"Baz! Let's rock!" She points to the ceiling, and he nods, jumping over the last pile of books and grabbing her hand. Together, they raise their arms and direct their joint earth energy overhead. A slab of rock peels away from the ceiling, pancaking the two mages before they even realize what hit them.

From the corner of my eye, I catch a swirl of black robes vanishing around the corner and up the stairs.

"They're getting away!" I shout, pulling myself to my feet.

"Let them go." Casey puts her hands on her knees and bends over, trying to catch her breath. "We need to get you and Quintana out of here before this whole place comes down. You okay?"

"I will be."

"Good. Because as soon as you've regained your strength, I'm going to kick your ass." With that, she returns to her partner, who's just coming back to consciousness.

"What... happened?" he mumbles, glancing around at the war zone as Casey helps him to his feet. He sways, then leans against her shoulder, his eyes wide with horror. "The essence—"

"It's gone, James." Casey pulls his arm over her shoulder, steadying him. "It was a smash and grab—black-mirror magick with a whole lot of special effects. The first two hit us and took the boxes, leaving their associates to finish the job. You okay?"

"I'm fine." He jerks out of her hold, anger fueling a quick recovery. "Which is more than we can say for the students who just lost their magick for the *second* time."

"We'll find them," she says. "The essences were stolen, not destroyed, which means they probably believe the magick is still viable."

"We don't even know who *they* are," he says. "And what about Phaines?"

"Buried," Baz says. "Probably incinerated too. Kirin and I were down there when the first blast came through. I portaled us out just before the room collapsed."

"You can portal on command?" Casey asks, her eyes wide.

"Rock magick, baby." Baz grins. "You might not realize this, Case, but I'm kind of handy in a jam."

"Noted. I don't suppose you can use some of that jam-handy rock magick to Humpty-Dumpty this place back together again?"

"I can stabilize the outer bedrock to keep it from caving in, but the walls and floor are toast. No one's using the basement again without a total remodel, that's for sure. Which means you're gonna need one hell of a cover story."

"It's your call, Case," Quintana says.

She nods, then lets out a deep sigh. "Okay. We stick with the original plan and call it in. We were here investigating the anonymous tip. We found the body and the essences from the student victims, but before we could remove it all, we were attacked by unknown assailants."

"Assailants most likely under orders from our back-stabbing dickhead of a boss," he says.

"Agreed, but the minute he knows we're onto him, we're putting the entire Academy at risk."

"I'm sorry," Baz says, "but did anyone else see those cloak-and-dagger mages that nearly killed us? Some of whom escaped, and are probably heading back to their dark holes to plot their next attack? We passed 'at risk' a long time ago."

Casey shakes her head. "We have to call it in. At this point, our only advantage is that Eastman thinks he's getting away with it."

"Newsflash," I say. "If you don't report him, he *is* getting away with it."

"We just started building the case against him," she says. "We don't have enough evidence to move forward with charges, let alone to secure a conviction. And he's clearly got people on campus working for him now. Students, faculty, other outsiders... We have no idea how deep this runs."

"And Trello?" Baz asks. "What's her involvement?"

"I can't get into that right now, but again, she's not the bad guy here."

"What about the London office?" Quintana asks. "If we go straight to the top—"

"There's no way we can report Eastman without him finding out first. He's got too many friends there, all up and down the chain of command. I had to cash in a ton of favors just to get the help we needed from the lab, and now—"

"What lab?" I ask.

Casey sighs and pushes her hands through her hair, the stress of the night finally catching up with her. "Kirin, as I explained before, there's a *lot* you don't know."

"So you keep saying. Why don't you enlighten us?"

Ignoring this, she turns back to Quintana. "Even if we could find a way to get a message to someone at London HQ, there's no guarantee they can help us, and certainly not quickly. I don't know if you've noticed this, guys, but the world is kind of a shit show right now."

Baz opens his arms, gesturing across the rubble formerly known as the library storage room. "You think?"

"London has their hands full," she says, "trying to keep witches and mages from being executed en masse by mundane law enforcement and vigilante mobs whose idea of fun is hacking into the magickal registration database and torching the homes of anyone on record."

I let out a gasp. "Are you serious?"

"That's the latest report from outside," Quintana confirms, his voice grim. He kicks a chunk of concrete, sending it across the room. "Casey's right—London can't help us. If we want to take Eastman down and protect Arcana Academy, that's on us."

"Awesome." Baz grins and rubs his hands together. "When do we get guns?"

"*You* don't," Casey says, glaring daggers at us both. "You two need to get back to Red Sands Canyon and wait for us there. I mean it this time. You nearly got yourselves killed tonight." Then, through the ghost of a smile I haven't seen in so long I almost forgot what it looks like, she says, "But thanks for the assist."

I raise an eyebrow. "Assist?"

"All right, fine. The save. Thanks for the save. Happy now?"

"Happy enough," I say, stopping just short of hugging her.

"Glad to hear it." Casey's smile drops, and she points toward the exit, all business once again. "Now I want you and rock-boy here to get the hell back to Red Sands before I kill you both and write it up as an accident."

SIXTEEN

STEVIE

I open my eyes to find Doc kneeling on the floor beside the bed in nothing but his boxers, my hand in a vice grip, his head bowed as if he's praying.

Not wanting to startle him, I squeeze his hand gently and whisper his name.

"Stevie?" He blinks up at me, sleep and confusion still marring his gaze. But then it comes all at once—a sudden clearing of his eyes, a smile breaking across his lips, relief flooding his energy.

He kisses my palm, my arm, my neck, all the way up to my mouth. Then, taking my face between his hands, he shakes his head and whispers, "I was sure I'd lost you."

"How long have you been awake?" I ask.

"Twenty of the longest minutes of my life. I couldn't risk trying to wake you. I thought maybe you'd gone back looking for Ani, or that you'd... That the river had finally…" He closes his eyes as a shudder rolls through him. "Goddess, you scared me half to death."

"I'm right here." I lean up and press another kiss to his lips. "We're both here. It's okay."

"Dark Judgment ordered you to drink from the Chalice. I saw the blood on your face, and then you were falling, and I couldn't reach you. I swam as hard and fast as I could, but it wasn't enough… His voice just kept echoing in my skull. 'You did this, Cassius Devane. You did this to her.'"

A tear tracks down his cheek, but I swipe it away with my thumb.

"It wasn't Judgment who gave me the Chalice, Doc. It was my Princess of Cups. At least, that's how it happened in my version. But I figured it must've been different for you—I saw his mark on your chest."

"Tell me everything," he says.

"Well, you and I were walking along the riverbank when we found that weird glowing cave. That part you remember, right?"

"Yes, but then you vanished. You literally vanished out of my grasp. I searched all along the river for you."

"In my version, I never left you, Doc. We were talking, and then you just… You got this glazed look in your eyes. Then your whole face twisted in pure agony. I could sense your pain, but I didn't know what to do. That's when the mark appeared. You fell to your knees—you were basically catatonic."

Now I'm the one trembling, the memories too fresh, too real.

That feeling of helplessness… Goddess, it was awful. I didn't know how to help him. I could see the mark blazing on his chest, and I knew Judgment had gotten a hold of him. But the enemy himself was nowhere in sight. It took every ounce of willpower I possessed to calm myself enough to think clearly. To ask for the right kind of help without alerting the entire Dark Arcana army to our whereabouts.

"I focused all of my energy," I explain. "I thought about all the air magick lessons Kirin ever gave me, all the things he said about connecting with my familiar, and I did it, Doc. I called on my owl."

"I saw him!" he says excitedly. "He was there with me. It felt like… like he carried your scent on the breeze."

"I still can't believe he actually came to me. I can't wait to tell Kirin about it. He's going to freak out!"

Doc smiles, tucking an errant curl behind my ear.

"Anyway, the owl showed up, and when I told him what was happening—don't ask how he understood me— he took off again. Moments later, he returned, the Princess of Cups following after him. She helped me bring you inside the cave, where the owl kept watch. I didn't want to leave you, but at the same time, something told me I *had* to —that it was the only way to save us."

"What about your Princess?"

"She led me deeper into the cave. She never spoke—not with words—but instinctively, I knew she was taking me somewhere important. It felt like we were walking for days, but I never got tired or hungry. I had a single mission—

follow her dark red cape. I kept it in my sights at all times, through darkness so all-encompassing I couldn't see my own hands in front of my face. But I could *always* see her cape.

"Eventually, we reached a massive, dark pool so far underground I thought we must be in the literal belly of the earth. It was magickal, Doc. Like… like a giant bowl full of stars. We kneeled at the water's edge and put our hands in it, and the starlight or whatever it was… it just filled me up. The darkness and fear in my heart left me, and the light took its place. That's the best way I can describe it."

"Incredible," he whispers, his eyes filling with wonder.

"In that moment, I just knew I was supposed to find that place. To be there with her, for whatever reason. A sense of deep peace washed over me, like nothing I've ever felt before. All my worries drained away. Suddenly, I had complete faith that you were going to be okay, and that we'd make it back home together. That Ani would come back to us in his own time. That Baz would heal. That Kirin would reconnect with his sister and forgive himself for the past. That *all* of us would forgive ourselves… Goddess, it just went on and on. Tears streamed down my face, and my whole body was shaking, but I couldn't stop smiling."

Fresh tears glaze my eyes as the same peaceful energy flows through me again, soft and warm and all-encompassing. The Princess flickers in my mind too, her red-gold hair fluttering, a silver crescent-moon circlet winking on her crown.

You are loved and you are love, she whispers now, just like she did at the pool. *Never doubt it.*

"When we stood up," I continue, "the Princess was holding her chalice. She drank from it, then presented it to me like a gift, just as she did the first time I ever saw her—in my vision in Trello's office when you first brought me to the Academy. But this time, it wasn't the old-fashioned gold cup she usually carries. It was *the* Chalice. I knew it the moment I touched it."

"Were you concerned about drinking from it?" he asks.

"How could I be? I was in such a state of peace. I knew no harm would come to me. And I was right—as soon as the liquid touched my lips, I was back at the mouth of the cave with you and the owl. And once again, I just… *knew*. I knew what to say. I knew how to break Judgment's hold on you."

Doc's eyes flicker with pain, then warmth, shining with new emotion as he traces the edge of my jaw. "You told me to come back to you. That it wasn't real. I could smell you. I could feel your touch."

"The mark on your chest faded. You finally opened your eyes, and you drew me close. You kissed me. That's the last thing I remember before… well, before I woke up just now."

"Goddess, what a marvel," he says, voice heavy with awe. "How is it that we had such different experiences? Such different visions? I swear I thought he was going to end us both, Stevie. There was so much blood…"

"I can't pretend to understand the dream realm. Every

time I visit, intentionally or not, it's different. But my gut tells me it's got something to do with love and forgiveness."

"How do you mean?"

"Dark Judgment preys on our deepest regrets. He mines our memories, panning for guilt instead of gold. And when he finds it, he twists and amplifies it like a weapon. It's the ultimate mental manipulation, and it works, because in all his twisted machinations, there's a kernel of truth. Like, logically I know I'm not responsible for my parents' deaths. But the fact is, if I'd stayed with them on the trail, if I hadn't argued and stomped off on my own, we would've been clear of the canyons long before the flood hit."

"Stevie, you can't—"

"Blame myself. I know. If we'd left on time and avoided the flood, they could've just as easily died in a car crash on the drive home. The point is, that kernel will always be there. For Kirin, it's his guilt over something that happened with his family a decade ago. Baz has a lot of unresolved family issues too. Ani blames himself for his parents' divorce. And you... You're still dealing with things, and..."

I let my words trail off, not wanting to dredge up Doc's past again. He just told me about Elizabeth last night. And I still don't know how his brother died, but obviously, there's plenty of fertile soil in Doc's psyche for Judgment to dig through.

"Anyway," I continue, "the more guilt and shame we carry, the easier it is for Judgment to hurt us. I think that's why Baz is so torn up right now. Whatever happened in his past was so terrible, he can't see his way through it, and

Judgment thrives on that. Whereas Kirin is starting to open up to his sister again, to mend those old wounds. I suspect that's why he's not having the same side effects as Baz."

"And what about you, my Star?" Doc asks softly. "Have you forgiven yourself?"

"Not entirely. But I'm getting closer, Doc." I reach up and cup his face, stroking his cheek with my thumb. "Before we found that cave, when you ripped the dress?"

"Sorry, but it needed to go."

"Yes, it did. And you helped me get rid of it—that's my point. You literally tore it off my body, but it was more than that. You helped me feel worthy. You helped me trust my own magick, my own light. It was a small step, but an important one. And for the rest of the dream, I never once encountered Judgment. I didn't relive my past tragedies and guilt. I felt only love and peace, only acceptance. Judgment can't mess with that."

"All we need is love," he teases gently. "That's what you're saying?"

"Not exactly. I mean, a kickass magickal army would also help." I let out a soft sigh. "I don't know, Doc. We've still got a long road ahead of us. We don't know the Magician's full plan, and if Janelle and Casey proved anything, it's that any witch or mage in our vicinity could be working for him—either intentionally or under coercion. Outside, cities have fallen under military rule, and witches can't even light a stick of incense for fear of being accused of terrorism. I'm not naïve enough to say love can totally counter that kind of hate—not when people in power decide their personal beliefs are carte blanche for the murder and imprisonment of others." I look up at him again, tracing the line of his brow with my thumb, losing myself for a moment in the depths of his gray eyes. "But I *do* believe love is where we start."

Doc watches me closely for another beat, his gaze finally sweeping down to my lips, and then he lowers his head, kissing me with a soft, deep kiss that makes my toes curl.

He's already sliding out of his boxers and climbing back into bed for a *proper* good-morning greeting, and I want nothing more than to give it to him. But first...

I press my hand against his chest and shake my head. "One more thing."

"Is this about love?" He grins, hovering over me. "Because I *swear* I was about to shower you with it."

"It's more about... dating."

"Dating?"

"See, I get that they did things differently in *your* day, back before the invention of the wheel. But modern girls have certain preferences when it comes to dates."

"Hmm. Perhaps you should enlighten this prehistoric cave-beast, then, and I'll endeavor to do better."

"I certainly hope so. Because as much as I enjoy a night under the stars with a few exotic cocktails, maybe next time we can do it in the real world, with *slightly* less dire consequences and a better selection of souvenirs." I reach beneath the sheet and retrieve the souvenir in question, handing it over.

"The Chalice of Blood and Sorrow?" Doc leaps up from

the bed. "Goddess, you're brilliant. I can't believe you got it!"

"Doc. Did you honestly think I'd walk all that way and *not* bring this creepy-ass relic back for you?"

A smile breaks hard across his face. "With you, Miss Milan? I don't know *what* to think anymore."

"Good. I like keeping my men guessing."

"Where do we put it?" he asks, holding it up between us. Here in the morning light, the Chalice looks even more sinister than it did last night, the teeth around the edge protruding at odd angles, the inside blackened with old blood.

It needs to be hidden at the Fool's Grave with the other sacred objects, but we can't do that until Baz and Kirin return—the magickal boundary won't unlock without blood from all five of us. So for now, Doc and I do some quick illusion magick, using a similar Moon spell to the one he and Professor Maddox used to cloak the Pentacle and Sword. Then, we stash the Chalice in a dresser drawer under some T-shirts and socks.

"Remember, Doc," I say playfully, shutting the drawer with my hip. "This is a magickal skull, not a fashion accessory."

"Noted. In the meantime, where were we? Ah, yes." He steps closer, sliding his hands around my hips. "I was about to—"

"Wait. Is that... bacon?" I lift my nose in the air, tracking the scent. "They're cooking breakfast down there!"

Doc shakes his head, his eyes glinting with amusement.

"I guess this means I'm taking a rain check on tying you up again."

"It's a compelling offer." I slide my hands up his chest, curling them around his broad shoulders. "But…"

"I know, I know. There's bacon. I get it."

"Thanks for understanding." I stretch up on my toes and plant a kiss on his cheek. "But after that, I'm yours. I promise."

"You're *always* mine, Miss Milan." He reclaims my mouth and deepens our kiss, sliding his hands around my backside and lifting me up, just like he did last night. I wrap my thighs around him, his rock-hard heat throbbing urgently between us.

Goddess, what was I thinking? The bacon can wait.

We've just fallen back into bed again when a loud crash downstairs startles us both.

"Was that the front door?" I ask.

"Baz, no!" Carly shouts. "Wait!"

I bolt upright in bed. "They're back. Something's wrong."

We get dressed in record time, the commotion downstairs growing louder with each passing second.

"Fuck off, Kirin!" Baz shouts. "Move!"

There's another crash, then we're bolting out of the bedroom, taking the stairs two at a time.

The kitchen is a disaster, with pans scattered across the floor, half-cooked eggs spilled down the front of the stove, a carton of orange juice overturned on the counter.

Carly stands in the middle of it all, oven mitt and

spatula raised in surrender, Isla and Nat flanking her with spatulas and spoons of their own, as if they're all about to call on some ancient cooking goddess to save the day. Around the table, Kirin's circling Baz like he's trying to corner a wild animal.

Actually, *wild* doesn't even begin to describe him.

Feral comes a little closer, but even then... I barely recognize him. His red-brown eyes are crazed, his hair an unkempt mess. Black soot streaks his face, his clothes burned in places, torn in others. The smell of alcohol and singed magick is so strong it makes my eyes water. Kirin's in a similar state, but he seems to have his faculties, which is more than I can say for Baz.

"*Where is she?*" Baz's voice booms, so loud and horrifying it rattles my bones. Vengeance floods his energy, powerful and deadly, blocking everyone else from my senses.

Right now, there's only Baz. Only darkness. Only fury.

"Where is she?" he demands again, flipping one of the chairs. "*Where?*"

But he's not asking for me. He can't be. Not like this.

Down in the basement, Janelle cries out for him, her voice thick with anguish and confusion.

Baz's eyes darken with new rage. Hunger. Death.

"Baz," I say softly, reaching out for him. He takes one look at me, then storms right past, as if I'm not even there.

Instead, he reaches for the basement door, damn near tearing it off its hinges.

Doc strides toward him. "Baz, don't—"

But it's too late. The door slams and bolts behind him, a hot pulse of boundary magick sealing the deal.

"What's going on?" Doc turns to Kirin. "When did you get back?"

Kirin rights the chair Baz tipped and drops into it, bewildered and exhausted. "We literally just walked in the front door. He was fine. Totally fine. He was asking for Stevie. Then he just... I don't know. The switch flipped."

Carly tosses her spatula in the sink, her shoulders slumping.

"My mother," she says softly. "She heard them come home. She called out for him, and that's all it took. He couldn't tell exactly where it was coming from at first, but the sound of her voice... It did something to him. He's... he's going to kill her, Stevie. I can feel it. I *know* it."

Dread fills me up, head to toe. I want nothing more than to shatter that door, run down the stairs, take him into my arms, and stop whatever madness is about to unfold.

To stop Baz from racing down a path he'll *never* return from.

But I can't help him. Not with this. Not now. I know it, just like Carly knows he's going to kill her mother.

I pick my way across the mess in the kitchen and reach for Carly's hands.

She doesn't pull away.

"I don't know what to do," she whispers, more vulnerable and open than I've ever seen her. "What to say. I've never seen him like this."

I squeeze her hands and offer a small, encouraging

smile, drawing strength from my Princess of Cups. My brothers. My friends.

And from Carly herself, from the promises we made to each other in the café after Harvest Eve dinner. From our shared love for the man we're *all* going to lose if she can't find a way to reach him.

"You love him, Carly," I say simply, nodding toward the basement door, knowing I have to let her do this alone. "You'll figure it out."

SEVENTEEN

BAZ

They're banging on the door, but they won't get in. With a little help from the stone walls surrounding it, I made damn sure of that.

The basement is my domain. Rock and dirt and darkness, hell yes. All the better to hide the monsters—the ones we fight, the ones we become.

With every step down the stairs, the gaping wound in my chest burns a little hotter, hurts a little more. But this time it's not the red-hot blaze of Judgment's wand. No, this is *all* me—totally aware, totally lucid, totally in control.

I have a job to do. Something I've put off for far too long, telling myself its completion would make me evil.

Maybe I'm already there. Maybe I don't give a shit one way or the other.

Stevie…

Goddess, the pain this will cause her. The look of shock

and disgust it will put in her eyes. The thought of it damn near stops me.

But I can't stop. No matter how bright her light shines, I know it's not for me. There's *no* redemption for me. My blood is tainted, my fate sealed a hundred times over.

I'm the Devil, baby. I was born to burn in darkness.

"Baz…" Janelle's voice echoes against the stone walls. "Tell me it's really you, sweetness. Tell me I'm not dreaming."

"It's me." I approach the cot, barely able to contain my disgust at the vile piece of filth lying in it, delusional and nearly paralyzed. "Dreams really do come true, huh?"

She reaches for me, her eyes glazed and unfocused. But that's okay. She doesn't need focus. I've got plenty enough for both of us.

"Help me," she says softly, as close to begging as I've ever heard.

"Didn't you get the memo?" I flash her a wide grin, one that probably borders on maniacal, and take a seat in the rolling chair beside her cot. "I'm not here to help you. I'm here to end you."

"What… what are you talking about?"

"I used to fantasize about this, you know," I tell her, taking more pleasure in the confession than I probably should.

I laugh.

Should. What does that word even mean?

I *should* have had a better childhood, but I didn't.

The people who signed up to protect me—first, by

bringing me into this world, then by taking me into their home—*should* have done a better job, but they didn't.

Maybe the idea of cold-blooded murder *should* terrify me, but it doesn't. It calms me. Warms me. Gives me a sense of purpose—one without hope, only action. One where *I* control the outcome.

At the end of the cot, there's a table set up with various potions, ingredients, and a few other implements. I reach over and pick up a silver athame, twisting it before her eyes.

"This one's nice, don't you think?" I ask.

"Your... your brother..." she stammers, but this just makes me laugh again.

"My brother murdered a mage in cold blood. Tortured him. Burned him alive. None of that was my fault. Yet you were more than happy to let me believe it was."

"If I die... If I don't pay the guards... He'll suffer."

I press the tip of the blade to her throat and lean in close, so close I can count the crow's feet tracking around her eyes. "I. Don't. Care."

As soon as the words are out, I know they're true.

For so long, I've carried the weight of my brother's sins, the guilt over his imprisonment. I let that guilt fester into nightmares, into punishment, into a lifetime of victimhood.

But it's over now. It's done. The Ford Redgrave I once loved died long ago, and it's time I accept that.

Which means there's not a single thing Janelle can hold over my head anymore.

"But he's your family," she whines.

"No, Janelle. He isn't. My parents aren't. And you sure as hell didn't earn the right to call yourself a mother, either. *My* family? My *real* family?" I point the blade at the ceiling. "They're upstairs trying to figure out how to break down the goddess-damned door so I don't do something crazy, like slit your throat. But you know something? I have a feeling that even if I *do* go crazy down here, they won't turn their backs on me. I'm not saying they'll give me an award or anything, but they won't bail. Because unlike you and everyone who came before you, my real family knows the meaning of that word."

"Baz, you don't know what you're saying. We can... talk about this..."

"No more talking, Janelle. Only throat-slitting." I twist the athame in my hand, admiring the silver blade, salivating at the thought of seeing it drip with her blood.

But then a new idea dawns. Better. Darker. Way more satisfying.

"On second thought? I won't be needing this after all." I set the athame back on the table and gaze down at my hands. "Call me a purist, Janelle, but I think I'd rather *feel* the life leaving your body."

I lean forward and wrap my hands around her throat, just testing it out. She claws at my arms, but she's so weak and groggy, it's like a gnat facing down an elephant.

Closing my eyes, I take a moment to soak it all in. The warm pulse, rapidly thrumming beneath my grip. Her paper-thin skin, soft and wrinkly. Her scrawny neck, as breakable as a bird's bone.

"Baz, please... Don't... Don't do this."

"Give me a reason." I release the pressure on her throat and open my eyes, watching the tears leak down her cheeks, waiting to hear the words I've waited to hear since I was a scared fucking kid trapped in her house of horrors.

Because I was wrong to hurt you.

Because I was the sick one, not you.

Because I'm sorry, Baz. I'm so sorry for what I did to you.

Hell, at this point, I'd even take one *word* if I believed she meant it. One shit-ass little "sorry," and I'd walk away from this moment, letting her keep whatever pathetic life she's got left.

But when Janelle finally finds her words, the ones that spill out are as twisted and ugly as her soul.

"You've always been an ungrateful bastard," she says, taking a deep breath and doing her best to put some fire behind it. "Your parents were right to abandon you. And that spirit-blessed bitch you call your girlfriend? She'll abandon you too."

She narrows her eyes, her lips twitching into a smirk, as though she's waiting for me to crumble, to fall at her feet, to beg her forgiveness.

But all I can do is shake my head.

"You have no power over me, Janelle Kirkpatrick. You are *nothing*. I could end you, or I could walk away right now, and your life would *still* be over. Because then you'd have to spend the rest of your wretched existence knowing that the boy you tried to control, to manipulate, to crush... Knowing that he grew up to be a man. That he found love and friendship and acceptance. That he was *never* broken. That he never needed you. That *no* one needs you."

She opens and closes her mouth like a fish, but no more words escape.

"Lucky for you, I'm not interested in making you suffer with that burden," I say, my hands itching with the need to finish this. I tighten them around her throat again, offering one last grin. "I'd rather just choke you to death. Goodbye, Janelle."

I press my thumbs against her windpipe.

"Baz!" she coughs out. "Don't!"

"Sorry, what's that? I can't hear you." I press harder, power coursing through my veins. Not magick, but power. Dark and hungry and ready to feed.

Kill her. Crush her. Take your revenge...

An explosion of stone and wood overhead shakes me out of my killing trance. Before I can even process what the fuck just happened, Carly's standing in front of me.

"How the fuck did you get through my wards?"

"Magick," she snaps. "Now come back upstairs with me. Stevie's making tea—we can all talk about this like adults."

"Adults. Right. So you and Stevie are friends now? What's that all about?"

"At the moment, it's all about saving you from making the biggest dumb-ass mistake of your entire dumb-ass life."

"Thanks, but I'll pass. I liked it better when you two wanted to claw each other's eyes out." I turn back to

Janelle, eager to get the job done, but Carly's not giving up so easily.

She steps in front of me, wedging herself between me and her mother's cot, her hands firm on my chest.

"Listen to me, Baz. I don't blame you for wanting her dead. Hell, *I* want her dead. But—"

"Carly," Janelle whispers. "Baby, do something."

Ignoring this, Carly pushes against my chest. "Just come back upstairs. We don't have to talk or drink tea if you don't want to. We can just—"

"Baby, *please*," Janelle croaks. "He's crazy. He's—"

In a move I couldn't have predicted with all the psychic power in the Academy, Carly straight up sucker-punches her mother in the mouth, knocking the bitch out cold.

"Goddess, I thought she'd never shut up." She shakes out her hand, flexing her fingers. "Wow, that really hurt. They never tell you that, do they?"

I stare, open-mouthed. "Did you just... Did you seriously just punch your mom?"

"Says the guy who was about thirty seconds from killing her?"

"Yeah, but I'm an asshole."

"And I'm not?"

"Fair point, but Carly, *you*? You don't go around punching people. You roll your eyes and make snarky comments and critique people's wardrobe choices."

She puffs up her chest. "Maybe there's more to me than meets the eye."

"So it seems." I can't help my smile—I mean, seriously,

that punch was pretty epic—but the levity doesn't last. This whole situation is so beyond fucked, they haven't even invented a curse word that covers it.

"Are you coming," she asks, "or do I have to sucker-punch you too?"

I blow out a breath and lean back against the table, crossing my arms over my chest. Most of the fight in me is gone, the hunger for vengeance subsiding. I don't know whether to be grateful or pissed.

"What are you doing here, Carly? Really."

"I was with Stevie and those guys when they found Ani. They thought I'd be safer back at—"

"I don't mean here in this house. I mean here in this basement. Here with *me*, busting through my wards, trying to save my ass from the same fate that befell my fucked-up brother. Why?"

"Why do you *think*?" She rolls her eyes, a move I know all too well.

Goddess, I wish we didn't have to have this conversation. I wish we could just keep ignoring it until her infatuation finally burns out, or she finds a guy who can give her what she needs. What she deserves.

It's not me. No matter what kind of wishful thinking she's engaged in, she *has* to know that by now. Even if she ignores all the times I told her as much, all she has to do is watch me whenever Stevie walks into the room.

Even an idiot can see I'll never look at anyone the way I look at the woman I love.

"Carly, listen. I don't know what your deal is with

Stevie. One minute you're warning me not to get involved with her, the next minute you and your mean girl posse are damn near trying to drown her, now all of a sudden you're buddied up on this rescue mission... My head is fucking spinning, okay?"

"I know it's... unexpected. But Stevie and I—"

I hold up my hand, cutting her off. "There's only one thing I need to know, and for once in your life, I need you to be totally fucking honest with me. Do you think you can manage that?"

She crosses her arms over her chest and nods, lowering her eyes.

"Look at me," I say. "Please."

Reluctantly, she does as I ask.

"I'm just gonna come out and say it." I keep my gaze fixed on hers, hoping like hell this is the right call. "Do you... do you love me?"

EIGHTEEN

BAZ

To my surprise, Carly doesn't laugh or look away, doesn't tell me how ridiculous I am, doesn't hit me with any of her patented snark.

She stares at me in uncomfortable silence for so long I start to worry I broke her.

I'm just about to go check for a pulse when she finally finds her voice again.

"Do you remember when you first came to live with us, and you found me crying in the basement?" she asks.

I nod, frowning at the memory. She kept asking her father to play this X-Box racing game with her, but he kept shooing her away. She skipped out on our first "family" dinner, which was just as well—Charles was on his phone the whole time, and Janelle got piss-drunk, blathering on about how happy she was to finally have another man in the house.

I found Carly after dinner, all alone in the basement rec

room, trying to figure out that stupid racing game. All along, I'd always assumed she had it made—two parents, rich as fuck, nice house, all of it. But in that moment, she looked so lost and lonely and broken, I could hardly stand it.

Despite the animosity and games between us, part of me will always see her as that sad little girl. And deep down, though I'd never admit it out loud, I'll always ache for her. Janelle might not have tortured her daughter the same way she tortured me, but that doesn't mean Carly got off easy.

For people who thrive on manipulation, one victim is rarely enough.

"You looked heartbroken," I say softly. "I'll never forget it."

"Honestly? I *was* heartbroken. I had no friends to speak of. And my parents... Goddess, all I really wanted was for someone to play X-Box with me."

"Someone to teach you *how* to play, more like." I smile, remembering how terrible she was at that racing game. "It took months of training to make you an even *remotely* worthy opponent."

"Hey!" Carly laughs. "For your information, I totally let you win."

"Right. Feeling sorry for the orphan, I get it."

"Something like that." She crosses over to me and takes my hand, holding it in both of hers. I flinch at first, but I don't pull away. For once, the gesture doesn't feel like a scheme, and when she looks up and meets my eyes again, I know that whatever she says next is going to be the truth, whether I'm ready for it or not.

"You asked me if I love you," she says, "and you wanted honesty. Well, here it is, Baz Redgrave. Yes, I love you. I've loved you since that moment in my parents' basement when you picked up the game controller, sat down on the couch next to me, and asked me what level we were on."

I don't know what I expected, but the bare truth of her confession pokes at something soft and tender inside me.

Goddess, I wish I didn't have to hurt her. For all her bullshit, she really did deserve better. Better from her parents. Better from her friends. Better from me. But she didn't get that, and I can't give it to her now, either.

"I never meant to hurt you, Carly. I just don't feel the same way. I—"

"Oh, I'm not done." She glares at me, squeezing my hand. "I've loved you—*still* love you—as the boy who saved me from loneliness. As the boy who looked out for me, even when no one was looking out for him. I loved you as my big brother then, and I love you as my big brother now. Nothing more."

I gape at her, all the oxygen in the room evaporating, spinning me in circles until it finally sets me upright again.

"I don't... What?" I ask.

"Okay, you're obviously having a hard time processing the fact that a woman in your presence doesn't have romantic feelings for you, so let me spell it out a little more clearly. I love you, but I'm not *in* love with you, Baz. I've *never* been in love with you." She smiles up at me, but it's sad as hell. "To tell you the truth, I'm pretty sure I don't even like guys, but that's a story for another day—assuming we live that long."

My jaw hits the ground.

None of this makes any sense. No, not because I can't bear the thought of a woman not falling head over heels in my presence. But because for years, Carly was damn near banging a drum on the campaign trail, telling everyone within screaming distance that she was my girlfriend. That I was off-limits. That she and I were quote-unquote *meant to be*.

"You okay there, champ?" She releases my hand and slaps me lightly on the cheek. "You look a little pale."

"I just… If you don't have feelings for me like that, why torment Stevie? Why act like a raving psycho around any woman who's ever shown an interest? Why tell your parents we're together? Your mother thought I was cheating on you with Stevie. She threatened to tell you about it and fuck with my brother…" I shake my head, trying to make a *shred* of sense out of this. "So now you're basically admitting—what? That you're just petty and jealous? That you don't want me having other female friends?"

"Nothing could be farther from the truth, Baz."

"Then what *is* the truth? That's what I'm trying to understand. Goddess, Carly. There's a witch upstairs that I'm *crazy* in love with. So fucking crazy I'm about to throw myself at her feet and beg for forgiveness for everything I've put her through this week alone. And you tormented her for *months*!"

"I know. I'm sorry. I just—"

"Why? Why would you do that? Just for kicks?"

She shakes her head, fresh tears sliding down her cheeks.

"All right," I say. "You win. I'm not going to kill your psycho mother. I'll go upstairs and drink my tea like a good little mage. But you and me? This bullshit? The games? We're done. We're not friends. We're not pseudo-siblings. We're *nothing*." I turn my back on the Kirkpatrick women, more than ready to leave this bullshit in the rearview. But before I can take a single step, Carly grabs my hand again, stopping me in my tracks.

She steps in front of me and puts her hands on my chest, looking up with eyes so haunted it sends a chill to my very bones.

"Wait. Just wait. I need to say this. I…" Carly takes a deep breath, then balls her hands into fists against my chest, her voice dropping to a whisper. "I know, Baz. I know what she did to you."

Even at a whisper, the words slam into me one at a time, like tiny wrecking balls to the gut.

I

Know

What

She

Did

To

You…

I don't have to ask her what she means. I don't think I can handle hearing her spell it out, either.

Shame rushes through my body, making me hot and itchy and pissed off all over again. I turn my back on her, not wanting her to see the truth in my eyes. The confirmation. The disgust.

"It was the only way I could think of to stop her," she continues. "I thought if Mom believed we were together—that I was in love with you—maybe she'd let you go. Maybe she'd stop doing... everything she did. But it turns out my mother didn't love either one of us enough for that."

Carly's still talking, but the words don't even make sense anymore. My head is spinning again, my ears ringing, my brain reshaping itself to try to make room for this.

All this time, she was trying to protect me from Janelle.

All this time, she knew. And she had to live with it too, just like I did. The secrets and shame. The disgust. The unspoken agreement that her father could never find out. The soul-crushing fear of living with a monster in the house —one we could never defeat, because this monster fed us and clothed us and went by the name of Mom.

"I should've done more," Carly says. "I should've told someone, or... I don't know. Something. I'm so sorry, Baz. I didn't know how else to—"

"It's not your fault." I head over to the cot again, staring down at the monster we lived with for so long, her jaw swollen, her mouth hanging slack. "I don't accept your apology, Carly, because it's not yours to make. It's not your fucking fault."

"It's not your fault, either. It never was." She comes to stand on the other side of the cot, glaring down at her mother with the same contempt I feel. "I get why you want her dead, Baz. I told you—I want her dead too."

"Then why the fuck are you working so hard to save her?"

"She's not the one I'm trying to save." She glances up and meets my gaze. "If you want to do this, I can't stop you. Hell, part of me wants to just stand aside and tell you to go for it. It's not like she deserves to live."

"You should listen to that part. It's the smart half."

"Baz, killing someone, even if they deserve it... It *will* destroy you, inside and out. You don't need to be clairsentient to know that."

I open my mouth to argue, but she's right. Taking someone's life? There's a cost, and it's a hell of a lot heavier than just going to jail.

I don't have to climb very far up the family tree for a shining example of *that* little truism.

"You don't have to talk to me about this," she says. "Not now, not tomorrow, not ever. But there is *someone* you should open up to—if and when you're ready." She wipes the last of the tears from her eyes and offers a soft smile. "Stevie loves you, Baz. She may have terrible taste in fashion, and we definitely have our differences—and also, what is going on with that *hair*? Seriously. But... but I've never doubted how much she cares about you. And you're obviously in it to win it with her, so if I were you, I'd commence the throwing-yourself-upon-her-feet thing as soon as possible. Witches like Stevie don't come around more than once in a lifetime."

"Carly. Did you just… Did you say something decent about Stevie?" I crack a smile. "Now I *know* the world is ending."

"If you tell her, I'll deny it."

"I would expect nothing less."

She returns my smile, and in her eyes, something softens.

An understanding passes between us.

Everything about this day has sucked.

But this… She brought a little light back in.

"Thank you," I whisper.

"Yeah, yeah. Go talk to your girl, jerk-off." She glances down again at the breathing corpse she once called her mother, her lip curling. "I've got a few things I need to get off my chest here."

"As much as I'd love to go talk to my girl, I *don't* love the idea of leaving you alone with her. You sure you're okay?"

"I'm not that little girl you found crying in the basement anymore." She kicks the edge of the cot, jolting Janelle back into consciousness. "And this bitch is about to learn that lesson too."

"Right. So, not to rain on your badass parade, but you literally *just* talked me out of killing her."

"Maybe I just didn't want you to have all the fun."

"Carly—"

"Goddess, drama king. I'm not going to *kill* her." She heads to the supply table, selecting a few choice ingredients from the remaining stash and dropping them into one of the empty potion bottles. Then, swirling the contents until everything glows bright green, she grins and says, "Mommy Dearest and I are just going to have a little chat about boundaries."

NINETEEN

BAZ

After making Carly promise she won't do anything crazy—at least, not the kind of crazy I was about to engage in—I go off in search of my girl, hoping like hell I can make things right. That I won't fall apart before I get the chance. That I won't fuck it up like I've done with everything else that's ever meant something to me in this damn life.

No pressure, dickhead.

But when I get back up to the main level of the house, she's in the guest room singing to Ani. The sound of her sweet, off-key voice is enough to break my heart, but I leave her to it, taking the opportunity to dump myself into a scalding hot shower.

She's still with him when I finish, so I head outside for some air and a walk into the desert area beyond the backyard, clearing my head and burning off the last of the fury smoldering in my gut.

When I return from the outing, she's locked away in her

bedroom with Kirin. After that, she's on a video chat with Jessa, and I'm about thirty seconds from losing my mind. I drink a beer. I take another shower. Pace. Crawl up and down the damn walls.

Goddess, it's all still such a jumble inside me, but one thing's for sure—Carly's right. I need to talk to Stevie. No matter how hard it is, no matter how long I have to wait.

I've been waiting years to get this out. A few more minutes or hours or even days won't kill me.

Just when I start to think I'm wrong about that, I finally get my big break. Gazing out the back window, I spot her outside, no other people or technology in sight. She's on her knees in the yard, fingers raking through the dirt like she's searching for some long-buried treasure.

It's nearly dinner time now, the sun hanging low in the sky, and I leave the crew inside, half of them sorting through the wine stash, the rest helping Isla with some spicy Caribbean dish she's cooking up.

Outside, Stevie's so focused on her task, she doesn't hear my approach.

So I stand there like an asswipe and watch her for a little while, wondering if I should lead with the apology or a joke or a question or the wise words of another man from another time, because surely I don't have the smarts or the strength to manage this on my own.

"You're welcome to stand there all night," she says suddenly, "but I'm afraid this is about as exciting as it's gonna get."

"How did you know I—right. Never mind." Of course

she knows. She always senses us, always knows when we're in her sphere. When we're happy, when we're in pain, when all we want to do is smother her with kisses. It's one of the things I love about her, as much as it makes me feel raw and exposed.

"How's Ani?" I ask. "I heard you singing to him earlier. Aerosmith, I believe?"

"Greatest hits." She lets out a soft laugh, still digging in the dirt. "The singing... That's kind of our thing, you know? I figured it might remind him of home."

"I'm sure it does."

I wait for her to turn around, but she doesn't. Just keeps pushing the dirt back and forth with her fingers, back and forth, back and forth.

"Looking for something?" I ask.

"We might be here at the house for a while, so I figured I should make it more homey. I'm thinking of planting a garden. Just some herbs, or... I don't know. Things I can use in my tea. Honestly, I just kind of felt like digging. But it turns out it's not so easy without tools."

"That all depends on who you ask." I send a pulse of magick her way, and the ground before her splits into wider tracks, the tiny stones and debris hovering in mid-air for just a moment before I let it all fall again. "I can teach you, if you'd like."

At this, she finally turns to look at me over her shoulder. The sight of those big blue eyes kicks me right in the chest, and I have to fight not to run to her and fall at her feet, right there in the dirt.

"If you want to," she says. Her voice is weary, her eyes uncertain, but I *do* want to. More than anything.

Nodding, I gesture for her to get to her feet, then move closer to her, careful not to overwhelm her. As much as I want to pull her close, I can't blame her for being a little skittish. The last couple of times she saw me, I was acting like a raving lunatic, looking right past her like she didn't even exist.

"What do I do now?" she asks, holding her hands out over the dirt, as if it's ready to jump at her command.

"Earth magick is one of the easiest to tap into. The key is staying grounded." Standing behind her, I guide her feet apart, positioning them about shoulder-width. "You can do this while you're sitting too, but that's usually during a ritual or meditation. A lot of times you'll want to call on earth magick in the moment—say, during a fight or skirmish, or some other on-the-fly situation. That's why I like to teach it standing up."

"Makes sense," she says. "But how is this different from Kirin's air magick? He can move rocks too."

"Air magick is less predictable in this kind of situation because you're relying on the currents of air to act upon the rocks. You don't have as much control. But with earth magick..." I lift her hands a little higher and send out a pulse of magick, and the dirt rises, hovering before us in a delicate dance. "See? You're calling on the objects themselves. We're communicating with the rocks, our energy interacting with theirs. It's a direct bond between our bodies and the earth, and in return, we get a direct response."

"Whoa, I can feel it!" Stevie lets out a breathless laugh, the dirt still suspended before us. "Their energy is moving through my hands!"

"Exactly. Now just tell them where you want them to go."

"*Tell* them? Just like that? Like, hey rocks! Go left!"

"Words, intent, visualization… There are as many ways to direct the energy as there are witches and mages. You have to find the method that works best for you. But so far, it looks like you've got their attention."

The earth shifts to the left, just like she asked it too.

With another laugh, she says, "Okay, let's move right."

On command, the rocks and dirt move to the right.

Stevie looks at me over her shoulder again, her face full of wonder, her smile endless. I don't have my camera, but I take a picture with my mind, memorizing the light in her eyes, the pure joy.

"This is amazing! Look!" She swirls her hands in a delicate arc, sending the debris into a similar pattern. "I feel like a magnet. Or… I don't know. Like I'm connected to it all."

"You are. It's magick. It's energy. All of it."

She plays with it a bit longer, trying new patterns and heights, even picking up a little more dirt from the ground, shaping it into a series of flowing waves before finally settling her hands again, letting it hover mid-air.

Taking a chance, I press a delicate kiss to the side of her neck, breathing in her sweet scent.

"I missed you," she whispers.

"I know. I missed you too."

She relaxes back into me and sighs, and I circle my arms around her waist, burying my face in her hair. All around us, the crickets sing their delicate lullabies, and a warm breeze ghosts across the yard, carrying with it the subtle scents of the desert.

Years of living in Arizona, in the magickal spaces between worlds, and I'm still not totally used to the climate here. Southwestern winters are so different from the crisp, stark winters on the east coast, the harsh Decembers that so often made me feel trapped and abandoned.

Inhaling deeply, I hold those warm sensations inside me, mingling with Stevie's honeysuckle-and-heaven scent, and for a full minute, I just live in it. The moment. The air. The magick. The love. *Her* love.

It's so perfect. So safe. And here, in the space between before and after, the words finally find a way out.

"I was fourteen the first time it happened," I whisper.

Stevie gasps, the rocks and dirt dropping instantly to the ground. Her body stiffens in my arms. She knows I'm not talking about magick.

She tries to turn around to face me, but I tighten my grip.

"Don't," I whisper into her hair, lips brushing the silky strands. "Please, Stevie. I need to get this out and I can't... I can't look at you. Not yet."

She seems to understand this, and I feel her relax into my arms once again, despite the banging of her heart behind her ribs. She presses my hands against her belly, giving them a tight squeeze and silently encouraging me to continue.

I don't speak again right away. I'm not even sure where to start. But she doesn't push me. Doesn't prod. She just... exists. Just loves.

After an eternity, I take another deep breath. And then I begin in earnest.

"She told me houses as nice as ours don't just pay for themselves," I say. "That everyone has a job to do, and this would be mine. I was lucky, she said, because it was a *special* job—one I was going to really love. And if I didn't love it, well... I'd be keeping the critiques to myself, unless I wanted to be out on the street, and for my brother to be executed."

She's silent as I tell her the story—every sick and twisted thing that bitch ever said to me, every night she crept through the shadows into my room, every night I spent crying myself to sleep afterward, wishing I could bathe in bleach.

Beneath my touch, Stevie's body trembles. With rage, with sadness, with frustration, with shock... All of it, all at once. She wants to turn around. I can feel the tension in her muscles, spring-loaded and ready.

But I can't let her see me like this.

"For so long I blamed myself," I continue, "even after I left that horrible house and came to the Academy. At Iron and Bone, I finally had my own space, doors that locked, a bed I didn't have to share with anyone I didn't invite. But I still couldn't escape her. Night after night, I relived her torment, berating myself for not figuring out a way to save myself. For not asking for help. For not setting up cameras or some other way to catch her in the act. I should've been smarter, stronger, braver. I should've known better. So many 'shoulds' I started to wonder if maybe I *did* want it, just like she said. That maybe I *was* sick and broken. Maybe I was the reason my parents left, the reason my brother went mad, the reason Janelle had to keep punishing me. But I wasn't broken. Just a little lost. Scared. Fucked up in more ways than I could count. And she preyed on it."

By the time I get all the words out and put them together in some kind of order that makes sense outside my own crazy fucking head, the sky is streaked orange with the last rays of the sunset, my throat hurts from talking, and my whole body feels like it was run over by a freight train.

But somehow, I feel light. Clear. Like I can fucking breathe for the first time in years.

I let out a deep sigh. There's nothing left. Just the breeze and the crickets, the soft sound of her breath, the steady beat of her heart.

Finally, I release my arms, letting her know she can turn around. But I haven't looked at her since I started talking, and now that I'm done, I still can't force my eyes to meet her gaze.

The last time I saw those blue eyes, she was looking at me with joy and wonder, marveling at the magick I'd just taught her.

I'd rather remember her that way.

I keep my gaze firmly on the dirt.

"Look at me, Baz," she says softly.

"I can't. Not yet."

"Then listen to me instead. Can you do that?"

I pull her close and rest my forehead on her shoulder, my hands on her hips. "As long as you're not gonna tell me how sorry you are."

"No sorries," she promises, sliding her hands up my arms. "Only this. You're the same man I knew an hour ago. The same man I knew last week. The same man I first met outside Iron and Bone, acting like a total dickhead but making me laugh anyway. And most importantly, you're the same man I fell in love with. Nothing about your past can ever change that. So we can talk about this as much or as little as you want, but please believe me when I tell you that *nothing* will change how I feel about you."

"I never wanted to talk about it at *all*—that's the thing. I never wanted you to see my ghosts. But all the stuff going on with me lately—the blackouts and the disappearing act —it's all part of this. It's like Judgment's in my head constantly, digging through the worst memories and bringing them to life. I can't control when it happens. One minute I'm here, and then there's this ice-cold dread washing through me, and I'm gone. That's what happened the night you and Kirin and I were together. And again after Harvest Eve."

"And with Janelle today?" she asks gently.

"Janelle... that was different. When I got to the house this morning, all I wanted to do was see you. But then I heard Janelle downstairs, and that was it. It unlocked the monster inside my mind again—but no, not Judgment. It was like something in me suddenly just... *decided*. I *had* to end it. If Carly hadn't come down when she did, I know I would've killed her."

"Carly sensed as much."

"Fucked up, right? Even though some part of me knew it was wrong, a bigger part of me didn't care. In that moment, the bigger part almost won out."

"And now?" she asks, but there's no judgment in her voice. Only softness. Only compassion.

"I wish Janelle Kirkpatrick was dead," I say. "I won't lie to you about that. But... no. I don't want her fucking blood on my hands. She doesn't deserve to take up any more space in my head *or* my life."

"That's probably the right call."

"She makes me feel weak." I tighten my hands on Stevie's hips, still unable to lift my head to look at her. "I feel like she's got this hold over me, and no matter what I say or do, she'll always be there. I can talk all the shit I want, threaten her when she's practically in a coma. Yeah, real big man, right? But when it comes down to it, I'll never be whole—that's how it feels. And not even *you* can fix that, Stevie."

"Baz, I don't... *Goddess*. I know you guys think I want to fix you—like maybe I have all this Star magick to make everything okay again. But the truth is, I can't take away your pain. I can't go back in time and undo all the horrible things Janelle did to you, or the things your parents did before that. And I'm damn well not going to tell you how to feel about it. But I will tell you this." She steps back and cups my face, gently tilting it up toward hers, and even though I keep my eyes closed, I feel her gaze on me, warm and kind, full of love.

"When I look at you," she says softly, "when I feel your heartbeat, when I taste your kiss, when you hold me close, when I see you fight for your brothers, when I think of *everything* we've shared together… I don't see weakness. The man standing before me now? He's a fucking warrior, Baz Redgrave. And if you don't believe that yet, I'll keep the faith for the both of us, for as long as you need me to."

Behind my closed lids, tears gather, my throat tight, my heart damn near exploding. Stevie's the empath here, but at her words, her touch, I feel her love wrap around me and sink in deep, filling all the cold and empty spaces inside me.

Sharing this story, making this confession… It hollowed me out inside. But by some miracle, she's managed to fill me back up again, just by being Stevie. Just by being the woman I love. Just by being my Little Bird.

And here, beneath the blaze-orange Arizona sky, I finally find the strength to look at her. Hell, maybe it's not even *my* strength—maybe it's all hers, borrowed by a broken man who may never fully heal. But maybe some part of the warrior she sees is still here too. Maybe we can co-exist, he and I. Starting right now.

Her eyes shine with emotion, and I take her face in my hands, holding it like it's the most precious gift, marveling at the impossibility of it all. Billions of souls in this world, thousands of lifetimes into which she could've come to this earth, and she chose now. She chose us. She chose *me*.

"I love you, Starla Milan," I whisper. "You're my light. My heart. My goddess. And I promise you, I'll spend the rest of my life—"

"Okay, could this *get* any more disgusting?" Carly barges into our perfect moment like a cold rain, standing on the back deck and glaring at us, her nose wrinkled, arms crossed, hip jutting out, her eyes about five seconds from rolling right out of her damn head. "Seriously. I think I've just lost my appetite."

Stevie cracks up, the last of the fading sun setting her eyes on fire, and in that moment, not even Carly's bad timing and badder attitude can ruin things.

"Can we help you, Carly?" I ask, but there's no malice there. Only friendship. Only gratitude. Only the possibility that comes from finally being honest with the people I care about and living to tell the tale.

Despite her mock sneer, I suspect Carly senses it too. New beginnings. Potential. And, dare I say… hope.

"Isla asked me to tell you dinner's ready," Carly says. "She cooked her Nana's jerk chicken. Apparently it's the— and I quote—bomb dot com. I mean, who even says that? Honestly."

Keeping my gaze locked on Stevie's, I grin and say, "You tell Isla to save us some leftovers. Stevie and I have plans tonight." I lean in close and whisper the rest, just for my girl. "*Disgusting* ones."

TWENTY

STEVIE

Baz and I never do make it to dinner—not even for the left-overs, or for Professor Broome's famous Prosperity Cake, or for the signature cocktails Carly and Nat created to compliment the whole meal.

Hours after our backyard reunion, we're still lying together in the darkness of my Red Sands bedroom, moonlight caressing our bare skin as we gaze into each other's eyes, fingers trailing softly over dips and curves, kisses lingering.

Tonight isn't about recreating all the crazy, passionate moments we've already shared—moments that will be waiting for us whenever we're ready. It's simply about feeling safe and whole. About being in the presence of love without fear, without manipulation, without judgment.

It's about picking up the broken pieces and making something new with them—something even stronger and more beautiful than before.

So that's just what we do.

One touch, one kiss, one whispered *I love you* at a time until we finally drift off to the incomparable lullabies of crickets and the soft desert breeze fluttering through the curtains, knowing that in this room, between Cernunnos and his Star, there is only love.

The next morning, we're up before the rest of the house, slipping into the guest room downstairs to give Professor Broome a break and spend some time with Ani. He hasn't awoken yet, but his color is looking better, his breathing soft and even. When I lay my head on his chest, the strong, steady beat of his heart thumps against my ear, and it fills me with the same sense of comfort and peace I felt in the cave with my Princess of Cups.

"He'll be home soon," I tell Baz. "I have no doubts."

"Then neither do I." Baz leans in and kisses Ani's forehead, the gesture so soft and tender it makes my heart melt. "You hear that, Gingersnap? Get your ass home."

We stay with him a little longer, taking turns reading him passages from the *very* naughty vampire romance novel Professor Broome inadvertently left on the night table. We've just finished up a particularly juicy scene that leaves us both a little breathless when our phones ping with an official Academy alert.

Baz digs out his phone, his face falling. "It's from Trello."

"What's it say?"

"Esteemed students and colleagues," he begins. "I regret to inform you that due to recent unforeseen circumstances, we have made the difficult decision to end our winter semester, effective immediately. Final exams have been canceled, and all grades will be determined based on work and class participation to date. Feel free to contact your professors directly if you have any questions about individual grading policies."

"I can almost hear the collective cheers on campus." I let out a sigh, leaning back on the bed next to Ani. "Honestly, I'm surprised she waited this long to shut things down. It's just not safe, especially if Eastman turns out to be a traitor."

"There's more," he says, continuing. "Unfortunately, given the volatile and often violent situation escalating outside our boundaries, students will not be permitted to return home at this time. All students will be required to remain on campus, under the sole direction and supervision of Agent Eastman of the APOA, who will be implementing new safety protocols to ensure your safety. While these protocols may feel restrictive, rest assured they are designed for your safety and will be lifted as soon as possible. Until that time, we are requiring all students to remain within their assigned dorm buildings. With the exception of Hot Shots, which was damaged recently after a gas leak, restaurants and stores will remain open and accessible within each building, as will the common rooms. Students are not permitted to visit other dorms or access any outdoor spaces. The Promenade is also closed at this time."

"Holy shit," I say. "She's going into full lockdown mode. People are going to freak out."

He scrolls a bit farther down the message, his brow pinched with concern. "Most of you are aware of the ongoing investigation involving our former head librarian, Professor Phaines. I am pleased to announce that the investigation has come to a close, and I can personally assure you that Phaines poses no additional threat, as he is deceased."

"Murdered, incinerated, *and* buried," I say, happy to remind myself of my attacker's multi-part brutal demise.

"Due to the diligent efforts of the APOA," Baz continues, "in coordination with key faculty and staff, Phaines was discovered taking refuge in the basement storage area of the library, aided and abetted by interim librarian Janelle Kirkpatrick. All indications are that they were using the area as a makeshift magick lab, conducting unregulated and illegal experiments. In the late hours after Harvest Eve, the lab suffered a massive explosion, damaging much of the library's foundation. Kirkpatrick has been apprehended by the authorities. Phaines was pronounced dead on the scene. Thankfully, no students or faculty were hurt, but several offices, along with some of our most prized collections, were destroyed. The library will remain closed for repairs for the foreseeable future and is, as are all non-dorm buildings, off-limits to students and faculty alike."

"Goddess. There's so much spin in that message, it's making me dizzy."

"Eastman's all over this," he says. "Casey told us as

much. I don't know why Trello would put him in charge, especially if she's on our side."

"I'm still not totally on Team Trello *or* Team Casey, for that matter. But let's say they're actually legit. Maybe Trello didn't have a choice. Kirin said Eastman doesn't know the other agents are on to him, and they're trying to keep it that way."

"Yeah, I get that. But this whole 'keep your enemies close' thing might come back to bite us all in the ass. It usually does."

"Did Trello say anything about the missing magickal essences?"

Baz skims through the rest of the message, shaking his head. "Just a bunch of platitudes about how we're stronger together and we'll get through this as a family, Arcana Academy pride, blah blah blah."

"There's no way I'm going back to Iron and Bone. I'm not leaving you guys, and I'm not leaving Nat and Isla, either. Or Carly. Or the professors."

"Pretty sure the rules don't apply to us anymore." Baz puts away his phone and leans down for a kiss. Then, with a devious smirk, "And if anyone tries to take you away from me, I'll bury them alive. Done and done."

"The best part about having an earth-mage boyfriend is the ability to bury bodies without leaving fingerprints. Who would've thought?"

"No, Little Bird. The best part is this." He claims me in another kiss and climbs on top of me, his fingers already working the buttons on my shirt.

"Not to ruin your big moment here, earth mage, but should we really be doing this next to Ani, especially when he's not even conscious for the fun?"

"I was thinking we could give him a little more incentive to come home." He presses another searing-hot kiss to my lips. "Maybe he'll make it back before the grand finale."

I laugh and wrap my legs around his hips, deciding I'm totally on board with that kind of logic. But before we can implement a full-on reenactment of the vampire novel as a beacon for Ani's homecoming, Kirin barges into the room.

"You want in on this, brother?" Baz asks, looking at Kirin over his shoulder. "We're trying to entice our boy into coming home. Emphasis on coming."

Kirin's face turns red, a flash of intrigue brightening his energy. "I, uh... Yes? Yes, I do want in on it very much? But... Shit." He rubs a hand over his head, then sighs. "Casey and Quintana are here. Time for a family meeting."

Baz curses, then climbs off me, offering a hand to pull me up.

I lean down and kiss Ani's lips, soft and sweet. "See you later, Sunshine."

"Keep the bed warm for us, Gingersnap." Baz ruffles his hair. "We'll be back."

TWENTY-ONE

STEVIE

Out in the main area of the house, most everyone is already gathered in the big living room, passing around plates of bagels and muffins and cut fruit. But from the serious look on Professor Broome's face, it's clear I'm going to need more caffeine for this conversation, so I make a quick detour into the kitchen.

Doc is standing at the coffeemaker, dressed in an impeccable dark gray shirt-and-slacks combo that has me drooling.

Damn, that man looks good in a button-down.

Damn, that man looks good *out* of button-down too, but now is not the time for fantasizing about hot sex with my mental magicks professor. Especially since I'm still halfway into a hot sex fantasy involving Baz, Kirin, and Ani.

Yeah, Doc *really* needs to reconsider that 'no sharing' thing…

"Sleep well? Or did Baz's snoring keep you up?" He

winks at me, eyes sparkling, energy pulsing with a mix of warmth, pleasure, and a hint of jealousy.

After a quick scan to make sure the other professors aren't watching, I stretch up on my toes for a kiss.

"Careful, Doc," I whisper. "Your possessive streak is showing."

"*You* be careful, Miss Milan," he whispers back. "Or we'll be having another talk about your... insubordination." His knuckles graze my nipple, lips teasing the shell of my ear, hot breath driving me wild.

"I see you're wearing the belt," I say, tracing the top edge of it with my fingers. Beneath my touch, his cock is just starting to bulge.

"Hmm. I'd rather see *you* wearing it. In fact—"

"You guys ready out there?" Casey calls impatiently from the living room, earning another point on my shit list.

"Be right with you, Agents." Doc pulls away from me, reaching behind him for a mug of freshly poured coffee and handing it over.

"What is this dark potion?" I ask.

"It's called coffee. Perhaps you're familiar?"

"Where's the lightly whipped foam?" I take a whiff, wrinkling my nose at the bitter assault. "And the honey? And the cinnamon? Kirin would *never* try to pass off this sludge as coffee."

"Just black today. Trust me, you're going to need it."

On *that* super fun note, we head into the living room and find seats, Doc taking a chair in front of the huge fireplace, me snuggling in between Isla and Carly on the big leather couch.

Perched in an armchair directly across from me is none other than the gun-waving, hostage-taking, kiss-interrupting Casey Appleton, flanked on either side by Kirin and Agent Quintana, hovering over her like sentries.

I glance up at Kirin, and he smiles softly, as if to tell me everything is okay.

If only it were that easy for me to believe it.

Baz told me the whole story about what happened during the library attack, and I *am* glad that Kirin's finally making some inroads with his family. But for me, the wounds are still fresh. Possession or not, I won't soon forget the image of Casey pointing a gun at Ani's head. Just thinking about it again now fills me with so much rage, I'm practically making my coffee boil.

"Stevie," Casey says, offering a pained smile. "Nice to see you again. I'm glad you're... well."

Is she serious? *Well?* Oh, yes. I'm fabulous. We're trapped in Red Sands Canyon, the world is rapidly becoming a total war zone, and one of the men I love is in a magickal coma in the next room—a disastrous link in a long chain of events Casey herself began the night she held a gun to his head.

If she thinks she can make it go away with a fake-ass compliment and a smile, she's certifiably insane.

"Kirin says you have an update?" I say, keeping the rest of those thoughts to myself.

Casey's energy flickers with regret, but she nods and

gets to her feet, looking at each of us in turn as if she's about to make some big, epic sales pitch.

Or drop a shit-ton of bad news.

Goddess, Doc was right. I *do* need black coffee for this meeting. I take a sip and force it down, willing it to work its magick on my bloodstream as quickly as possible.

"I know Baz and Kirin told you all about what happened at the library the other night," she begins, "including the fact that we can no longer count Agent Eastman among our allies. And you've all seen Headmistress Trello's announcement, yes?"

Baz scoffs. "The one where she put our not-ally Eastman in charge of the Academy?"

"That's the one." Casey gestures toward Quintana. "We wanted to give some more background on that, and give you an update on how we—with Anna Trello's help—plan to proceed. Agent?"

Quintana nods, taking point. "During a review of the exterior suite camera footage from the Iron and Bone dorms, our satellite computer lab in New York found some anomalies."

"What kind of anomalies?" Doc asks.

"For starters, it looks like Eastman intentionally altered some of the footage on the security feed outside Stevie's suite."

"But Eastman was the one who set up the new system in the first place," I say. "He showed up at my suite after Trello sent out the security emails, saying he had to update everything. I watched him do it."

"That's precisely when he made his move," Quintana says. "He manipulated the video from your system to make it look like Janelle Kirkpatrick was casting spy runes outside your door."

"We found Janelle's lipstick out there, though," Baz says. "You're saying he planted it?"

"No. We saw Janelle on the repaired footage—she *did* pay Stevie a visit earlier that morning. We don't know why —Stevie didn't answer the door. But Eastman himself cast the rune. Somehow he transposed the images to make it look like it was Janelle."

"But why was Eastman spying on my suite?" Alarm shoots through my chest. Baz and Kirin checked everything out after we saw Janelle on the feed, and Baz set up protective crystal grids to counteract any future magick. But still, the whole idea leaves me uneasy.

"Fucking perv," Carly says. "Let's castrate him."

I squeeze her knee, grateful for the solidarity, but I'm pretty sure Eastman wasn't looking for a few post-shower boob shots.

"We don't believe the suite was his primary objective," Casey says. "He didn't even complete the rune properly. He was likely trying to cast doubt on Janelle—she's been his scapegoat all along. His main goal was always the archives."

"How did my mother get involved with Eastman?" Carly asks.

"It's a complex web," Casey says with a tired sigh. "One

we're still trying to untangle. Our working theory is that Eastman and Janelle's connecting point is Phaines."

The coffee turns to lead in my stomach.

All roads lead back to the Dark Arcana. To the mage who nearly killed me.

"Can we back up a moment?" Professor Maddox asks. "Why did you begin to suspect Agent Eastman in the first place? I'm not well-versed in APOA politics, but I was under the impression he's one of the most well-respected agents on staff. Many of us were surprised he'd even been assigned to the Academy."

"As were we," Casey says. "Which, in hindsight, was the first red flag. Normally, they just send field grunts out for this sort of thing, especially for the preliminary investigations. But when word came through that the Academy needed our help, he assigned himself immediately."

"And no one questioned this?" Maddox asks.

"He's been my boss and mentor for many years. I trusted him. I figured he had a plan."

"He sure did," I say. "Just not the one you were hoping for."

Casey nods. "After the student attacks, I asked him about enhanced security, but the idea made him jumpy. Agent Quintana and I also started feeling like he wasn't taking our concerns seriously—evidence was dismissed or downplayed as coincidence, and our requests for additional agent support on campus were repeatedly denied, even when it became clear we were dealing with something much more serious than we initially believed.

"On a hunch, I sent some security footage to my source at the lab and asked him to analyze the feeds for any inconsistencies. I wasn't expecting him to implicate Eastman directly—at most, I thought maybe Eastman was covering up a mistake, hiding his own incompetence. That would've been shocking enough, but what we discovered was just... It was appalling."

"As you've probably deduced," Quintana says, "it wasn't the explosion at the library that damaged the archives. That was all Eastman's doing—I'd bet my magick on it."

Kirin shakes his head, his shoulders slumping. "I always assumed the archives lab was one of the safest and most well-guarded places on campus. I designed the enhanced security protocols myself."

"Eastman is very clever," Casey says. "Once he realized what you and Stevie were working on, he made it his mission to break those protocols. He used every tool at his disposal to do so."

"But why?" I ask. "Does he have some grand plans to steal the Arcana objects and take control of magick? If that's the case, he'd better take a number."

"He's not interested in stealing or controlling magick," Casey says. "He wants to dismantle it. He believes—militantly—that humans were never meant to have magick, and that the prophecies—something that could help us protect and nurture magick for future generations—shouldn't be translated at *all*."

She drops back into her chair, eyes flashing with

genuine anger. I feel it in her energy, a hot and prickly wave mixed with a deep sense of betrayal and a good dose of self-blame.

"After my contact at the lab discovered the video doctoring," she continues, "he went through a virtual backdoor into Eastman's online backups and network activity. He found a *trove* of anti-magick propaganda, including pseudonymous memberships on some of the most extremist anti-magick forums in existence. Worse, he found evidence tying Eastman to high-level non-magickal authorities working to stamp out magick. Unless it's all part of some elaborate frame job, William Eastman has been ratting out magickal practitioners throughout the country for years —including some of the very families who work for him."

The enormity of that settles in, weighing heavy on us all.

Nat, who'd been quietly twisting and untwisting her multi-colored hair, finally pipes up. "Why the fuck does he still have a job? What he's doing *has* to be illegal, right?"

"*Legal* is a term reserved for non-magickal authorities," Casey says, "and he's helping those authorities. In terms of APOA ethics, yes, he's breaching every last one. But my contact is still working on securing admissible evidence. Unfortunately, most of APOA has their hands full protecting the larger community from the ongoing attacks and false arrests."

"If Eastman is so bent on destroying magick," Baz says, "and he's working to frame witches and mages in the community at large, why is he bothering with us?"

"He wants to *end* magick," Casey replies. "Completely.

What better place to start than the academy responsible for honing the minds and magickal skills of the best and brightest witches and mages in the country? If one of his aims is to dismantle magickal institutions from the inside out, you guys are basically the source."

I gulp down some more of the bitter, black coffee, hoping it will counterbalance the cold sense of doom crawling over my skin. As if we don't have enough to worry about with the Dark Arcana and the outside authorities, now we've got Eastman fucking us from the inside, all under the guise of protecting and serving.

"Evil," Nat says, giving up on her hair and reaching for a chocolate cappuccino muffin instead. "There's no other word for it."

"Yes," Casey says, "and like most truly evil people, Eastman believes his intentions are a hundred percent noble. In his mind, magick itself is what harms students, and by destroying it, he's saving them. Saving all of us. That's why he was able to get through the Academy portals —the magick didn't perceive him as a threat, because down to his very core, he believes he's a savior."

"But he's a mage," I say. "One of us. He's basically condemning himself."

"According to what we found in his online records," Casey says, "he believes he's going to hell, and his only chance at salvation is to destroy the very thing that makes him unworthy."

Unworthy. The word makes my insides burn.

"That is the most fucked-up thing I've heard all week,"

Baz says. "And believe me, I've heard a lot of fucked-up shit lately."

Professor Maddox shakes her head, her eyes shining. "We've seen this sort of fanatical behavior in many other contexts, but the root is always the same: a deep, unsettling hatred of self. Unfortunately, it rarely ends with the self. That kind of darkness spreads like nuclear fallout, sickening everyone it touches."

"Getting back to Phaines," Doc says, coming to stand behind me. He touches my shoulder, giving it a gentle, reassuring squeeze. "How does he tie into this?"

"And Anna Trello?" Professor Broome asks.

"And my mother?" Carly reaches for the last chocolate cappuccino muffin, breaking it in half and passing the other part to me.

Soon we're all talking at once, everyone asking a million questions, the energy in the room rising to a fevered pitch of fear, anger, and determination.

"One at a time," Casey finally says, shouting over the din to get our attention. We settle down again, waiting for her and Quintana to continue unraveling a conspiracy so many levels deep, it makes Area 51 look like a kiddie playground.

"Carly," Quintana says, "it will come as no surprise to you that your mother's primary interest here was the Arcana artifacts."

"Nothing about my mother's crazy schemes surprises me anymore," Carly says. "But yes, she's been chasing that golden ticket for decades."

"In our investigation of Phaines, we learned that he and your mother had been working together for many years, predating his known crimes and her arrival on campus."

"He was a so-called friend of the family," Carly says. "We've known him forever."

"Your mother believed he had knowledge about the objects, including maps and manuscripts that could ultimately reveal their exact locations. That was her only interest in Phaines, as far as we could tell."

Carly nods.

"For his part, Phaines—who was chasing after the same legends—believed your mother could help him through her connections to other wealthy treasure hunters as well as additional financial resources for his ongoing magickal experiments."

"I'm intimately familiar with those," Carly says. "Turns out I was one of them."

"As was your mother," Casey says. "Phaines's possession formed a mental link between Janelle and me, giving me glimpses of their relationship. Apparently, through similar but lower-level possessions and other spells, he'd been using her—with her consent—to spy on your magickal development for many years."

Carly's so angry she's shaking. I reach for her hand, trying to send her calming vibes. Across the room, Baz meets my gaze, his energy flaring with concern for her, trumping even his own hatred for the woman who caused them both so much pain.

"Apparently, he believed he could perfect his siphoning spells and eventually access your psychic gifts," Casey says.

"Like he did to those other students," I say. "Basically, stealing their magick."

"And my mother was involved in all of it." Carly closes her eyes and shakes her head, another wave of fury rolling through her. "Again, I'm not surprised. Disgusted, but not surprised."

"Once Janelle was appointed interim librarian," Quintana says, "Phaines had a personal spy on campus. One who could access his research and keep him apprised of any new developments with the Melissa Milan prophecies."

I glance up at Kirin, his eyes filling with pain and regret. It's not his fault my mother's work was stolen from the archives, but he hasn't stopped apologizing since he first told me about the attack at the library. At this point, I'm less concerned about the memento of my mother's work and more concerned about what Eastman wants to do with it.

"So Anna Trello has been asleep at the wheel this entire time," Professor Broome says, shaking her head in disdain. "We've certainly locked horns a few times over the years, but I still respected the woman. I never expected such complacency."

"Or duplicity," Professor Maddox says.

"Trello's been in league with Phaines from the start," I say, unable to keep the bitterness from my voice. "She murdered him to cover her tracks. She knew he was stealing students' magick. She knew about the fairy's breath and the possessions. She was obviously working with him

—she said their agreement was over. That they'd come to the end of the road."

"I don't know what agreements they had in place before my arrival," Casey admits. "But I assure you—she was working with *us*."

"How so?" I ask.

"After the first wave of student attacks, Trello immediately suspected Phaines. She sensed his dark magick at work, but she didn't know whether he'd been hiding on campus the entire time, or somehow found a way back through the security portals."

"Yet she still assured everyone on campus that he wasn't a threat," I say.

"As I've said before, I don't always agree with her decisions or communication tactics, but I do know she has the Academy's best interests at heart."

I give her an eye-roll that would make Carly proud.

"Anyway," Casey says, "not long after Janelle's arrival, Trello caught her messing with the security cameras outside the library storage area. Soon after, even though Janelle had a house here in Red Sands, she discovered Janelle had been sleeping in Phaines's old office. So one night, after confirming Janelle was asleep, Trello headed down into the basement, hoping to uncover the reason for her new librarian's shady behavior."

"She found it," Quintana says. "The whole setup. In that moment, she knew Janelle was harboring Phaines, keeping him alive, and helping with his experiments."

"Goddess," Carly says with a bitter laugh. "If that

woman had put *half* as much effort into being a mother instead of an evil henchwoman, I might not need so much therapy."

Casey offers a sympathetic smile. "Your mother wasn't working alone, Carly. After Trello's grim discovery, she brought her suspicions to Agent Quintana and me. From there, we pored over the myriad findings from our contact in New York and determined that Eastman was also involved in supporting Phaines. Apparently he'd learned about Phaines's experiments through his online connections, and saw an opportunity. We don't know how it all came together, but at some point, Eastman made contact with Phaines and struck up a deal of his own. He wanted access to Phaines's siphoning magick, and Phaines wanted to be back on campus. Eastman figured out how to break the portal security and bring him back in, and from there, they joined forces with Janelle. Eastman and Janelle kept Phaines alive and helped coordinate the attacks. It seems they also managed to convert a few other students and faculty to their cause."

"Like the dark mages who attacked us in the library," Kirin says.

"Exactly," Casey says.

"We had all these theories," Quintana says, "but no hard proof. Until the brilliant Agent Appleton decided to go in as bait—an idea I opposed from the start."

"So did Trello," Casey says. "But ultimately you both knew it was the best way to get the irrefutable proof we needed."

"So you broke protocol and set yourself up for an attack." He glares at Casey something fierce, but his energy is nothing but protective.

"We knew the attack pattern," Casey explains. "Late at night, students walking in more remote areas. So, I put on an Arcana Academy hoodie and took a solo jog out behind Flame and Fury. Two cloaked mages nabbed me right away. I figured they'd try to siphon my magick—I had an undetectable counterspell in place for protection. But instead, they shot me full of Fairy's Breath and let Phaines take my mind and body for a joyride."

"We all know how well *that* worked out," Quintana says.

"Fast forward to my and Janelle's capture," Casey says. "Trello was already worried my plan would get me killed. When Dr. Devane showed up at Trello's place, demanding access to a vehicle and a remote house in the Red Sands community, she put the pieces together and decided Phaines had to be eliminated. She wasn't willing to risk my life any more than we already had, or to risk more attacks on students."

"And Eastman?" I ask. "How does he come back into play?"

"Trello contacted him to report Janelle and Casey missing," Agent Quintana says. "She expressed concern that the women had been kidnapped or harmed, though of course she knew they were here with Dr. Devane."

"Being kidnapped and harmed," Casey adds, shooting a death glare at Doc.

"I was a complete professional," Doc says.

"A professional kidnapper is nothing to brag about," she quips. Then, with a resigned sigh, "But in the end, I would've done the same to protect the people I love."

Her attention shifts toward Kirin, her energy warming.

"When Eastman learned Phaines was dead," she says, "he sent in his minions to collect the essences and related research from the library storage—that's his prize in all this. Finding a way to eliminate magick from the population without eliminating the population itself."

A shiver rolls down my spine. "And this is the man with ultimate authority at the Academy now? Where a forced lockdown prevents people from leaving or even interacting beyond their own dorms? I can't believe you guys are okay with that."

"Far from it," Quintana says. "But we need more time to get the evidence together. Besides, with Phaines dead and Janelle out of the picture, Eastman is on his own now."

"Along with his shadow-mage minions and whoever else he's charmed into joining his savior mission," Kirin says. "We fought those guys, Case. I don't want to go up against them again."

Casey shakes her head. "Eastman needs time to regroup. He doesn't want to ring any alarm bells. His whole plan relies on secrecy—he needs the students to remain calm and to trust his authority. That will buy us a little more time."

"Where's Trello now?" Baz asks. "If she's so high-and-mighty in all this, why hasn't she made an appearance?"

"A question I've been asking since I enrolled here," I say.

"She is off-campus following another lead," Casey says. "I'm waiting for her to make contact again with more information, but from what little she's told me, it's important."

"What little she's told you," Doc says. "That's a theme with Anna Trello—one you'd be wise to examine rather than taking her at her word."

We spend the next hour asking questions and rehashing everything we've just learned. By the time the agents are done putting together all the known puzzle pieces—along with a good deal of speculation about the still-missing ones—the bagels and pastries are gone, the only fruit left is the universally hated cantaloupe, and my head's about to go nuclear from the overdose of keyed-up energy in the room.

"So to recap," I finally say, "the Magician wants to reclaim magick as his birthright, killing us all in the process. The government wants to kill us just for existing. A high-ranking APOA agent who's now calling the shots at our Academy wants to strip us of our power and throw us to the wolves, despite the fact that he himself is a mage. And our traitorous headmistress is actually a double-agent working in the shadows to keep us all safe."

"That about sums it up." Casey glances at her phone, then nods at Quintana.

Apparently, story time has come to an end.

"Listen, guys," she says, rising from her chair. "I know the news is grim. It may not feel like it, but the Academy—including the Red Sands community—is the safest place for everyone. The magick will protect you, as much as anything can. I'm just asking you to give us a little more time and a little more trust before doing anything else."

"That's just it though," Carly says. "If what you're saying is true, we need just as much protection from what's happening *inside* the Academy as we do outside of it."

"We're picking the lesser of two evils," Casey says.

"Always a good strategy, Case," Baz says, flashing her a sarcastic thumbs-up.

Ignoring the dig, Casey turns back to Carly. "Carly, this may be difficult to process, but I need to tell you... Agent Quintana and I are taking custody of your mother today."

"What does that mean, exactly?" she asks.

"Janelle is being charged with aiding and abetting a fugitive, multiple counts of assault, attempted murder, fraud, and conspiracy to steal student magick, among other things. She'll be questioned at length by APOA. Depending on the outcome, she'll face either a trial or—"

"Or a death sentence." Carly glances at Baz, a deep understanding passing between them. He comes to stand next to her, putting a hand on her shoulder while Casey continues.

"She left some things in her Red Sands house," Casey says gently. "It's not far from here. If you'd like, I can come back later and take you to—"

"I appreciate your kindness, Agent Appleton." Carly flips her long raven hair, her smile brightening right along with her energy. "But I've already taken everything I need from Janelle Kirkpatrick."

I glance at her, arching an eyebrow at the smug satisfaction emanating from her being.

"Oh, and Agents?" She taps her lips, pretending to be deep in thought. "I should probably warn you—Janelle might look a *little* different than you remember."

Casey narrows her eyes. "How so?"

"The thing is… My mother knew how to siphon too. Not magick, but life essence." Carly shrugs. "She always said I kept her young. She meant that literally."

"Fucking bitch," Baz mutters.

"It's all good now. Mom and I cleared the air yesterday." Carly smirks, waggling her brows. "Also, I totally spelled her ass."

"Let me guess," Baz says. "The little chat you had about boundaries?"

"It's funny what happens when your daughter decides to take her youthful glow back," she says, smoothing a hand over her shiny hair. Now that she mentions it, she *does* look a little perkier today, her skin glowing, her eyes bright. "I left her down there with a mirror. I don't think she's too happy with me right now."

"You are awesome and terrifying," I say.

"Remember that next time you try to get on my bad side, Twink."

With renewed urgency, Casey gestures for Quintana to head down to the basement to see what monstrosity awaits them. Before she follows him, she pulls me aside, her voice low and serious.

"Stevie, I just wanted you to know how sorry I am for

my part in what happened at Breath and Blade. I know I hurt you, and you're all still dealing with the repercussions of that night—especially Ani."

I cross my arms over my chest and wait for her to continue, to insist it wasn't her fault, to remind me that Phaines was in the driver's seat, that she didn't understand what was happening…

But she doesn't.

"I understand trust has to be earned," she says instead. "I promise I'll do what I can to earn yours, no matter how long it takes."

My respect for her goes up a few notches. I'm not ready to invite her to the next Witch-'N-Bitch or anything, but I no longer want to bury her up to the neck in the backyard and let the scorpions find her, so that's progress.

None of us wants to see Janelle again, so we all head outside until the agents are finished transporting her out. Once the coast is clear, Doc quietly calls the brotherhood into Ani's room.

"I know we promised the agents we'd stay within the protective boundaries of the house," he says as we gather around the bed, "but there's one more errand we need to take care of first."

He's talking about the Chalice. After we pulled it out of the realm, we spelled it and hid it in the dresser, but that was just a temporary solution.

"You want to take it the Fool's Grave," Baz says.

"But how?" Kirin asks. "The magickal boundary protecting the objects will only open with all five of us present. We have to wait for Ani to come back. He doesn't have control of his body right now."

"We don't need Ani's body to unlock the magick." Doc reaches for Ani's arm, his energy resigned and apologetic. In his free hand, he holds a syringe, the sharp needle glinting in the sunlight. "Only his blood."

TWENTY-TWO

STEVIE

Hours later, when the house is silent save for the hum of the fridge and the soft snores drifting from the upstairs bedrooms, we make our escape.

"Stay alert," Doc whispers as we pile into the SUV.

Snugly seat-belted into the passenger seat, I clutch my Eye of Horus pendant and whisper a prayer of protection— to my parents, to the goddesses, to the entire universe. Then, with a vial of Ani's blood secured in Doc's bag and the Chalice of Blood and Sorrow secured in mine, we drive out into the starry-eyed darkness.

Our destination is over an hour away—a forgotten desert outpost in the middle of nowhere, featuring an abandoned convenience store and gas station that looks like it hasn't done business since the 1970s. The old pumps are rusted and hollow, the hoses disintegrated long ago.

"This place was built by mages to mark the path to the energy vortex behind it," Doc explains as he drives onto the cracked pavement and kills the engine. "We need it to create a portal back to campus."

I nod, hefting my bag over my shoulder. Portaling directly from Red Sands would've been more convenient, but at what risk? If this goes sideways tonight, the last thing we want is anyone—or any*thing*—following us back through the portal to our house.

"I feel like we've got a giant target painted on our backs," I say, peering into the ghostly remnants of the convenience store. Actually, "store" is a bit generous; it's more like a large shack, its few shelves and coolers overrun with tumbleweeds.

Doc squeezes the back of my neck. "We'll be home before you know it."

Home. The word wraps around my heart like a blanket, filling my mind with visions of a future we haven't yet secured, but one that gives me hope and strength nevertheless.

Is it even possible? A home with the men I've come to respect, to trust, to love?

"She's smiling," Baz says, leaning in to kiss my cheek. "We're all the way out here in Apocalypsetown on a stealth mission that might just get us killed, and this woman is smiling."

"It's called *hope*," I tell him, grinning until my cheeks hurt. "And right now, I'll take that over freaking out like a little bitch *any* day."

"Are you saying I'm freaking out?" he teases.

"No," Kirin replies. "I think she's saying you're a little bitch."

"Fair enough." Baz laughs, stealing another kiss before heading into the lonely desert beyond.

We fall in beside him, following the pull of the energy vortex about a half-mile out to a flat, sandy area encircled with scrub brush. The magick is too faint for most regular humans to sense, but to me it's undeniable, like an invisible water current gently dragging us in.

I hold out my hands, letting the magick wash over them, warm and comforting. "This is definitely the spot."

Doc kneels down on the ground and removes the Academy pin from his bag—the same one he used to wear on his ties. "This portal will get us into the Petrified Forest of Iron and Bone," he says. "From there, Baz will create a second portal to take us to the caves. Our goal tonight is the Fool's Grave—get in, hide the Chalice, and get out. Agreed?"

"Agreed," we all reply.

Gathering behind Doc, we watch in silence as he performs the same portal ritual I first witnessed behind Lala's house. He pricks his finger with the tie pin, then draws a sigil into the earth with his blood, whispering a spell.

The sigil blazes white, then sinks into the ground, calling up the portal—a swirling, shimmering mass of bright blue and white light, pulsing with strong magick.

"I'll take point," Kirin says. "If anything's waiting for us on the other side, I'm bringing the whole damn sky down on their asses."

"Let's hope it doesn't come to that." Doc gets to his feet and gestures for Kirin to go ahead, then Baz. He grabs my hand last, and the two of us step through together, spilling out into the Forest.

All around us, petrified trees glow like white stone monoliths in the moonlight, a sight as eerie as it is beautiful.

With no time to waste, we all link arms, then Baz uses his earth magick to portal us the remaining distance, leaving us off at the mouth of the narrow passageway that leads into the caves.

"And speaking of hope..." Kirin points up at the sky, his smile bright. "Looks like we've got some backup tonight."

I glance up and catch the graceful white arc of my snowy owl familiar, swooping down and then circling, keeping watch.

"Hey... you!" I wave up at the night sky, my grin stretching wide.

"You really need to name him," Kirin says.

"I know. I'm just waiting for inspiration—it hasn't come to me yet."

"Don't wait too long," Kirin says. "Naming him will further solidify your bond."

"He's definitely just here for backup, right?" Doc says, concern tightening his voice. "Not as some kind of omen?"

Goosebumps erupt across my arms, but I ignore them, shooting Doc a warning glare. "Hope, Doc. Remember? That's the theme tonight. Try to keep up."

Doc grunts out a meager laugh, but I'd be lying if I said I didn't share his concern. The silence of the forest is so all-encompassing, it almost feels like a movie set. No crickets, no night birds, no ground creatures scuttling about. Even the breeze seems to have evaporated, leaving us in a strange sort of in-between that feels neither natural nor safe.

The doom-vibes only intensify as we make our way to the inner cave, a deep chill running down my spine. Its icy fingers refuse to lessen their grip, even when we reach the stone altar inside.

"The energy is off." I finally succumb to the urge to rub my arms. "I can't pinpoint it exactly, but something about this doesn't feel right."

"*Everything* about this doesn't feel right," Doc says, retrieving the Book of Reckoning from its hiding place. "Let's just get it over with and get back to Red Sands."

We perform the now-familiar Keepers of the Grave ritual, slicing our palms over the altar and calling on the King of Swords for guidance and clarity, our deeds recorded in the book for posterity.

Opening rites complete, we proceed to the antechamber, calling on our blood once again—this time spilling it on the ground where we bound the first two Arcana objects. Doc adds the vial of Ani's blood, and together, we recite the short opening spell:

Blood that binds, blood that shields
At our command, the magick yields

At first, nothing happens. We repeat the spell two more times, squeezing a little more blood into the mix, those icy fingers of dread digging deeper into my chest.

Even with my healing magick, my hand is throbbing, the sight of the blood making me uncharacteristically queasy.

Everything about this night is conspiring to push me off-balance.

"Stevie?" Doc glances my way. "Are you all right? You look a bit pale."

Nausea rolls through my gut, hot and fast, and a low hum vibrates across the ground, a gentle purr that quickly builds into a rumble.

"It's working," Kirin whispers. "Thank the goddess."

Doc comes to stand at my side, his arm strong and comforting around my waist, but the nausea is only getting worse. I feel like I'm on a boat, the ground swaying beneath my feet.

Before us, a magickal dome rises like a bubble in a cauldron, our blood streaming down the sides in thick, red strips. It looks like a candy apple, bright and glossy, the sight stirring up long-buried memories of carnivals and hell-hot summers, the taste of cinnamon and sugar, the crisp bite of a tart apple, my sticky hand reaching for my dad's as the Ferris wheel spins us to the very top of the world...

"Stevie?" Kirin says. "Cass, she doesn't look so hot."

His light touch on the small of my back brings me out of the memory, and I blink rapidly, taking in a big gulp of air as Kirin and Doc scrutinize my face. Beneath my ribcage, my heart bangs a desperate beat.

Remember your life, child. Cherish it. For it will end before the sun rises...

The voice echoes in my mind, faint and disembodied, the words fading before I can even make sense of them.

"I'm... I'm good," I assure them. "Just need a little space." I take a step backward, stomping my feet to dissipate the last of the weird energy. I've already forgotten the strange message; all that's left now is a vague sense of dread at the bottom of my stomach.

Doc scans my face, brow furrowed. "You sure?"

"Guess I just got a little woozy from the vibrations in the ground. I think it passed."

Before us, the magick bubble ripples once more, then vanishes, revealing the objects we spelled on our last visit: the Pentacle of Iron and Bone and the Sword of Breath and Blade, surrounded at the cardinal points by the four Princes of the Tarot.

"Get the Chalice from Stevie's bag," Doc tells Kirin. "We need to finish this."

I drop the bag from my shoulder and Kirin retrieves the skull, setting it in the dirt between the other two sacred objects. All three pulse with renewed magick, as if their very nearness gives them enhanced strength—a deep, unwavering sense of destiny and purpose that emanates outward in a million tiny shock waves, each one making my hands tingle, my fingers desperately reaching for the sword...

I grasp it tightly, pointing it at my opponent as I prepare to make my last stand.

"We will end you, Little Star," the woman shouts, her auburn hair snapping in the wind like a flag. She stands tall in her golden chariot, eyes wild with hatred and hunger, her feral horses charging forth as if they're running straight from the mouth of hell.

She's bearing down hard, dark magick giving her speed and strength. Hooves pound the earth, sending clouds of red dirt billowing in their wake, rising like smoke to obscure the landscape.

All around me, the Petrified Forest trembles.

I stand my ground, raising my sword, calling on the strength of my Princesses and all the magick in my veins, power crackling through me like lightning. "Come for it, bitch!"

"You will die before the night is over…"

"Stevie?" a voice calls. Urgent. Scared.

Is it Baz? It sounds like him, but I don't remember…

"Fuck, I don't think she can hear us. *Stevie?*"

Hands grip my shoulders, a tsunami of fear hitting me from all sides.

"Come back to us, my Star." This voice is gentle but firm, hands sliding up to cup my face, warm breath tickling my lips. "Come back."

My eyelids flutter open, the cave slowly sliding back into focus. Before me, Doc's eyes soften, his breath escaping in a rush of relief.

"Vision?" he asks.

"I'm not… I'm not exactly sure." I close my eyes again,

SPELLS OF BLOOD AND SORROW

desperately trying to track down the images, but everything eludes me. I know I saw *something*—its ghost still lingers at the edges of my memory—but I can't see it.

All that remains now is the taste of scorched earth on my tongue and the faint impression of a sword gripped tightly in my hand.

"The Sword," I say. "It was calling to me. I'm pretty sure I was preparing to fight."

The guys exchange worried looks.

"You okay to do the rest of the ritual?" Baz asks.

I nod, glancing down at the real Sword and taking a deep breath. Its magick still sings to me, but it doesn't overwhelm me. Doesn't suck me into any weird visions.

Still. Whatever's going on here, it's clear we need to get the hell out—and soon.

Reaching for my bag, I pull out the obfuscation potion I recreated from Professor Broome's original spell. Quickly and efficiently, I pour the silver liquid in a circle around the objects, just like we did last time.

Then, acknowledging the four Tarot cards still in place at the cardinal points, I repeat the spell of protection three times:

> *Arcana princes, one and all*
> *We beseech you, hear our call*
> *Now the Chalice is protected*
> *When our foes are misdirected*

The silvery-white circle rises into an iridescent dome,

once again enclosing the objects inside. The magick pulses, a soft hum drifting across my fingers.

"Stevie, what is it?" Doc asks softly.

"I feel like we're in reaction mode," I admit. "Always one step behind, desperately trying to patch the holes in the dam when we don't even know where the river's coming from."

"We're doing the best we can with the information we have," Kirin says. "The legends, the manuscripts, your mother's interpretations, our own... It's an imprecise science at best."

"And we've been wrong about so much of it." I run my hands along the magick barrier, the Arcana objects glowing faintly in response. "There's still a lot we don't know. Will this barrier hold, and if so, for how long? Does Ani have the Wand? Does Judgment have *him*? With Phaines dead, what happened to the Hierophant energy? Did it reincarnate, or is he floating around the dream realm with the others, figuring out a way to break through and get to these objects? To us?" I rub my eyes, a wave of pure exhaustion barreling into me. "And now, most of Mom's original journals and notes are gone. All we're left with are Kirin's backups, a book she pulled out of the dream realm that's written in a language so old I'm not sure it even exists in our records, and a series of highly inconvenient visions I can't even remember half the time."

"People have done more with less," Kirin says. "So, whether we've got one book or even just one page, I'm not giving up."

"None of us are giving up," Baz says, all three of my mages drawing close, surrounding me in the warm, protective bubble of their love.

And if love were truly enough to save the day, our enemies wouldn't stand a chance.

But it isn't enough. Not for this war.

"We need to tell the others," I say, finally voicing the thoughts that've been on my mind since Doc's Harvest Eve toast about our ever-expanding family. "The professors, Carly, Nat, Isla… They're not just hanging out at Red Sands to hide from danger. They're with us—they put their lives on hold for us—because they believe in defending magick and one another, just like we do."

"They already know about the Dark Arcana," Doc says.

"And they deserve to know about the Light." I take his hands, smiling up into his gray eyes, his Moon energy filling me with a deep sense of wonder and magick. "They deserve to know *us*, Doc. Not just as elemental mages, a grumpy professor, and a spirit-blessed witch who makes a mean cup of tea. They deserve to know the Major Arcana who've sworn an oath to protect magick from all who seek to destroy it. Who've sworn an oath to fight for them."

Doc sighs, an argument poised on the tip of his tongue. But a deep acceptance threads through his energy, and he finally nods.

"I'm with Stevie on this one," Baz says. "We're all in this together now. Secrets between us are just going to end up as more weapons for the Dark Arcana."

"Secrets are what got us into this mess in the first place."

Kirin gestures at the sacred objects, still glittering beneath their protective dome. "Case in point."

"I never thought it would come to this, but..." Doc squeezes my hands. "You're right, Stevie. They deserve to know everything. We'll talk to them in the morning. Now, if you don't mind, I'd really like to get us the fuck home."

I laugh, some of the exhaustion fading as fresh hope rises.

We gather around the dome, watching in silent reverence until it fades back into the ground, the Arcana objects safely hidden once again.

Back in the main chamber, we've just closed out the ritual and put away the Book of Reckoning when another vision flickers at the edge of my awareness.

"The Princesses are here." I try to focus on them, to pick up on whatever message they've brought, but they fade out too quickly, replaced at once with a dark shadow that wraps around me like smoke, chilling me to the core.

I gasp, clutching my head as a searing pain slams through my skull, unlocking the images from my earlier vision in brutal, technicolor detail.

"It's... It's a warning," I grind out, fingers itching for the Sword we've just buried. "The Chariot... She's coming for us!"

"Here?" Doc hauls me to my feet, wrapping an arm around my waist and dragging me toward the exit. "The Forest?"

As if in response, the unmistakable sound of hoofbeats pounds across the top of the cave, relentless and powerful, louder and more ferocious than an entire herd of wild stallions.

The cave walls crack and tremble, rocks raining down from above.

"Move!" Kirin pushes us against a wall just as a huge section of the ceiling slams down behind us. "Baz, get us the *fuck* out of here!"

Baz links his arm in mine, attempting to call up his rock mojo. But the cave is too unstable, the walls crumbling down around us. He can't hold the magick long enough to fully cast the spell.

"I'm losing it!" he shouts. "The energy is too erratic! I can't—"

"Go! Now!" Doc shoves us out of the main cave about three seconds before the entire chamber collapses into a pile of dust, the impact reverberating beneath our feet. On either side of the passageway, rocks and debris cascade down the walls, filling the narrow space, quickly cutting off our exit.

"What do we do?" I shout. There's nowhere to run, no escape from the relentless pounding of hooves.

A thunderous boom detonates overhead, and in the span of one panicked heartbeat, the entire cave system crashes down.

There's no time to move, no time to even scream. On instinct, I shove my hands outward as if I can stop the collapse with sheer will alone.

But it's not my hands or even my will that saves us. A burst of white light explodes from my chest, a nuclear blast that decimates the surrounding rock walls, leveling the entire passageway. Sharp, heavy slabs of rock crash down around us, but nothing touches me or my mages, the magick of my powerful wings creating a protective force field.

Suddenly my perspective changes, granting me a bird's-eye view; down below, the mages crowd over me, trying to protect me from the falling debris. But I'm not with them—not anymore.

I'm in the sky, soaring across the Petrified Forest of Iron and Bone. Red dust covers the landscape, and far in the distance, two horses beat a hasty retreat—one black, one white—dragging a golden chariot and an auburn-haired woman, the tattered remnants of a green cape fluttering behind her.

The Chariot and her steeds flicker and fade, finally vanishing into the night. And I return to my body, to my mages, the magick inside me dissipating.

The cave is destroyed. By all rights, we should've been pulverized. But overhead, my snowy owl perches on a petrified stone formation, his mournful call reminding us that we're still alive. Still here.

The whole thing is over in no more than a minute or two, the Forest falling utterly silent once again.

Shell-shocked and bloodied, the four of us climb out of the ruins and immediately link arms, and Baz finally calls on his earth magick, spinning us back out into the starry night, far away from the caves. Doc quickly drops to his knees, pulls out his pin, and calls up the next portal, ushering us back to the abandoned gas station.

It's not until we're all back in the SUV, the engine revving, that I finally allow myself to breathe.

"What in the ever-loving fuckery was *that*?" I ask. But none of my mages has the answer. They all just stare at me, open-mouthed, a swell of pride and respect and awe coursing through their energy.

I'm about to tell them to cut it out when a flash of white snags my attention outside.

And there, preening from the top of a rusty gas pump, the owl looks on curiously.

I bolt out of the SUV, tears spilling down my cheeks.

"Thank you," I breathe, stopping just before the pump and holding out my arm. He flutters down to take the offered perch, nuzzling my hair. "I don't know how you did it, but thank you. You chased off that crazy-ass bitch and her psycho horses and got us out of that labyrinth…. I can't even imagine what would've happened if… Wait. Labyrinth! That's it!"

Kirin, who followed me out of the car, casts a dubious glare. "Stevie? What are you talking about?"

"From the movie!"

"The movie?" His brow furrows. "David Bowie in tights?"

"Yes, it's perfect!" I stroke the owl's head, a sense of profound rightness filling my heart. "You deserve a kingly name, my friend. A magickal name."

He cocks his owl head, letting out a soft hoot.

I'm taking that as a yes.

I smile, pressing a kiss to the top of his soft crown. Then, beaming up at Kirin, "Allow me to officially introduce my owl familiar. Kirin, meet Jareth. Jareth, I'm pretty sure I speak for us all when I say… Thank you for saving our nearly pancaked asses."

"Especially hers," Kirin says. Then, totally ignoring Jareth's hoots of protest, he hauls me against his chest and kisses the very last of the breath from my body.

* * *

After our ordeal at the Fool's Grave, I'm more than relieved to discover Jareth has decided to follow us home. He sails through the night sky overhead, keeping his ever-watchful eyes on us as we leave the outpost in the dust. I lose sight of him in the clouds for a little while, but the moment we're safely back at the house in Red Sands, he's just *there*, hanging out at the top of a sandstone tower just beyond the backyard.

Maybe it's a sign that my magick is getting stronger. Maybe Kirin was right and he was just waiting for the official appointment of his name. Either way, his kingly presence is a welcome one—especially after what happened tonight.

The Dark Arcana are growing stronger. They may not be able to fully manifest in physical form yet, but that doesn't mean they can't get to us. The status of the Arcana objects we worked so hard to protect is unknown; even if they survived the cave-in, we may not be able to get to them again, especially if the Chariot and her pack of Dark Arcana dickheads are watching the Petrified Forest or any of the lands around campus. And with Eastman given free rein at the Academy, screwing with the protective wards to suit his needs, the magick that keeps students safe from dark forces is weaker than ever.

Snuggling deeper into my blankets, I let out a long sigh. Even here, safely nestled in the protective embrace of Kirin and Baz, I can't seem to let my mind settle, endlessly plagued with a single racing thought:

We barely escaped tonight.

And something tells me that for the Dark Arcana, the attack that destroyed our most sacred place and nearly claimed our lives was nothing more than a practice run.

TWENTY-THREE

STEVIE

In the infamous words of Carly Kirkpatrick, "The end of the world is no time to settle for culinary mediocrity."

So, the morning after our covert mission, she and Baz team up to cook us a brunch fit for royalty: orange-glazed French toast stuffed with cinnamon cream cheese; baked apples and brie; fresh berry salad drizzled with honey; roasted potatoes with rosemary and olive oil; poached eggs over sautéed spinach; banana date pudding; lemon sunshine bread; and—bless their overachieving little hearts—enough bacon to fill a suitcase.

They make a great team in the kitchen, and their energy is downright infectious, full of laughter and newfound friendship. Watching the two of them rediscover the kind of sweet sibling bond they missed out on growing up… It's like getting a glimpse into a past that *should* have been. Now that Janelle's out of the picture, they're getting a second chance—not for a better past, but for a better right now.

Whether it's Janelle's exit, or Baz and Carly's teasing jokes as they chop and stir and sauté, or the fact that we survived a brutal magickal attack last night, or even just the sweet and savory smells of a damned good home-cooked meal, the vibe in the house this morning is light and happy, full of a promise as bright as the sun streaming through the open windows. Wrapping my hands around a mug of Earl Grey, vanilla bean, and rose petal tea, I try to take it all in, to hold on to the warmth and joy, to store it deep in my heart.

For as perfect as this moment feels, I know it's fleeting. I know that until we can uncover and defeat our enemies, *no* happiness is secure, *no* future is promised.

But before I can sink too deeply into those dark thoughts, Baz is leaning in to steal a kiss, his soft moan of pleasure temporarily eradicating my worries.

"Good morning, beautiful," he says. "You snuck away this morning before I could ravage you."

"Maybe I had a better offer," I tease.

"Is that so? From who?"

My gaze darts toward the kitchen entryway, where Doc has just made his first appearance of the day, his hair uncharacteristically tussled, his eyes still a bit glazed. I'm not sure he'll ever recover from the surprise visit I paid him this morning.

"Nice of you to join us, Dr. Devane." I smile at him, wide-eyed and innocent. "Trouble sleeping?"

"Cass?" Baz shakes his head, his mischievous grin

stretching wide. "*He's* your better offer? Oh, you've *got* to be shitting me."

"Maybe you should talk to him, Baz," I say, keeping my voice low. "He's got this no-sharing rule, but I'm thinking mornings could be better for everyone involved if he bends it, just a little. Don't you agree?"

"Miss Milan," Doc warns, looming over us both, "do *not* get on my bad side. You won't like the consequences."

I stretch up on my toes and nip his earlobe. "Oh, I think I'd like the consequences *very* much."

"So anyway," Baz says, clearing his throat, "brunch is ready. Get it while it's hot. Preferably without making the rest of us sick." He gives Doc a playful smack on the chest. "And we'll talk about sleeping arrangements later."

On that note, the rest of the house files into the kitchen, and together we descend upon the counter like locusts, loading up our plates from the impressive spread set out before us.

"Don't forget the mimosa bar," Carly says. "We've got pineapple juice, tangerine, orange, mango, pineapple orange mango, grapefruit, and for those of you who need a little more fiber in your diet—looking at you, professors—there's some prune juice."

"Cass," Baz says, "I think she means you."

"Right. I think I'll be sticking to whiskey for all my digestive needs." He grabs the bottle from the stash of booze on the counter and pours a shot into his coffee, then takes a seat at the table, right next to me.

It's a perfect meal, and as the morning stretches into the

afternoon, we luxuriate in the delicious food and drink, the excellent company, the warm sunshine spilling across the kitchen. It feels like we're in a bubble, safe and protected and loved, and part of me wishes we could stay inside it forever.

But as the final pieces of bacon disappear and the sun rises high in the afternoon sky, the Arcana mages and I know we can't put off our revelations any longer.

"Professors and friends," Doc begins. "Now that we're all sated, Stevie, Baz, Kirin, and I have a few things we'd like to share with you."

"Starting with where you all snuck off to last night?" Carly shoots me an all-knowing smirk. Goddess, living with a clairsentient witch is definitely not all it's cracked up to be.

"Starting," Doc says, covertly squeezing my hand under the table, "with the fact that our Dark enemies are not the only ones blessed with the power of the Major Arcana."

"Wait, don't tell me." Carly presses her fingers to her temples as if she's trying to predict the punchline, clearly assuming this is a joke. "Stevie's the Star. *Starla* Milan. Star... Get it?"

She glances at me, the smile frozen on her face as she waits for the rest of us to laugh.

But all I can do is shrug and grin. "Guess you really *do* know everything, Carly."

* * *

The guys and I let Doc do most of the talking, filling in the blanks on the history of the Brotherhood, including my mother's involvement as the World Arcana and Phaines's role as the Dark Hierophant. Out of respect for Lala's privacy, we don't mention her by name, saying only that the High Priestess has been assisting us inside the dream realm, helping us unravel some of the mysteries about how the Arcana energies manifest in physical form and what—if anything—we can do to stop them from carrying out their mission.

We tell them about finding the Chalice of Blood and Sorrow, and about last night's crazy adventure, including my visions of the Chariot, the attack we suffered at the Fool's Grave, and Jareth swooping in to save us from certain doom.

It seems like hours before we get the whole story out, each of us taking turns to share our gifts and our nature, the legends and lore we've pieced together so far, my mother's prophecies. But no matter how crazy it all sounds, the witches gathered here—Professor Maddox, Professor Broome, Nat, Isla, and Carly—take it all in stride, their energy swirling with amazement and curiosity and a deep, unwavering respect.

Even Carly, who insists she's still calling me Twink, no matter how powerful I become, can't hide the fact that she's a hundred percent in our corner. In *my* corner.

As I sip my pineapple mimosa and look around at the witches and mages surrounding me, it's hard for me to remember a time when I *didn't* have magickal friends.

When I actually believed magick was a curse, no matter how deeply I craved this knowledge. Since I enrolled at the Academy, my life has changed so much—and I owe it all to magick. To the path that was hidden from me for so long, finally revealed.

Despite the challenges, the dangers, the threats still looming, I wouldn't choose another path for anything. I *belong* here, and I'll do whatever it takes to keep my friends safe.

To protect the ones I love, no matter what the cost.

Finally, when the telling is complete, the barrage of questions answered, and the last of the champagne popped and poured, Doc clinks a fork against his glass, calling for a toast.

"As an Arcana mage and member of the Keepers of the Grave, it is my sworn duty and honor to protect magick and all those who are blessed with it," he says, lifting his glass. "I renew that vow today, in the presence of everyone gathered here, every one of whom I'm proud to call a friend."

"And as your friends," Professor Maddox says, raising her glass to join his, "we take your vow as our own. I pledge my service to protect magick and all who are blessed with it, for all of you and for all the generations of mages and witches to come."

The other witches follow suit, solemnly repeating her words and raising their glasses, solidifying a promise that will echo in my heart for the rest of eternity.

"To magick and friendship," Professor Maddox says.

"To magick and friendship," comes the unanimous reply, all of us clinking our glasses and drinking in solidarity. In friendship. In love.

Finished with her mimosa, Professor Maddox sets down her glass and rises from her chair, a familiar psychotic light dancing in her eyes—one that tells me *she's* about to start dancing on desks again... and *we're* about to get homework.

"I'll get the markers and poster board," she says, beaming with renewed energy and a fiery sense of purpose I haven't seen since the Academy canceled classes. "We've got big plans to make, witches. *Big* plans."

TWENTY-FOUR

STEVIE

"Good afternoon, my Gingersnap." I set a plate of lemon sunshine bread on the table next to Ani's bed and climb in beside him, burying my face in the crook of his neck. Even in a magickal coma, he still smells like my Ani, warm and sweet and full of summer. Closing my eyes, I take a few moments just breathing him in, visualizing a time when he's back with us, when our enemies have been defeated, when witches and mages no longer have to fear for our lives just for being who we are.

The rest of the house is buzzing with activity as Professor Maddox sketches out a training plan and doles out assignments, and I give Ani the full report.

"Professor Broome is going to work with us on protective as well as offensive potions and charms. Maddox plans to kick our Tarot education into high gear—she wants us to have a better grasp on how to harness the energies of each suit to create more effective spells." I reach for his hand, lacing our fingers together. "Doc's got mental magicks covered, of course. Baz is on earth magick, Kirin on air. As first years, the girls and I have a lot to learn about tapping into and controlling our magick, but we're ready for it. I've already learned some cool earth and air tricks, and Doc's going to show me how to harness water energy. I just need my favorite fire mage to wake up, and I'll be all set."

I smile and close my eyes, still breathing him in.

"I know. It's a lot, right? And here I thought we'd be getting a break with Trello ending the semester early, but nope. No such luck. On top of the elemental magick stuff, Kirin and I are supposed to hit the figurative books again tomorrow—our *actual* books were stolen, but there's still a lot to work with on his backups, and he's got access to some online databases full of Tarot lore."

The more I tell Ani, the more daunting it all sounds. A handful of witches and mages trying to scrape together a curriculum of magickal learning while researching lore and plotting defensive and offensive maneuvers against the Dark Arcana, the non-magickal authorities who wish we'd all stop breathing, and legions of corrupt mages and witches who don't know *whose* side they're on?

What kind of odds are those?

Still, something Kirin said last night really stuck with me. Whether we've got an entire library, a single book, or a single page, we're not giving up. And we've got so much more than that. We've got each other, and the promises we made today. No matter how hard things get, all I have to do is think about the people who sat around that table and held up their glasses today, and I'm ready to fight to the death for every single one of them.

I spend a few more minutes catching Ani up on all the news, and then I tell him about my hopes for the future—all the things I still want to learn at the Academy, all the places I want to explore with him, all the songs and games and sweet, sultry kisses I plan to share with him.

Then, rising from the bed, I light a yellow candle behind the plate of lemon sunshine bread, then place a fist-sized citrine crystal before it, right on top of the Sun card.

The spell comes to me easily, flowing directly from my heart, out through my lips, and right out into the universe, where I picture it sailing across the realms to Ani, lighting his pathway back to us.

> *Mage of sunshine, mage of fire*
> *Hear my words and know my desire*
> *Wherever you wander, wherever you roam*
> *May the light of our love guide you back home*

I repeat the spell three times, then kiss my fingertips and press them to the card, sealing the spell with the most powerful magick there is: love.

"Okay, now that we're all caught up… I've got another concert queued up for you. If you're not in the mood for my singing, just say so." I wait a few beats, then lean closer, cupping my hand around my ear. "Nothing? Okay, I'm taking your silence as permission to continue."

Cracking up at my own stupid joke, I grab the karaoke

mic and my phone, flipping through the playlists until I find what I'm looking for.

"Prepare yourself for the Stevie Milan Bon Jovi remix," I say. Then I take a deep breath, hit the button, and light up the stage.

I sing my heart out for every song, shaking my hips, bobbing my head, working it until I'm damn near exhausted and the yellow candle sputters out, filling the air with the scent of candle wax and lemon bread and the big-haired, air-guitar-shredding nostalgia of the eighties.

I've just wrapped up the last song—an epic rendition of *I'll Be There for You*—when the impossible happens.

The citrine crystal cracks in half.

And Ani says my name.

TWENTY-FIVE

ANSEL

Stevie... Stevie...

The name is on my lips, the sound of it bringing flashes of another life to my mind. A woman with wild, curly hair and eyes the color of the sky. She's running down a red dirt path toward me, her hair flowing out behind her, her smile as bright as the sun itself.

Stevie...

She glows like an angel, reaching for me, still smiling, her words echoing in my mind, again and again and again.

> *Mage of sunshine, mage of fire*
> *Hear my words and know my desire*
> *Wherever you wander, wherever you roam*
> *May the light of our love guide you back home*

I reach for her, the magick between us building,

conspiring to bring us together. I feel it pulling me closer, pulling *her* closer...

> *Mage of sunshine, mage of fire*
> *Hear my words and know my desire*
> *Wherever you wander, wherever you roam*
> *May the light of our love guide you back home*

My heart beats a frantic rhythm, the air around me superheated with magick and fire. If I could only touch her, feel her in my arms, maybe I would remember...

> *Mage of sunshine, mage of fire*
> *Hear my words and know my desire*
> *Wherever you wander, wherever you roam*
> *May the light of our love guide you back home*

Home. Yes, she is my home. She must be. I can feel it, deep inside. A sense of rightness and completion. Joy. A light that can't be dimmed.

I push harder, running faster and farther, determined to reach her. She's closer now, so close I can almost taste the sweetness of her skin. I stretch out my arms, and she does the same, our fingertips brushing for the briefest instant...

Lightning explodes overhead, ripping the very fabric of space and time, tearing her from my grasp. I reach for her again, desperate, lost, but my wild-haired angel is already fading, vanishing into nothingness.

Stevie...

Who was she? Do I know her? Did I ever?

The hollow ache in my chest tells me I do. But the harder I try to remember her, the faster the feeling dissipates. In its place, a new feeling dawns, hot and electric, full of power. Full of promise. Full of everything I could ever want.

"Come back, Ansel," a voice calls, so unlike my angel. This one is dark and certain, full of fire and smoke and death. "You know where you belong. Return to me now, my Black Sun."

At his command, the hollow inside me fills with purpose, with a deep desire to please him. To forget all else that came before, and forsake all that will come after.

There is only him. Only power. Only fire.

I blink away the momentary confusion, and my vision sharpens. Before me, the dark druid stands tall, the Wand of Flame and Fury gripped tightly in his hand.

I bow to him, dropping to my knees.

"Forgive me," I say.

"It is done." He touches the Wand to my chest, the uncomfortable heat of it urging me back to my feet. "They don't understand our great need, Ansel. The purity of our mission is like a blinding light, chasing away their inner darkness. They recoil from it in shame. Only fire will set them free."

"I understand."

"So you've said, yet part of you recoils as well."

"What must I do?"

"We must separate that which prevents you from

fulfilling your destiny. From achieving your ultimate power."

I nod, willing to do whatever it takes to please him. To earn his trust.

The druid steps aside, revealing the red dirt path where I first saw the woman. But instead of an angel, another woman awaits in the distance now, standing inside a golden chariot led by two magnificent horses—one black, one white.

"You mustn't move, Ansel," he warns. "Not until the ritual is complete."

I promise to obey, and the druid's eyes sparkle with something that looks like malice, but I know that can't be true. He loves me. He *saved* me. He sees my true potential. He will not fail me.

Stepping off the path, he raises the Wand toward the sky, his powerful magick igniting the wood, burning so hot it's nearly white.

Far in the distance, the charioteer whips her horses into action, driving them hard and fast toward us.

Toward me.

The druid closes his eyes and speaks his dark enchantment:

> *Flame and fury, will and might*
> *Rend the shadow from the light*
> *Dark desires now revealed*
> *Heart and soul shall be concealed*

His voice grows louder and more menacing at every recitation, magick crackling in the air around him, silver-white flames licking the wooden staff. The horses pummel the dirt path, the sound of it like the ancient, unstoppable heartbeat of the earth itself, thudding up through the ground, rattling my bones.

The charioteer is relentless, driving her horses harder and faster, every crack of her whip making me flinch. Their speed is almost impossible to comprehend; two horses blur into a single gray beast, powerful and massive, unstoppable.

The druid continues to shout his spell, and a single tear slips down my cheek.

I am awestruck.

I am paralyzed.

I am unworthy.

A bolt of lightning strikes the earth before me, and the Chariot and her massive steeds barrel into me, *through* me, an explosion of fire and magick that rips me in two.

The pain is like nothing I've ever felt—burning and tearing, a loss so deep and fathomless I'm certain I won't survive. I don't *want* to survive. I fall to my knees and clutch my head, howling in agony, begging for death.

The pain is too much, too vast, too *everything*...

And then it stops.

Suddenly I feel... nothing. Absolutely nothing.

I open my eyes to find myself standing on the dirt path again, unharmed, unbroken. Before me, another man stands. The same red hair, the same golden-brown eyes. He is my mirror.

But where I am full of shadows, he is goodness and joy, childlike wonder, happiness. White light emanates from his very being, nearly blinding me.

He reaches out for me, his smile compassionate, his eyes holding a hint of sadness in an otherwise serene face.

But there's nothing he can offer me now, nothing he can promise.

"Ansel, it is time." The druid presents me with the gift I've longed for my entire life.

My hand wraps around the Wand, my magick instantly fusing with it, reverberating back to me with a sense of completion and wholeness.

Instinctively, I know what must be done.

Gripping the Wand tightly, I call on my fire magick.

What comes next is easy. Fated. Written in the stars.

I point the Wand toward the man standing before me— my twin. Then, I let my magick fly.

His shoes ignite first, the brutal witchfire eating a quick path up his legs, his torso, his face.

I watch in fascination as he burns, his skin glowing bright red like a smoldering ember, then blackening. I watch as it turns the color of bone. I watch as he collapses in a pile of ash and memory.

"Begone, Ansel McCauley," I whisper, and the breeze heeds my call, picking him up and carrying him away.

"Where is he?" I ask the druid once he's gone, more curious than concerned.

"He has been called to atone. You needn't concern your-self with him anymore. You have other work—greater work —to accomplish now."

"What must I do?"

"First, tell me what you recall of the life of Ansel McCauley."

I close my eyes, trying to give his request the considera-tion it deserves.

Ansel McCauley... Did I know him?

Images flash through my mind like a movie—a child-hood by the ocean, the scent of cocoa butter and sticky cherry popsicles, the warmth of the summer sun on fair skin. A chubby little girl stomping through sandcastles, squealing with delight as the waves chased her along the shoreline.

I shake my head, and the ocean blurs into a house. An ear pressed to the wall as a man and a woman threaten and scream, beg and shout. Accusations of infidelity, of a young ginger-haired mage, unwanted and unloved.

Everything ends, everything begins again.

The house blurs into a campus. School. Witches and mages. The Academy. Friends that call themselves brothers. There are classes and professors, a bar where students sing karaoke. There's a woman too, with crazy hair and a terrible singing voice, her skin as sweet as honeysuckle.

She's singing to me, calling me home... Her eyes are the deepest shade of... blue? Hazel? I'm losing the image. Losing the feel of her touch in my hair. Losing the taste of her kiss.

In its place, I taste fire. Power.

Everything ends, everything begins again.

The last of the images finally fades, and moments later, blinking up at the druid, I can't even remember what I was thinking about.

"Nothing," I say honestly. "I recall nothing."

This seems to please him greatly. He gestures behind me, and the charioteer steps forward, her tattered green cape fluttering in the breeze.

"We have a task for you," the druid says to me. "A test, if you will."

"Does it involve…" I smirk at them, unable to contain the inner joy bubbling to the surface. The word hovers on the tip of my tongue, as bold and sweet as candy. "…*fire?*"

They beam at me like proud parents.

I beam too. I laugh. I'm nearly exploding with it. I've never felt so free, so alive.

"Oh yes, my Black Sun." The druid places his hand on my shoulder, his eyes alight with the same brilliant heat coursing through my heart. "More fire than you can *ever* imagine."

TWENTY-SIX

STEVIE

Cities kneel before the flames
Thus begins the deadly game
When hope is lost the Star shall fall
As Death arrives to conquer all

From the ashes, called to rise
With blackened hearts and golden eyes
Souls imprisoned in a tomb
Soldiers marching for our doom

"Well, that's an uplifting piece, isn't it?" Biting back a sigh, I set down the page and flip through the rest of the printouts from Kirin's backups, looking for anything that might give us a clue about Ani's condition.

It's been two weeks. Two weeks since he said my name, and not another word since. Not a groan, not a twitch of his eyelid, nothing. Physically, he's completely healthy. Professor Broome has him on a magickal IV, and she's keeping him in a magickal stasis to prevent his body from atrophying, constantly monitoring him for any signs of distress.

He looks like Ani. He *feels* like Ani.

But he's completely unreachable.

Even at a high dose, the dream potion shouldn't have rendered him comatose—not like this. And while we may not know exactly what's causing his condition, it's not hard to see the hands of the Dark Arcana at work.

Unfortunately, Mom's prophecies are about as clear as the red mud at the River of Blood and Sorrow, and after weeks of research, Kirin and I are no closer to helping Ani than we are to figuring out how to defeat our enemies.

"Your mother isn't exactly known for her uplifting poetry," Kirin teases, gently massaging the knots from my shoulders. He's sitting behind me in an armchair near the fireplace, and I'm on the floor in front of him, trying to relax into his warm touch. His hands are powerful and precise, and at any other time, I'd kill for a back rub like this.

But with every verse I read, my muscles grow tighter, the tension inside me coiling like a serpent.

When hope is lost the Star shall fall…

I glare at the words on the first page again, wishing they didn't affect me so strongly, but how could they not? The phrase is a bone-chilling reminder of the prophecy Lala shared about my so-called suicide, and I can't help but take it as a warning.

Thus her ache shall find no ease, so shall the daughter of The World surrender to the emptiness, to the void within and without. By her own hand, of her own volition, The Star shall fall. Henceforth she shall take her eternal breath in utter darkness...

As confusing as Mom's prophecies have been, none of them have come to me by accident. The fact that this latest one references the falling Star, along with the arrival of Death and golden-eyed soldiers rising from the ashes? To call it a "doomsday prophecy" doesn't even scratch the surface.

It feels a lot like some of my visions—an army of ghoul-like mages swarming the campus, incinerating anyone in their path. Is this what we're facing now? Is this the future waiting for us on the next horizon, the last great loss in a chain of hundreds more, the ache that will finally—if Mom and Lala are right—push me over the edge?

And what of my Arcana brothers? I would *never* leave them. Even at the end of the world, if only *one* of the men I loved remained standing, I wouldn't leave his side for anything. Me surrendering to the emptiness? Willingly ending my life? That could only mean one thing: the men I love are doomed to die.

Souls imprisoned in a tomb... Soldiers marching for our doom...

I blink back tears, the words blurring like tiny ants scuttling across the page.

"What do you think it means?" Kirin peers down over my shoulder. "All that fire imagery is a little intense."

"What it means is my mother was fucking stoned when

273

she wrote this." I grab the stack of papers and chuck them across the room, frustration and helplessness colliding inside me, pushing me to my feet. "I am *so* done with this emo Arcana poetry. Fire, flames, death-death-death. Why couldn't she just write about sex and breakups like everyone else? Maybe include a few guitar chords, make a few songs out of it. What good is a tragedy if you can't turn it into a musical?"

"Fair point, but sex and breakups aren't going to help us beat the Dark Arcana."

"Neither is this shit if we can't decipher it."

"We can, though. *You* can." He pushes his glasses up his nose, offering an encouraging smile. "Stevie, you're doing amazing. Even without the original material, you've translated so much in a short time. Under extreme duress, I might add."

"But the translations don't make any sense!"

"Not yet, but it will come to you. It always does." He shifts in the chair, motioning for me to come sit with him, but I'm too amped up. I pace the room, trying to work off the anxiety running through my veins.

"Goddess, my mother's mind is like a maze with no way out." I pick up the scattered papers, stacking them on the coffee table, flipping over the top page so I don't have to look at it anymore. "That verse... Is it about the fires that happened a couple of months back when they first started rounding up all those witches and accusing them of arson? Is it a clue about future attacks? The whole thing about the flames and rising from the ashes reminds me of Judgment, but beyond that? I don't know what to make of it. For all I know, it's completely unrelated to any of this. And that's the problem, Kirin. It all comes down to *my* interpretation of my *mother's* interpretations of whatever messages she was channeling at the time. There's a *lot* of room for error here, and we don't have the luxury of getting it wrong. People's lives are at stake."

"You're saying you want to give up on the prophecies? After all the work we've put in, all the late nights, all the breakthroughs? You want to forget about it and go back to the textbooks instead?"

"I... No. Of course not." I blow out a breath, my frustration no match for Kirin's calm, steady presence. With a soft smile, I join him again, sitting in his lap and drawing my knees up to my chest. His strong embrace is like a reset button, and I rest my head on his shoulder, sinking into his warmth. "I guess I just want all the answers, and no one has them, and Ani's still trapped in the dream realm, and everyone here is working so hard to master their magick, and we have no idea whether the Arcana objects are safe, or what the Dark Magician is planning, or whether Judgment can still get to us... Goddess, Kirin. For all we know, he's holding Ani hostage, and that's why he can't return to us."

"Shh." He pulls me closer, pressing a kiss to the top of my head. "Don't speculate like that. We may not understand what's happening in his mind, but Ani is physically stable. I'm taking that as a positive sign."

"Maybe we should work in Ani's room today. He might call for me again."

"It's been two weeks," Kirin says gently, his breath stirring my hair. "We can't keep putting everything else on hold, pacing his bedroom and just hoping it happens again."

"It *will* happen again. He just needs more time."

"Yes, and in the meantime, *we* need to keep moving forward. That means you can keep working on this research with me, or you can practice your mental magicks with Cass, or potions with Professor Broome, or elemental magick with the girls, or any of the other magickal skills you still need to learn. But you *can't* keep climbing the walls, waiting in limbo for Ani to come back to us. That won't help anyone."

"I can't just leave him like that. He's..." I trail off, my words lost to the wave of emotion rising inside me.

"We won't leave him," he says, stroking my back. "Never. We just need to keep working on the prophecies until... Baz?"

Kirin's energy shifts so quickly I barely have time to process it—hopeful and encouraging to raw, unchecked fear in a heartbeat.

"What's going on?" I glance up just as Baz barrels into the room, keyed up like a live wire. Totally ignoring us, he digs the remote out from between the couch cushions and clicks on the TV.

"We're working in here," I say, but he holds up his hand

to shush me, eyes glued to the newscaster who just appeared on screen.

"…reporting live outside Moonlight Bay Beach, California," she says grimly, "where authorities say an explosion of unknown origin has decimated the entire city."

She's standing on some sort of dock, and behind her, gray smoke billows across the horizon, the blackened skeletons of buildings barely discernible through the haze.

"This is a rapidly evolving situation," she continues, "but initial estimates place the death toll in the hundreds, with scores more grievously injured. The explosion occurred at approximately two p.m. Pacific Standard time, when… Wait, we're getting an update…" She presses her fingers against her earpiece, nodding as she processes the new info. "We've just confirmed that the explosion was both intentional and magickal in nature. I'm being told that the FBI's Magickal Enforcement Unit has arrived on the scene via military escort."

"Holy shit." I rise from Kirin's lap and stand next to Baz, reaching for his hand as the others flood into the living room.

"Guys!" Isla says. "Did you hear?"

"What's going on?" Nat's face is pinched with worry. "I just saw something on my phone about an explosion in California?"

Doc comes to stand at my other side, wrapping a protective hand around the back of my neck as the reporter approaches a fire chief and a group of police officers, all of them black with soot, their eyes haunted.

"Excuse me, can any of you tell us whether you've made contact with the survivors? Are rescue operations underway?"

The group exchange tense glances, shaking their heads. The fire chief removes his helmet and drops his gaze. "There are no survivors, ma'am."

"You mean..." She shakes her head rapidly, as if she can't even comprehend his words.

"The people inside city limits at the time of the attack," he says, "they were..." He clears his throat, barely holding onto his composure. "They were incinerated."

"Everyone?" she gasps.

"Incinerated," he repeats.

"Incinerated." I swallow hard, the word carving a deep gash in my heart.

All of us watch the unfolding coverage in stunned silence, unable to move, unable to draw breath as the screen fills with devastating video shared by passersby and people who were lucky enough to be out on their boats rather than inside the blast radius when the explosion hit.

An entire town, filled with businesses and restaurants and homes and cookie shops and daycare centers and gardens and swimming pools and libraries and ocean views that stretched on for miles...

It's all just gone. Smoldering. Incinerated.

"Cities kneel before the flames," I finally whisper, glancing over at Kirin, who hasn't moved from the chair. "Thus begins the deadly game."

Could this be the beginning Mom foretold? One of the Dark Magician's tricks?

"Our information is still limited at this time," the reporter says, "but they're now saying the confirmed death toll is already over…" She closes her eyes, the skin between her brows pulled into a deep crease as she tries to maintain her professional detachment. When she speaks again, her words are barely audible over the bustle of police activity around her. "North of four thousand."

"*People*?" I exclaim, as if the number is too vast to comprehend, too ridiculous. Surely she means four thousand cockroaches, or windows, or boat docks. But people?

"Many others are still unaccounted for," she says. "Sadly, we expect that number to rise as the evening wears on. Judging from the visual extent of the damage, it's clear that anyone who was within city limits at the time of the explosion is now presumed dead. We realize this is a very difficult time for all those affected, but authorities are asking anyone with loved ones in the area to stay away and keep the emergency phone lines clear. We will continue to provide updates as more information becomes available."

Baz switches the channel to another newscast, a different angle on the same billowing smoke and haunting black metal frames, this time with an alarming news ticker scrolling along the bottom in bold red letters.

WITCHCRAFT BLAMED FOR DEADLY ATTACK ON PEACEFUL CALIFORNIA BEACH COMMUNITY… THOUSANDS MURDERED BY ACT OF MAGICKAL TERRORISM… ALL WITCHES AND MAGES MUST REPORT TO LOCAL FBI CENTERS FOR QUESTIONING…

"...now confirming that a group of mages calling themselves the Soldiers of Light have claimed responsibility for the attack," a voiceover pipes in over the horrifying images. "Information on the group is limited, but authorities believe they may have connections to the Arcana Academy of the Arts, a magickal university headquartered in London with campuses overseas as well as in the southwestern United States. Anyone with information about the Soldiers of Light is asked to contact the FBI immediately."

"Soldiers of Light?" Professor Maddox says. "I've never heard of such a group. Certainly not in association with the Academy."

"That's because they likely don't exist," Doc says. "It's a setup. It must be."

Again, Mom's prophecy echoes in my mind.

Soldiers marching for our doom...

"Regardless of current legal status," the voiceover continues, "all witches and mages in the United States are required to report to local authorities for immediate questioning. Any magickal persons who do not report within the next twenty-four hours will be considered fugitives."

"Are they fucking serious right now?" Carly asks. "They can't do that."

"They can, and they are." Baz clicks to another channel, this one showing footage from stoplight and retail security cameras capturing the precise moment of the so-called attack. One minute, everything is normal—people walking down the sunny streets with ice cream cones and shopping bags, a pack of motorcycles racing by, a guy on the corner dressed like a clown, waving a big sign about cell phone deals inside. Then, out of nowhere, streaks of silver-blue light tear across the pavement, one right after another, igniting an inferno that burns so hot it literally melts the pavement.

And everyone on it.

My stomach churns, my knees nearly buckling. It happens so fast—maybe three seconds onscreen—and then the image cuts out.

The security cameras were destroyed.

The screen switches to an aerial view, a traffic helicopter catching the same moment. From the sky, it looks like a nuclear attack—a flash of bright white light, then nothing but fire as far as the eye can see.

All around me, the energy in the room turns to ice. Panic and dread, confusion, fear, sickness.

"It's so much like that night at Breath and Blade," Doc finally says. "I can't get it out of my mind."

"It really is an uncanny resemblance," Professor Broome says.

"What night?" I ask. "What are you talking about?"

Isla clutches her teardrop pendant, her eyes wide and watery. Even her braids seem to be trembling.

"Ani," she says softly. "The night Ani unleashed his witchfire to save us all from Janelle and Casey."

Still standing at my side, Baz shakes his head. "It wasn't him."

"Baz," Doc says, "you didn't see him that night. The fire, the intensity, the scorched ground... Other than the scale of this attack, it looks identical to what Ani conjured at Breath and Blade."

Baz drops my hand, folding his arms over his chest. "So you're saying Ani just... what? Magicked himself out to California while we were asleep, and lit the whole place on fire?"

"We can't rule it out," Doc says.

"Yeah, Cass. We sure as fuck can." Baz points toward the guest bedroom. "Ani is in a fucking *coma*. In *that* bedroom, where he hasn't moved from since Harvest Eve. He'll be lucky if he can even remember his own name after this, let alone mastermind devious plots to incinerate entire cities. He's practically a vegetable, and—"

"He's *not* a vegetable," I snap, Baz's grim pronouncement igniting my anger. "He's alive, and some part of him is fighting like hell to get back to us. He said my name, Baz. Goddess, what is *wrong* with you?"

"Maybe you misheard him, Stevie." He gives an exaggerated shrug. "Or maybe these guys are right, and Ani's totally fine, calling your name and coordinating magickal attacks against innocent people while the rest of us stand around with our thumbs up our asses, casting spells and praying to the goddesses that we somehow survive this shit."

"You know as well as I do Ani didn't cause that." I jab my finger at the television, anger spilling over in hot, fresh tears. "And he's not a vegetable, and he *will* wake up, and if you have any doubts about either of those two things, you can go *fuck* yourself."

"Stevie, listen to me." Doc grabs my shoulders, pinning me with a gaze so full of sadness and fear, it nearly steals my breath. "You have to understand—"

"It wasn't him, Doc. We're talking about Ani. *Ani*! And you're acting like Ani's the cause of this random act of violence, when there's no way he even—"

"What happened today," he continues, his voice breaking. "It wasn't random. Moonlight Bay Beach? That's... that's Ani's hometown."

I blink up at him, the words banging around in my mind, trying to stick.

Moonlight Bay Beach. Ani's hometown. Not random...

No matter how hard I try to hold on to them, to make sense of what Doc told me, I just can't. Sure, maybe this senseless, gruesome attack is happening in Ani's hometown, but I can't believe he has any connection to the violence playing out on the screen behind us. To the devastation that will echo across the country for years and decades to come.

Over four thousand dead.

Scores more missing, others from just outside the blast area fighting for their lives.

A nationwide roundup of witches and mages—a roundup few will ever escape.

It's all too much to comprehend. Too much death, too much fear, too much sadness filling up the house. Filling up my head.

"Air," I finally gasp, pulling out of Doc's hold. "I need air."

The room spins, bile rising in my throat. Ignoring the sound of my name and the weight of their oppressive energy, I bolt for the door, throwing myself out into the wide-open space where I promptly and unceremoniously drop to my knees and retch.

TWENTY-SEVEN

STEVIE

I'm only outside a few moments when a calm, stately presence washes over me, and Jareth swoops down from his hiding place, perching on a waist-high sandstone slab in the backyard.

"I knew you'd come," I tell him, wiping away my tears. "You always know when I need you, huh?"

In response, he lifts a wing, inspecting his plumage as if he couldn't care less about my predicament one way or the other.

But I know he senses my pain. Just like I can sense his presence now, always close to me, always watching.

"Yes, you're quite handsome," I confirm. "There's no denying it."

This gets a little hoot of acknowledgment, and I laugh, some of the weight lifting from my chest.

Taking my first deep breath in what feels like an hour, I reach out and stroke his head, my energy immediately settling. Out here in the dusty backyard, fresh air caressing my skin, the golden sun hanging over the horizon, the grounding energy of the red rocks steadying me, it's almost impossible to feel anything but peace and contentment.

Even when it seems like the rest of the world is on fire.

"There's no way that was Ani," I tell Jareth. "Now, I'm not saying it's coincidence—how could it be? But if his hometown was attacked by witchfire, my guess is someone's setting him up. Doc was on the right track with that. Soldiers of Light? No, that's bullshit. Even if there *was* a group of mages that wanted to wreak havoc on the human world, they certainly wouldn't go around bragging about it."

Another hoot. A flutter of wings.

"I'm thinking it was Judgment—he's the most likely candidate here, what with his obsession with the Wand and fire and tormenting souls. Possibly with a big assist from Agent Eastman and his merry band of conspiracy theorists too, right? Because guys like that? They want us *all* to burn in hell, even if it means sending a few of their own into the fiery pits in the process."

Jareth watches me closely, blinking his bright, golden eyes.

"Goddess, I really wish you could talk to me," I say, tracing the soft edge of his wing. "What would you say, I wonder?"

"I'd probably start with an apology," comes the gravelly reply.

Jareth takes off at the approach of a new visitor, and

when I turn around, it's Baz I find standing before me, his eyes red, his mouth pulled into a deep frown.

"You're right," he says. "You don't even have to say it. I'm an asshole. The biggest fucking asshole this side of the apocalypse."

I let out a sigh. "Baz, you just—"

"You've always known that about me, though, so you can't exactly claim false advertising. I'm thinking this works in my favor, because at the very least, you know I'm not a liar." He hooks his fingers into the waistband of my jeans and pulls me close, locking me in a fierce gaze, knuckles brushing the bare skin of my belly. "A world-class dickhead, maybe, but not a liar. So when I tell you I'm sorry, please, *please* know it's the truth."

Here in the setting sun, his red-brown eyes are on fire, the heat from his fingers radiating against my skin as he slides his hands along my waistband, stopping to rest at the small of my back.

"I never should've said that shit," he continues. "I swear I didn't mean it. I *know* Ani's still with us. He said your name, Stevie. Trust me—I've been holding onto that fact like a lifeline for weeks. I'm just..." He closes his eyes and shakes his head, emotion choking his words. "I fucking miss him. I want him back here with us where he belongs. I'm going out of my fucking mind."

I lock my hands behind his neck and lay my head against his chest, timing my breaths to the strong, familiar beat of his heart.

"I love you," he whispers, and I tighten my hold, feeling

like he's the only thing anchoring me here right now. The only thing keeping me from spiraling and spinning right out into space.

"It wasn't him," I say against his chest, fresh tears leaking from my eyes and soaking his T-shirt. "All those people, the fire… Please tell me it wasn't him."

Baz rests his cheek on the top of my head and sighs, his hands winding into my hair, his heart beating like a drum against my ear.

He doesn't answer me.

He *can't* answer me.

Because for all his faults, Baz Redgrave—truth in advertising—is not a liar.

TWENTY-EIGHT

STEVIE

It's well after midnight, and I'm lying awake in Ani's bed, running my fingers through his soft, coppery hair, watching him sleep. I've been here since we finished dinner—a somber affair of soup and salad, none of us able to speak more than a few polite words in the wake of the devastating news coming out of California.

We are truly fugitives now, a house full of witches and mages with no legal rights, no country, no home but the one we make together.

The enormity of it hasn't even hit me yet. And it can't—not now. Because if I let myself think about it for more than one minute at a time—*really* think about it—I'll crumble.

So for now, I close my eyes and focus on the sound of his steady breathing, singing him a lullaby of eighties rock ballads until I finally drift off to sleep.

* * *

I'm dreaming. I must be. Because when I open my eyes again, a flickering candle burns on the night table, the golden flame reflected in a pair of the most beautiful caramel eyes I've ever seen, peering down at me over a smile as big as the sky.

"Ani?" I gasp, my heart banging inside my chest. I don't move. Don't even blink. Because if I do, and he vanishes...

"How's it going, Stevie Boo-Boo?" He laughs, then scoops me into his arms, rolling on top of me in a crushing hug, suffocating me with a kiss so sweet it makes my chest ache.

"I'm dreaming," I say, pulling back to take his face between my hands. His hair is wet, dark and curling around his ears, his skin carrying the scents of soap and sunshine, as if he's just stepped out of the shower. "And you're... naked?"

The hard evidence becomes more apparent—and, well, *hard*—the longer he lies on top of me, nothing more than a sheet and my T-shirt and underwear separating us.

"Maybe *I'm* the one who's dreaming." He lets out another soft laugh. "On second thought, scratch that. I've had enough dreams to last a lifetime. Right now, I'm only here for what's real."

"Did you shower? When? Should you be walking around just yet?" I try to sit up and turn on the nightstand light, but Ani claims me in another kiss, pushing me back down against the pillow.

I don't fight him. The kiss is too delicious. Too sweet. Too real.

Goddess, it's really him. He's here. He's home. He's mine.

Tears spill unbidden, and Ani pulls back, brushing them away with his thumbs.

"I feel fine, Stevie. Seriously. Stronger than ever. Whatever you guys did to take care of me? A-plus, five stars, would recommend."

"Magick," I whisper, gazing up at him with awe and wonder. "We should...We should get up. Everyone will want to see you."

"Yes, but *I* only want to see *you*. You're way hotter than the rest of those scrubs."

I laugh. "I'm not sure our Arcana brothers would appreciate being called scrubs. Especially—"

"Stevie? I'm not sure I care." He slides his hands into my hair and lowers his mouth again, his weight settling perfectly between my thighs as he steals a deeply seductive kiss that has me damn near moaning into his mouth.

After all the shyness, all the sweet and subtle gestures along the winding path of our relationship, I have to admit... This new, assertive Ani is pretty damn sexy, his demanding kisses igniting a fire low in my belly.

For the briefest instant, my mind flashes back to the news that broke tonight, to the haunted faces of journalists and firemen and police officers, to the fires still burning through the streets of Moonlight Bay Beach.

But I can't bring myself to tell him about it just yet. The news will still be there when we wake up tomorrow, just as heartbreaking as it was tonight. And right now, in the aftermath of so much death and destruction, suddenly all I want is to feel whole and alive. To live in this moment, and this moment alone, falling in love with the mage who beat the odds and fought his way back home to me.

But that thought unleashes another one, and I can't hold back my worry. Not even for Ani's deliciously hot kisses.

"Wait." I press my hands against his bare chest. "Are you... Are you feeling okay? Are you sure you want this right now?"

"I'm sure I want this. More than anything. Right now, tomorrow, the next day... Hell, I've wanted this since you kissed me in Kirin's office that night." He nudges my cheek with his nose. "Don't you?"

"Are you kidding me? I've wanted this since... I don't know. Probably since you took me up to the top of the Cauldron and gave me the sunrise, if I'm being totally honest."

"Then what's wrong?"

"I'm just a little worried about you. You were basically in a coma for two weeks, and now—"

"And now I'm not." He flashes another big grin. "Look, I can't explain it any more than you can. All I know is I spent an eternity in hell. Absolute hell, Stevie. And the only thing that kept me alive was focusing on *this* moment. On you. On the knowledge that if I could just find a way to make it back here, to follow the sound of your voice, I'd have the chance to hold you again. To kiss you. To taste you."

"You heard me?" I ask. "I knew it! I sang to you every day!"

"All the best of the seventies, eighties, and nineties," he says, beaming. "But now I'd rather you leave the music behind and put that beautiful mouth to work on something else."

My resolve is weakening, my body heating up at the idea of touching him. Taking him inside me. Sealing our bond in the way I've been dreaming about since I first started falling for him.

I don't respond right away though, and Ani rolls onto his back beside me, his naked body glowing in the candlelight.

"You don't have to do anything if you're not into it," he says, his voice soft and seductive. "But I can't make any promises for myself."

His hand slides down his chest, down the smooth planes of his abs, and he fists his cock, giving himself a gentle stroke.

I swallow hard, my gaze transfixed on the curve of his hand, the steel-hard length of him growing even harder beneath his touch.

That should be *my* touch.

My *mouth*, actually. That's what I want first.

Desire blooms inside me, making my mouth water for the taste of him.

"You okay?" he teases, still touching himself.

Goddess, he's driving me mad, and I can't take another minute of it.

I strip out of my clothes, then climb on top to straddle him, grabbing his hands and pushing them back against the pillow. His cock is hot and hard between my thighs, a tease I've got no power to resist.

"You're officially the *worst*," I whisper. "But you're *my* worst, and I'm not letting you go."

Then I lean down and kiss that smug, sunshiney smile right off his face.

He moans into my mouth, breaking free of my hold to bring his hands to my thighs, stroking my skin with a featherlight touch that sends shivers rippling across my body. But I'm not ready to let him *really* touch me.

Not until I've had *my* fill.

I break our kiss, trailing my mouth down his chest, kissing every ridge and hollow as I follow the enticing trail of dark red hair down to his smooth, perfect cock.

Wrapping my hand around the base, I take him into my mouth, teasing the tip with my tongue before taking him in deeper. Ani's soft moans are all the music I need, a seductive song that sends a flood of heat to my core and encourages me to take him deeper, sucking and licking, savoring the taste of every inch as it glides across my tongue.

"Stop," he finally breathes, gently tugging my hair. "Goddess, Stevie. If you keep doing that, I'm going to come."

"And that's a problem because…?" I lick a path up to the tip, sucking it between my lips again, flicking him with my tongue. Then I pull back, glancing up at him with wide, innocent eyes. "But if you *really* want me to stop…"

A whimper escapes his lips, and Ani shakes his head,

eyes rolling back as he grabs the headboard and sinks into the pleasure of my—*ahem*—deepest attentions.

I suck him harder now, bringing him in as deep as I can take him, then further still, his reactions unleashing a moan from the back of my throat.

"Stevie," he breathes, his hips rocking, ab muscles flexing, his whole body T-minus five seconds from losing complete control. "Don't stop," he begs. "Please don't stop. Goddess, yes. *Fuck…*"

Ani slides his hands into my hair, and I suck and tease, dragging my fingernails down his thighs, driving him to the absolute brink. I pull back once more, then go down hard, my tongue undulating against his cock, urging him to let it all go.

"Fuck! Stevie!" Ani bucks into my mouth, his body trembling, every bit of his pent-up desire finally exploding in a white-hot burst, slick and heavy as it slides down my throat.

I release him slowly, giving him a minute to catch his breath before I make my way back up, straddling him once again.

"Goddess, you're amazing," he says, eyes glazed with desire, heart beating wildly beneath my fingers.

"I really missed you," I say, still not totally certain he's real. But if this is a dream, I'm going to enjoy it for as long as I possibly can. "*Really* missed you."

"And I really missed you too." Keeping his caramel gaze locked on mine, Ani takes my hand and guides my fingers into his mouth, sucking them slowly, his hot, velvet tongue sending ripples of pleasure up my arm.

I let out a soft sigh, focusing on the warmth of his kiss, the pressure of his tongue, the heat pooling between my thighs.

Just when I think my body might burst into flames, he pulls my fingers free, then guides my hand down between my thighs.

Heat spreads across my cheeks, and I let out a nervous giggle. "Seriously?"

But Ani's not laughing. He's not even smiling.

"Touch yourself," he whispers, eyes blazing, his cock growing impossibly hard between my thighs. "Show me what you like."

"I... um... What?"

Normally I'm the first one to advocate for a little self-love—with or *without* battery-operated assistance—but I've never shared something like this with another person. The idea feels a lot like letting someone read your journal—intensely private, possibly mortifying.

Maybe even a little exhilarating.

Ani watches me, a red-hot dare flaming to life in his eyes.

I slide my fingers over my clit, unleashing a gasp from my lips.

"That's it," he whispers. "Show me."

Emboldened by his obvious excitement, I draw a slow circle, finding my rhythm.

Ani grips my thighs, shifting beneath me until he's perfectly positioned at my entrance.

"Are you good with this?" he asks, and I nod, biting back a nervous smile. Heat sizzles in the air around us, a crescendo slowly building to an inferno as my fiery ginger takes control.

He slides inside me, slow and torturous, sinfully delicious. I close my eyes and whisper his name, rocking forward against my hand as I take him in deeper, then pull back, slowly sinking down on him once again, every thrust sending ripples of pleasure across my nerves.

"More," he says, rocking his hips to a faster pace. "Goddess, I want more of you."

I always figured my Sun Arcana would be fun and playful in bed, but this hot, demanding side of Ani is completely unexpected—and a total turn-on. With every word, every move, every touch, he makes me feel wilder. More feverish.

I roll my hips and ride him harder, my fingers sliding faster over my clit, the dual sensations making me so hot, so wet.

Sliding his palms up my ribcage, Ani teases my nipples with his fingertips, eyes dark with desire. In a sexy, liquid voice I barely recognize, he says, "Is this how you touch yourself when you're alone in your bed, fantasizing about your Arcana brothers? Fantasizing about sharing us?"

"Goddess, yes," I breathe, the admission unlocking something inside me, bold and free and totally uninhibited.

"I know what *my* fantasy looks like," he murmurs.

"You're lying on your side, letting Baz fuck your soft, sweet mouth while Kirin eats this gorgeous pussy, and I take you from behind." He slides his hands down to my hips, then around my backside, fingers dipping down into forbidden territory with a light touch that has me desperate for more.

Another soft moan escapes my lips.

"Right here," he whispers, gently teasing the backdoor entrance, a heady promise of future nights together, dark desires yet to be unlocked. "So tight. So fucking perfect."

"Ani," I breathe, fire gathering between my thighs, pressure building at his every word.

"And what would the illustrious Dr. Devane say?" he teases. "Hmm. Would he join us, or would he stand back and touch himself, watching us with envy, still refusing to share as the rest of us fuck you senseless?"

"Ani, you're driving me crazy," I say, slowly increasing the pressure on my clit, his words painting a vivid picture in my mind—one I've been imagining for longer than I care to admit. Between my thighs, his cock grows harder in response, and I rub faster, fingers slipping across my super-heated flesh as I lose myself in the promise of Ani's seductive fantasy.

"Or maybe," he says, voice drunk with lust, "you'll take two of us at once, Kirin between your thighs, me fucking you from behind, making sure you feel every inch as we go deeper and deeper until you *melt*."

He grips my ass and arches his hips, grinding hard against me. His cock is so thick, so hard inside me, every deep thrust makes me gasp.

"I can't hold on," I pant, unable to control the frantic pulse of my fingers on my clit. "I'm right there. Goddess, Ani... I don't want to stop."

"Don't stop. Make yourself come for me," he demands. "I want to *feel* you lose control."

My muscles tighten, the heat spiraling out from deep inside, and suddenly I'm right on the edge, sliding over his cock, chasing the orgasm just out of reach. I cry out his name, but before I can utter another sound, Ani bolts upright, stealing the breath from my lips with a deep, devastating kiss. Hooking his hands around my shoulders, he grinds into me, his body shuddering as he comes inside me, hot and hard.

I hold my breath, still balanced on the precipice, my nerves on fire, when Ani shoves his hand between us, joining my own fevered stroking. His touch is like fire itself, hot and hungry, desperate, devouring...

And holy fucking hell, I'm gone.

"Fuck, Ani! Oh my *goddess!*" A white-hot starburst of pure, explosive pleasure detonates, and I shatter, my thighs trembling, my heart pounding, my whole body lit up from the inside.

It's so blinding, so deep, it feels like my soul is leaving, chased away by the intensity of it all...

Without warning, the bedroom vanishes, the hardwood floor and plaster walls turning into red sandstone, the sky stretching dark and wide overhead.

A vision. *Fuck.* I'm sucked into it so fast I don't even have time to warn Ani. One minute I'm riding out the

SARAH PIPER

blissful waves of my orgasm, the next I'm falling face-first into the dirt as a blaze of fire shoots over my head, so close it singes my hair.

I push up to my feet and whip around, bracing myself for another battle with Dark Judgment.

But the mage threatening me with the Wand of Flame and Fury isn't Judgment at all.

It's Ani. Dark and deadly. Empty inside.

His eyes are black, his smile dripping with blood.

"Ani!" I shout, reaching for him. "Let it go! It's killing you!"

The rocks vanish, and I'm back in the bedroom once again, warm and safe in the arms of the man I love.

The blood is gone. The Wand is gone. There's only Ani, his caramel eyes warm in the candlelight.

"Goddess, it's you," I breathe, reaching for his face.

But he flinches at my touch, his eyes turning cold and unforgiving. The fiery inferno that burned so hot between us mere seconds ago has turned to ice.

"What's wrong?" I whisper.

"What's wrong with *you*?" His cold eyes narrow, lip curling back over his teeth. "*Unworthy.*"

I'm out of the bed in a flash, backing up toward the window with the sheet clutched in my hands, desperate to put as much space between us as I can.

Ani's eyes clear, and he looks at me across the dimly lit room, his face falling. "What... what happened?"

I pull the sheet up to my chin, not moving from the window. My whole body is trembling. "I don't know. I

300

just... I saw something. A vision. You... you had the Wand."

He doesn't reply, just keeps staring at me, confused and uncertain.

"You were trying to hurt me," I say. "I know it wasn't real, but it—"

"You think I'd *ever* hurt you?"

Something new flashes in his eyes, but it's not sadness or concern. It's not confusion. It's not even a sense of betrayal at the idea that I might actually be scared of him.

It's rage.

His energy hits me at the same time I see it in his eyes— a fury so intense, so pure, I can almost feel its heat on my skin.

The lingering haze of lust burns away in an instant, and new questions slam through my mind. He mentioned Doc refusing to share—how did he know about that? And how, after all those months of shy, sweet jokes, did he become such a commanding dirty-talker? All that confidence, all that fire... I didn't expect it.

Because it wasn't Ani.

Not the Ani I fell in love with. Not the Ani who sang with me and made up funny Tarot stories and gave me the sunrise.

"What's happening?" I whisper, tears glazing my eyes.

"What's wrong, Starla?" he snaps, climbing out of the bed and stalking toward me. His steps are slow and deliberate, a lion stalking a gazelle. "Don't like a man who pushes back? You prefer them dumb and docile, is that it?"

"No, I..." I close my eyes and take a deep, steadying breath. I don't know what's going on, but this isn't Ani. Maybe it's some side effect from the dream realm or the potion, or some lingering brain fog from the whole ordeal, but it isn't him. "You've been through a lot, Ani. I think we all need to just take a step back and—"

"Step back right into Baz and Kirin's bed. That's what you mean, right? Or maybe Cass's? Anyone but good ol' Ani." He grabs the sheet and whips it out of my hands, tossing it onto the floor between us. His eyes are wild, his smile bordering on manic. "String me along for a laugh or two, some fashion advice, a few stupid karaoke songs, but I'll never be good enough for that pussy, right?"

His energy hits me again, all at once. Rejection, loneliness, self-loathing, darkness. I've barely tasted the full cocktail of it when the door bursts open, Doc and Baz barreling into the room.

Doc takes one look at the scene, then grabs Ani by the throat, pinning him against the wall. "Apologize to her. Now."

Ani's eyes blaze with new fire, but then it's like a wall goes up between us, cutting him off completely. I can't get a read on him, can't sense anything beyond a cold, dark numbness that makes my skin crawl.

Gaze locked on mine, Ani forces a smile I know he doesn't mean. "I apologize. I'm just a little... tired. After everything."

"Just... get some rest." Dropping my gaze, I grab the sheet and my clothes and head for the door, desperate to get as far away from that room as possible. Away from *him*.

Baz follows me out, closing the door behind him, leaving Doc to deal with Ani's post-realm mood swings.

"You okay?" Baz asks, holding up the sheet while I get into my T-shirt and underwear. No one else is around, but I appreciate the gesture nevertheless, especially since I feel like Ani just stripped me to the core.

"Thanks," I say, taking the sheet and wrapping it around myself. "I'm okay. Just a little rattled, I guess. I was so happy he woke up, and things got heated between us, and it just... Goddess, it happened so fast."

Baz scrutinizes my face, then shakes his head, pulling me in for a soft hug. He's trembling, I realize, unable to hide his anger.

"You're pissed at him," I say.

"After the way he talked to you? I wanted to put him through the wall." He pulls back, gazing into my eyes, his face tight with concern. "Didn't you?"

"No," I answer honestly. "I can't be mad at him, Baz. Not after what he's been through."

I close my eyes, burying my face against his chest.

The dream realm changed Baz. It changed Kirin. It changed all of us. I was a fool to think Ani would come through it unscathed, especially considering how long he was trapped there.

"He'll be okay," Baz says, rubbing my back. "Just give him some time."

I nod, but I can't bring myself to share his optimism. I

can't explain it, but this just feels different. Maybe it's because Ani was always so happy and warm, our Sun Arcana. But hearing those cruel words fall from his mouth, seeing the look of disgust in his eyes, *feeling* the repulsion in his energy…

I'll never forget it.

I glance back at the bedroom door as a new feeling blooms in my chest, hot and prickly.

Guilt.

Because whoever I just shared myself with in there, in all the hot, delicious ways that set my body and soul on fire?

It *wasn't* Ani. It only looked like him.

TWENTY-NINE

BAZ

She skipped lunch again. That was the first clue. I was willing to let it slide the day after the world started burning and Ani arose from the dead, talking all that nonsense. But by the fourth skipped lunch, I was officially worried.

Still am. Pretty sure she knows it too.

She manages to avoid me by sticking with the other witches for most of the afternoon, the whole lot of them concocting some scheme for later that sounds like it involves copious amounts of booze and cackling. But then, just after sunset, I find her alone in her bedroom, sitting on the bed and staring down at a Tarot card.

"Message from Mom?" I ask gently, sitting down beside her.

Thankfully, she doesn't toss my ass out.

"No," she says with a sad smile. "I pulled this one myself. I was hoping to get some advice."

"I'm no Dr. Phil, but something tells me your needs

aren't being met in that department." I wink, but Stevie's clearly in no mood for jokes. "What's going on, Little Bird?"

A long, heavy sigh floats from her lips, and when she looks up at me again, her eyes are shiny with tears. "Ani. That's what's going on."

"Stevie, the other night..." I shove a hand through my hair, not sure how to word this. I know what I *want* the answer to be, and if it's anything other than a firm *hell no*, we're going to have a serious problem on our hands. "Did Ani hurt you? Physically?"

"What? No, it wasn't anything like that. He just... He wasn't himself, Baz. And I'm not talking about him being tired or messed up after his ordeal. This is... something else."

"What do you mean?"

She tells me about their reunion, about some of the things he said to her, the changes in his demeanor. "At first, I was into it, you know? But then I had that vision, and he just... He reacted badly. I tried to tell him about it, and... I guess you guys heard what happened."

I nod, brushing a lock of her hair over her shoulder, my hand lingering on her back.

"And ever since then, he's just been super weird around me. Like, hot and cold. One minute, I think he's back. And then it's like he doesn't even know me and has to remind himself who I am. I haven't been alone with him since that night—I'm too scared to see that side of him again."

"Yeah, I don't blame you. I see it too—he's definitely not

acting like himself. But he was in the realm a long time, Stevie. He's having a rough re-entry. I'm sure it's just that."

"Has he talked to you guys about what happened there? What he saw, or whether he ran into Judgment?"

I shake my head. "Kirin and I tried to ask him about it the day after he woke up, but he didn't want to get into it. Just kept saying there wasn't much to tell. Cass got the same response the night we barged in on you guys and he hung back to talk to him—he said Ani just put a wall up, refusing to talk about the realm."

"When he first woke up," she says, "all he said to me was that it was absolute hell. But beyond that, nothing."

"What did the cards say?" I ask, but there's only one sitting on the bed before her.

The Sun, reversed.

"This is actually the eighth attempt," she says. "The first three spreads I did? All our old friends showed up. One, Five, Seven, Twenty—Magician, Hierophant, Chariot, Judgment—all reversed."

"Three times in a row? Statistically impossible."

"Yep. So I pulled them out of the deck, set them aside, and started over."

"Isn't that cheating?"

"Their energy was completely overpowering my readings. I felt like I needed a clean slate. But every time I turned another card, it was this one—Sun Reversed. I shuffled it back in, mixed up all the cards, tried again. Four more times. And each time, this card either dropped out on its own, or I pulled it on the first try."

"Any idea what it means?"

Her shoulders sink, her eyes filling with sadness and worry. "Do you remember the night I brought the black dahlias out of my nightmares?"

"Not something I'm going to forget anytime soon, believe me."

"Well, in that nightmare, Judgment called Ani the Black Sun."

I shudder, remembering when she told me about it. Judgment said something about how Ani would rule over the Dark armies that would usher in the new magickal order.

I can't lie. Seeing this card, hearing her interpretation, remembering the nightmare she told me about... Goddess, the very idea of Ani going dark is supremely fucked up, and supremely terrifying.

But I can't say it's impossible. Not after all the other shit we've seen.

"No way," I say anyway, shaking my head. "Ani came back to us. If he were dark, he'd be stuck in the realm with the rest of those assholes."

"Phaines wasn't stuck in the realm."

"But Ani came *back*," I say again, as if repeating it will make a damn bit of difference.

"But the Ani who came back... It *isn't* him, Baz. Not totally. He was in the dream realm longer than any of us. He won't talk about what happened there, or why he took the dream potion in the first place instead of just waiting for us. He hasn't said a single word about the news from his hometown, or whether he's worried about his little sister, or anything else going on outside the Academy. It's like he just wants to pretend that everything's totally normal—like we're all just here in this house for an extended winter break, partying together while the rest of the world is one lit match away from total annihilation."

"Are we interrupting?" a voice calls from the doorway. It's Cass, with Kirin bringing up the rear.

"Yes," I say, at the same time Stevie invites them in, scooting over to make room on the bed.

"We were just talking about Ani," she says, showing them the reversed Tarot card.

She tells them about her Black Sun theory, about Judgment's dire warnings from her nightmares.

"Maybe it *is* Judgment's influence," Doc says, "but that doesn't mean Ani's been turned. It's possible he's just haunted, not unlike Baz was after his return." He looks over at me. "How are you feeling, by the way?"

"I haven't seen the mark in a few weeks." I lift my shirt and show them the exact spot on my chest where the blazing XX used to appear, but there's nothing there now. "Maybe he's gone."

"*Exactly* a few weeks?" Kirin asks, narrowing his eyes. "Or roughly a few weeks."

"Does it matter?"

"Actually, yes. Three weeks ago, you came back to Red Sands and had it out with Janelle and Carly. I'm assuming it had something to do with whatever you saw in the realm, since it was Janelle's house we—"

"Yeah, we don't need to go there again." I glance at Stevie, her eyes softening.

"I just meant..." Kirin shrugs, pushing his glasses up his nose. "Look, we're assuming Judgment plays on our regrets and guilt, bad memories, all that stuff. The more we let things fester, the deeper the wounds, that's where he really digs in. So by confronting some part of your past, or talking about it, getting it out in the open... What if that's what keeps him at bay?"

"It makes sense," Stevie says to me. "The past doesn't have as much power over you now as it did in the realm. Which means you're cutting off his food supply."

"So long, walking buffet," I say, and Kirin nods.

"It also explains why it hasn't hit me as hard," Kirin says. "I was able to talk about some of my shit with Stevie in the realm, and it didn't follow me back here quite the same way."

Cass rises from the bed and heads to the window, gazing out into the abyss. I tell myself it's because he's just a broody-ass motherfucker, and not because he's experiencing any of Judgment's post-realm wrath for himself.

"Whatever he did to us in the realm," I continue, "it seems to have an echo effect here, triggered by our own personal guilt and shame. We all agree on that. So that begs the question..." I pick up the Sun card, turning it over between my fingers. "What's triggering Ani?"

"Goddess, and I thought *I* was the sensitive one around here." Ani blazes into the room and hops on the bed, his smile overly bright, his eyes glassy. "Who died? You all

310

look about one animal rescue commercial away from bursting into a group ugly cry."

"Ugly? Speak for yourself." I scowl, scrutinizing his all-too-happy face. If Professor Broome wasn't monitoring him so closely, I might think he was hopped up on another potion.

The fact that he's bouncing around like the Fool's puppy after being in a coma for two weeks doesn't sit well with me either, not to mention the aggression he showed toward Stevie the other night. We may be living with the Academy's most talented potion maker and healer, as well as a boatload of kickass witches and mages, but Ani's rapid recovery is just a little too far south of unnatural for my liking.

"Aww." He shoves my shoulder hard, still beaming at me with that shit-eating grin. "You can stop pouting now, Baz. I'm back."

"And looking pretty good for a guy who's been hibernating like a fucking bear half the month." I laugh, trying to keep my tone light. "Lemme guess. Green smoothies and meditation?"

"Maybe I'm just naturally resilient."

"Maybe you're just naturally a pain in my ass." I reach out and haul him in for a surprise hug. For all the freaky shit going on around here, I missed the sunshine-faced asshole. More than he even realizes.

But it seems Ani isn't in the mood for affections tonight —at least not from me. He shrugs me off and reaches for Stevie instead, pulling her close and nuzzling her neck.

When she doesn't respond, he moves in closer, going right for the kiss.

Stevie, shocking the hell out of all of us, turns away from him. Stone-cold gives him the back of her head, like she can't even bear the thought of his lips touching hers.

After months of watching the two of them make puppy-dog eyes at each other, singing their ridiculous songs, cuddling and cooing like a pair of lovesick kids, the sight of her flat-out rejection is more than unsettling.

But if Ani's fazed by it, he's doing a damn good job keeping up the happy-go-lucky sideshow.

"*Someone's* in a mood." He rolls his eyes, then picks up the deck of Tarot cards from the bed, shuffling them as hard and fast as a Vegas dealer, then flipping over the top five cards.

One, Five, Seven, Twenty, and his own, Trump Nineteen.

All reversed.

"*That* looks a bit ominous," he says, tossing the rest of the cards across the bed, a move so blatantly disrespectful I damn near smack him for it. "No wonder you're all so glum."

A knock on the doorframe catches our attention, and Carly peeks her head in. "Stevie? We're ready."

Stevie's sigh of relief is massive and undeniable.

Rising from the bed, she scoops up her Tarot deck, not sparing a second glance for any of us.

"First time all of us are in the same bed," Ani says, "and our girl bails. You believe this?"

I force another laugh, because the silence is getting pretty damn awkward. But no one else even cracks a smile.

"Where are you off to tonight, Miss Milan?" Cass asks.

"I've got plans." Stevie heads for the hallway. I'm about to follow her out when she turns around and glares at me. "With the *girls*."

"Is that a euphemism?" I let my gaze drift down to her breasts and cock a smirk, waggling my eyebrows, desperate to make her laugh. Desperate to see the light return to her eyes.

But my usual charms fall flat, and Stevie turns away without another word, vanishing down the stairs with Carly.

"*Rude.*" Ani folds his arms over his chest and pouts, but it's all an act, his bullshit running so thick we practically need shovels. "Was it something I said?"

"Maybe it's just your *face*, Gingersnap." I give him a playful shove right off the edge of the bed, but my mood is anything *but* playful.

Stevie was right. This *isn't* our Ani. Not all of him, anyway. Whether he's dark or not, some vital part of him, some spark that made him whole and made him ours...

It's gone.

And I don't know how—or even *if*—we'll ever get it back.

THIRTY

STEVIE

I've just lit the last candle on the back deck when Baz strolls out through the sliding door with Ani, the two of them laden with a platter of raw meat, several bags of munchies, and a cooler full of beer and hard lemonades.

"Excuse me," Carly says, hands on hips, shooting them both a death glare. "Where do you think you're going?"

"What?" Baz asks. "We were planning to barbecue tonight."

I head over and stand at Carly's side, crossing my arms over my chest and doubling up on the death glare. "Sorry, boys. Take your meat back inside—this space is a DFZ."

Ani cocks an eyebrow. "A *what* now?"

"Dick-Free Zone." I glare pointedly at his crotch. "Unless you want to sacrifice that thing to the goddess or see it roasted on the barbecue, I suggest you get the hell back inside."

"Oh, is that for us?" Nat saunters over, helping herself to the tray of meat in Baz's hands. "Thank you!"

"But I—"

"Music!" I say suddenly, reaching into Ani's pocket and stealing his phone. "You always have the *best* playlists."

"You brought alcohol too?" Isla relieves Ani of his cooler, flashing a broad grin. "You guys thought of everything! *Sooo* sweet! Thanks!" Her smile drops. "Now go away."

Baz blinks like a deer in headlights, reaching out for the long-lost tray of meat, but Nat's already setting pieces of chicken and beef onto the grill, slathering them with the jerk sauce Isla made, the smoke and sizzle promising an excellent meal.

"Was there something else?" Carly asks, tapping her foot impatiently. "Or did you need a live demo of the consequences of violating the DFZ?"

"Why does *he* get to stay?" Ani thumbs toward Jareth, who's preening on top of his favorite sandstone out back.

"Because unlike you guys, *he* doesn't talk back." I grab the bags of tortilla chips from the crook of Ani's arm, then shove both boys back inside, slamming the door behind them.

"And don't come back," Carly calls after them, "unless you'd like to learn the true definition of a weenie roast!"

"Damn, girl. You're a brutal bitch," I tell her. "I think I might marry you after all."

"Ehh, you're not my type. But when it comes to scaring away the boys, I've always got your back."

"Good to know."

"Goddess, I thought those boys would never leave." Professor Broome heads out through the doorway with an armload of brightly colored bottles of soap bubbles and wands, Professor Maddox following behind with a case of champagne and something that looks a lot like a saber.

"What's all this?" I ask.

"Bubbles, of course," Broome replies, her eyes sparkling. "For the stars-and-moon ceremony."

I grin, shaking my head. "And we need an ancient weapon for the stars-and-moon ceremony because…?"

"Oh, that's not for the ceremony," Maddox says. "That's for popping off champagne corks like a fucking *pirate*." She squints one eye at me. "*Arrrrgh!*"

"This night just got a *whole* lot extra," Isla says, "and I am *here* for it."

"Let's get it poppin'!" Maddox waggles her eyebrows, cracking up at her own corny joke as she unboxes the first bottle of champagne and removes the foil and outer seal. Then, holding the bottle in her left hand with the cork side pointing out toward the backyard, she grips the saber in her right hand, tells us to get ready, and *zings* the blade up the side, popping the top clean off—cork, glass, and all.

White foam spills out onto her feet, and she lets out a whoop, the rest of us cheering and clapping at the whole damn spectacle, already fighting over who gets to pop the next bottle.

It's the perfect, dick-free kickoff to the first official Witch-'N-Bitch at the new house, and just what I need to help me forget about the bad news, the Dark Arcana, and all the dicks in my life, just for a little while.

Girl time, live and uncut.

* * *

The bubbly flows for hours, the barbecue surpassing all expectations, the laughter loud enough to wake the dead. When the moon is high in the sky, and we're just drunk enough to stop questioning crazy ideas, Broome busts out *her* version of bubbly, ordering us all to strip down to our underwear, drop our fears and limiting beliefs on the deck, and take a bottle of soap bubbles out into the backyard.

Giggling like little girls, we do as she asks, marching in a half-naked line out back, forming a circle beneath the sky.

The moonlight shines down on us all, casting us in a silver-blue glow that looks like magick, filling me with hope and wonder on a night when I thought I'd almost lost both.

Professor Broome says a quick blessing over the moon, inviting us to set our intentions for the weeks ahead. Then, when we're ready, we open up our bubbles, take a collective breath, and blow our rainbow, soap-bubble wishes up to the stars.

I love everything about it. The warm air on my skin as we dance around in our underwear, blowing bubbles until we're dizzy. The sound of the true, unabashed laughter that comes from dropping all pretenses and just being completely silly. The feeling of lightness in my heart. The pure magick of it all.

"My turn with the saber!" I shout, suddenly inspired, charging back up to the deck and grabbing a fresh bottle. With everyone cheering me on, I whip the blade across the glass, popping off the top in a spray of champagne and laughter, foam dripping down my arms and onto my bare stomach.

"Why do you look like you're about to sacrifice someone in a barbaric ritual?" Baz asks, looming in the open doorway behind me.

I whip around to face him, bottle and saber in hand, and his eyes go wide, gaze trailing down over my bra to the foam dripping from my fingers.

"And holy shit," he says, lowering his voice. "Why the fuck am I so turned on right now? I'm pretty sure I just came. Only a little, but still."

I flash a smirk. "Didn't anyone ever teach you not to piss off a half-naked witch with a saber?"

"Apparently, I skipped that class. Are you gonna wear that outfit to bed later?"

I swing the saber between us, then touch the tip to his crotch, arching an eyebrow.

"DFZ. Right." He raises his hands in surrender. "Going back in the house now. Please don't hurt me."

"Good boy."

He flashes one last devilish grin. "But seriously, about that outfit…"

"Go!"

Boy chased off once again, I rejoin the girls, who've all taken up residence in the lounge chairs spread across the deck.

We sing along with the music, talk about our favorite Tarot cards, and Professor Maddox even shares a few funny memories about the trouble she and Mom used to get into together back in the day, running wild across campus, plotting epic spells, trading sweet-natured secrets like only best friends can.

For a while, it seems like nothing can touch us here.

It's a temporary bubble, but a beautiful one, and when Carly links her arm in mine and drags me out back to snap a selfie under the moon, I'm almost convinced everything really *is* okay. That nothing bad will happen to us—not tonight, not ever again.

But then there's a knock on the deck door from inside the house, and a cold ball of dread drops into the pit of my stomach.

"They're back again?" Nat asks. "Goddess, they really don't value those Ds, huh?"

I head back up to the deck and grab the saber, ready to threaten whichever *D* is about to invade our space.

But when I peer into the open doorway, the eyes peering back at me don't belong to Baz, Ani, Kirin, or Doc.

"*Casey?*" I glare at her with mild annoyance, wondering what the hell brought her out here tonight, totally unannounced, after weeks of radio silence.

She nods, then steps aside, revealing the true reason for

her visit—the one witch in the entire magickal universe who's *definitely* not on the Witch-'N-Bitch guest list.

I'm just drunk enough to be a total cunt about it too. And with *this* uninvited guest? Trust me, I've earned it.

"Good evening, Anna." I flash a wide grin, then swing the saber in a wide arc, touching the tip to her throat. "You've got thirty seconds to justify your existence before I pop your head off like a fucking cork."

THIRTY-ONE

STEVIE

She sits alone in the armchair next to the fireplace, sipping her tea like the Queen she believes she is, flames crackling in the hearth behind her. The whole scene is like something out of a nightmare fairytale, the kind they used to tell kids in the Victorian era to scare them into good behavior.

Her unexpected arrival ushered in a swift end to our Witch-'N-Bitch fun, chasing off the last of my buzz and popping our perfect little bubble of magickal miracles. As soon as the guys heard the confrontation unfolding outside, they came charging out en masse, more than eager to spell her ass right back to whatever shadowy alley she slithered out of tonight.

But in the end, I could neither send her away nor make good on my threat to decapitate her with a champagne saber.

Because Anna Trello brought me a peace offering—one I couldn't refuse.

Books.

Two of them, to be precise, now stacked on the table at her side, emanating a force of magick and power so welcoming, so intimate, there's no doubt in my mind they're authentic.

My mother's grimoire, and Journey Through the Void of Mist and Spirit. A collection I came to know—in my brief tenure as an Arcana Academy student and researcher of dark prophecies both ancient and modern—as the Book of Shadow and Mists.

My books, stolen by Professor Phaines the night he drugged, kidnapped, and tortured me. Stolen back by Anna Trello, presumably after his demise at her hand.

Now, seated on the sofa surrounded by Carly, Isla, and Nat, the guys and Casey Appleton an immovable wall behind us, Professors Maddox and Broome a formidable force hovering beside Trello, I give my former headmistress a glare that would set a lesser witch on fire.

But if she's intimidated at all by the show of magickal force, she doesn't reveal it; her energy is as cold and stoic as her eyes.

"Agent Eastman is no longer recognizing my position at Arcana Academy," she says now, teacup and saucer balanced primly in her lap. "I'm essentially a fugitive in his eyes, deemed unfit to lead and protect our students. My office has been overrun, my personal quarters sealed with magick I can't access. He's called in several others to support his claims, and I've spent the past few weeks off-campus, searching a vast network of underground magickal communities for any information that might help us."

"And?" Casey asks. For all their so-called partnering up, she doesn't seem too thrilled with Trello at the moment, either. "What did you learn?"

"Everyone is afraid to speak out," Trello says. "Which is exactly how they want us. Scared and docile. Easy to manipulate. More than willing to trade our basic freedoms for the perception of safety."

"So who's helping out Eastman?" I ask. "More APOA guys?"

Trello shakes her head. "These men are... They're different. They're all mages, clearly part of a formalized organization or network, but nothing legitimate as far as I can tell. They operate in secrecy and shadow, rarely speaking in the presence of outsiders. There's a darkness among them, an energy that chills the very blood."

"Do you think they've got any connection to the so-called Soldiers of Light?" Doc asks.

"I have no idea, Cassius. We don't even know whether the Soldiers exist or are merely a ploy by the true terrorists to further incriminate witches and mages. We don't know whether Eastman and his men are involved with them or with the attacks at large. Everything about this is a mystery —one that grows darker and deeper with each passing day."

"So that's it?" Ani smirks at her, pacing beside the couch like some kind of criminal prosecutor about to roast the star defense witness. Nothing about his demeanor feels familiar to me. He's a totally different person now, his ordeal in the dream realm stealing more than just time.

Behind me, Kirin squeezes my shoulder, and Carly shifts closer to me on the sofa, as if they both sense my unease.

If only Ani shared their perceptiveness.

"That's all you've got?" he presses. "A mystery that grows darker and deeper every day?" He barks out a harsh laugh, one so uncharacteristic, so unlike our light and happy Sun Arcana, it makes my skin crawl. "*Someone* is burning cities to the ground, incinerating children, destroying cultural landmarks, and blaming it all on your fellow witches and mages, and that's all you've got to say about it?" He clucks his tongue, shaking his head at her. "You don't know this, you don't know that... Honestly, Headmistress. With such a profound lack of knowledge, it's a wonder you achieved such an esteemed position at the Academy at all."

Trello's eyes blaze. "Do not presume, Mr. McCauley, that you know *anything* about my knowledge or experience, in this matter or any other. Classes may be on hold for the foreseeable future, but I am still your headmistress, and I demand your respect."

She takes another sip of her tea, her hands rock steady. But despite her cool demeanor, her energy has shifted, the ice fracturing just enough to reveal a hint of real emotion beneath.

Fear. Uncertainty. Regret.

Not a combination I've come to associate with the headmistress, that's for sure.

But as much as Ani's one-man, trial-by-fire circus act is giving me an ulcer the size of Arizona, he's right to question her.

If she doesn't know anything, what the hell is she doing here?

"Headmistress Trello," I finally say, "I appreciate you returning the books to me, but Ani has a point. If you don't know anything, there's nothing left to discuss. So if you don't mind, I'd really like to get back to my evening."

I mean, really. What did she expect? That she could just waltz in here with my books after months of cold-shouldering me, and I'd drop to the ground and kiss her feet?

I stand up from the sofa and collect her teacup and saucer, hoping she'll take the hint and see herself out. But Trello just keeps glaring at me like I'm a petulant, ridiculous child.

"You're wrong, Starla," she says. "There is *infinitely* more to discuss. So much, in fact, that I'm having trouble knowing where to start."

"How about your so-called undercover partnership with Professor Phaines?" Carly says. "The so-called agreement that went bad enough for you to murder him."

Trello exchanges a quick glance with Casey, who nods for the older woman to continue.

"You owe them an explanation, Anna," Casey says. "You owe *me* an explanation too."

Trello sighs, then gestures for me to return to my spot on the sofa.

"Starla, this is going to be very difficult for you to hear," she says. "And I know you have little reason to trust me. But I need you to sit down, and I need you—above all else —to listen."

I reach out for her energy, scouring it for any signs of treachery.

Again, I find the same mixture of fear and regret, this time topped off with a deep sorrow, an old loss from which she's never recovered.

I look into her eyes, and for a brief moment, her walls come down, revealing a sad, broken woman carrying a life-time of pain. Of grief. It rolls off her body in waves—a dark, familiar ache I've lived with ever since my parents left this plane.

Trello lowers her gaze, and the connection between us breaks.

But I know what I felt, and that shared pain—however brief—was enough to buy her a few more minutes of my attention.

I drop back onto the couch and gesture for her to continue, settling in between Carly and Isla, knowing— deep in my bones—that I'm going to need all the support they're able to offer.

"Your parents' death," Trello begins, and I suck in a sharp breath, gripping Carly and Isla's hands. "It wasn't an accident, Starla. It was a dark mage attack."

The shock of her statement punches me in the gut, stealing the rest of the breath from my lungs. I suck in more air, trying to force myself to breathe again, to speak, to move, but the only thing I can feel is my heart shattering.

All at once, the memories rush back, slamming through my skull, tearing me apart inside and out.

"But... but the flood," I stammer. "The water came out of nowhere, rushing into the canyon. It all happened so fast... I saw it. Dad pushed me into that cave and the water just... It swept them away. I watched that water steal them away from me."

And then it came back to finish the job, flooding the cave and cutting me off from the world. If it wasn't for Search and Rescue and a very patient, highly skilled dive team, I wouldn't be sitting here right now, enjoying the privilege of this pain.

I'd be dead, buried in a box beneath a granite headstone in Los Piñones Cemetery in Tres Búhos, Arizona, right alongside my parents.

Trello's steely eyes soften, her mouth pulling into a deep frown. "Yes, that was the official cause of death. The head injuries they sustained from the force of the floodwater."

I nod, wiping away familiar tears.

"But the cause of the flood itself?" Trello shakes her head, unleashing a deep sigh. "That was unnatural, Starla. It was dark magick at work. I knew it the moment it happened—I could sense it. More than that, your mother warned me it would happen that way, just as she warned me there was nothing I could do to stop it. It would be, in her words, the beginning of a prophecy eighteen years in the making. All I could do—all I continue to do, all these years later—was keep my promise to her."

"What promise?" I whisper, the "eighteen years in the

making" part ringing ominously in my head. I was eighteen when my parents died. Eighteen when that so-called prophecy began.

"To ensure that you enrolled at Arcana Academy five years later, when she predicted the next domino would fall. To provide you with access to her research, along with all the support we could offer. And most importantly, to protect you, by any means necessary and for as long as possible, from the destiny she knew would ultimately befall you." She turns her attention to Carly, her brows drawn into a deep V. "You asked about my involvement with Professor Phaines? He'd been part of the Academy for even longer than my tenure here. I'd known him a long time, and he seemed just as bereaved by the deaths of Connor and Melissa Milan as I was. But soon after Starla's arrival on campus, I began to suspect Phaines had some sort of knowledge of the mage attack. The things he said about Starla, the questions he asked me, the renewed interest in Melissa's prophecies after so many years... It didn't add up."

"He tried to murder Stevie," Carly reminds her. "Because he thought her blood would give him access to the Arcana objects."

Trello nods, not bothering to deny her knowledge of the objects or the reasons behind his attack. "Phaines fled to escape prosecution for his crimes, but I knew that if I let him disappear completely, I'd lose my chance at getting the answers about the mages who attacked the Milans—mages who could very well come after their daughter. So I tracked him down and offered him a deal: in exchange for information about the dark mage attack, I would provide information about the activities of the Arcana Brotherhood and your progress with the prophecies and the search for the sacred objects."

"You *knew*?" I ask. Of all the things she's unloaded on us so far tonight, that little revelation is by far the most astonishing. That she knew about our Brotherhood, that she knew about our mission, that she was willing to sell us all out to a man she already suspected was involved in my parents' murder...

Red. All I see is red.

I rocket to my feet, launching myself at her. I don't even think about it. All I want is to claw her eyes out, to carve up that stoic, smug face with my bare hands...

Kirin's on me in a heartbeat, wrapping his arms around me, pulling me back from the would-be assault.

"Breathe," he says softly, lips close to my ear. "Just breathe."

I relax into his hold, the anger receding just a little, leaving me trembling and anxious. I try to sit down again, but Kirin shakes his head, refusing to let me go.

"I needed Phaines to share information," Trello continues, as if I didn't just nearly attack her. "For that, I needed him to trust me. I pretended to be equally unscrupulous. But as part of our arrangement, I also required him to remain off-campus and avoid all contact with Starla or any other Academy students."

"And he accepted these terms?" Doc asks.

"With a few caveats—namely, that we appoint Janelle Kirkpatrick as interim librarian in his stead."

"Motherfucker," Baz says. "Janelle Kirkpatrick, who was already working as his personal spy."

"I agreed to it," Trello says, "but with a counter-caveat of my own." She nods toward Casey. "I called in APOA, knowing that your presence would help keep students safe and ensure Phaines stayed off-campus. Sadly, that didn't work out as planned. Phaines returned to campus with the help of Agent Eastman, and you all know how the rest of that story unfolded."

"So after all this wheeling and dealing," I say, unable to keep the venom from my voice, even as Kirin's arms tighten around me, "did it work? Did Phaines finally confess all his secret knowledge about the dark mages that killed my parents?"

"Regrettably, he did not." Trello folds her hands in her lap and sighs again. "I had to kill him before he got that chance. He'd already assaulted you, barely sparing your life. He attacked other students. And then he possessed Casey. Her life was in imminent danger, and I couldn't let things progress."

"And you're telling me you weren't part of all that too?" I ask. "That you're just an innocent bystander in all this?"

"I've never claimed to be innocent. But no, Starla. I was never part of Phaines's plans to harm you and the other students, nor to attempt to steal the Arcana objects for the Dark Magician."

"Yet all of those things happened during your so-called

arrangement with him," I say. "All because you claim he had information about my parents' death—a death you couldn't even be bothered to acknowledge by attending the funeral or offering the most meager of condolences."

Her eyes blaze again, her energy flooding with anger and indignation. "There is so much more to this story than you could *ever* imagine."

"Then I suggest you get to it, Headmistress," Doc says, coming to stand beside me and Kirin. "Despite your tenure and title—not to mention your masterful manipulation techniques—you're on *our* turf now. I think I speak for Stevie and everyone else assembled here when I say, with utmost respect, we are sick and tired of your bullshit. So say your piece, then get the fuck out."

Inside, my heart leaps with pride, a smile tugging the corners of my mouth. If Kirin didn't have my arms pinned at my sides, I might just throw myself upon Doc's mercy, kissing him until we obliterated every last line of professional decorum.

That's my hot, commanding, control freak of a mental magicks professor, y'all.

Trello, for all her bullshit, doesn't flinch. She looks me dead in the eyes and says, "There's something you need to understand about your origins. Your conception."

"Is this the part where you tell me how close you were to my mother?" I ask. "How she trusted you with her most intimate thoughts? How you cared so deeply about her and my father?"

A shudder runs through her body, head to toe, and a

chill washes over the room. Suddenly, it's not just her energy revealing her true feelings, but her whole facade, the aloofness finally crumbling away, revealing a broken woman full of pain and regret—a woman I wish I never had to see.

Because the woman sitting before us now—nothing like the smug, self-satisfied bitch who waltzed in here tonight—is clearly harboring something so dark and painful, so earth-shattering, it's going to break more than just my heart.

"No, Starla," she says softly, dropping her gaze into her lap. Her hands, calm and steady throughout our entire interrogation, finally begin to tremble. "This is the part where I tell you your mother sealed your fate the day she made a blood deal with the Dark Magician to bring you into this world."

THIRTY-TWO

STEVIE

Forward and backward through time and space
Past present future, all boundaries erased
Memories show us what oaths have kept hidden
Reveal our truths, unbound and unbidden

Soft and steady in the quiet darkness of the kitchen, Doc speaks the enchantment, the Moon card glowing silver-bright on the table. On its face, seven drops of blood merge into one—three of mine, three of Trello's, and one from Doc, binding us to his Moon magick, sealing the spell's power.

On either side of the card, two silver candles anointed with mugwort flicker in the darkness, casting us all in an eerie orange glow.

The rest of the house is silent. After barely saying good-night, Ani went to bed, content to leave us to our own unfolding dramas. But the others are waiting in the living room, giving us the space we need to complete this task. To reveal the last of Trello's secrets, and possibly my mother's as well.

To turn my world on its head.

"The spell will essentially allow us to walk back in time through the landscape of Anna's memories," Doc explains. "As she draws the Tarot cards and weaves her story, you and I will be able to see those memories unfolding in our own minds."

"But memories are faulty," I say. "How do we know we're getting the truth?"

"Some of the details may be inaccurate or hazy, but the magick prevents her from outright lying to us." He turns to Trello, the warning clear in his eyes. "You may begin. And Anna? If you attempt to manipulate us tonight, I assure you —it will be your last attempt at *anything*."

Trello makes her promise with a firm nod, her gaze stern and severe across the table, the angles of her face even sharper in the flickering candlelight. She draws the first card from her deck, setting it on the table before her—a pregnant woman seated in an elaborately carved wooden throne, clutching a bundle of wheat and a cornucopia overflowing with fruit and flowers. One foot rests on a rock, while the other dips into a flowing stream.

The Empress can mean many things—creativity, abundance, self-love, and so much more. But tonight, the image speaks to me very clearly of the literal pregnancy depicted, and of a deep desire for motherhood and boundless love.

In my mind's eye, the face of the Empress turns into my mother's face, young and buoyant, her eyes dancing with hope as she chatters about her desire to bring a child into this world.

She's talking to a friend over a cup of tea.

She's talking to Anna Trello.

"I see her," I say, the memory spell taking hold.

"Young and in love," Trello continues, "your parents were eager to start their own family. But as badly as they wanted a child, it just wasn't meant to be."

She turns the next card—the Three of Swords, featuring a stone heart situated at the base of a tree. Three swords balance on the stone, pointing up at three scars carved deep into the tree's bark.

The scene in my mind shifts, my mother's eyes now full of heartache and anguish, her tea turning cold as she confesses her worries. I hear her voice, almost as if I'm sitting at the next table over, eavesdropping.

We've tried everything, Anna. Spells, potions, herbs... Even mundane medical intervention. Nothing's working. I don't understand...

"Your mother could not conceive," Trello says. "She was so desperate for a child, Starla. For *you*. For in her mind, she'd already made you—already fallen in love with you. She was distraught about her situation, yes. But a witch as determined and headstrong as Melissa Milan would never let something like biology stand in her way. So after exhausting all other avenues, when even your father was ready to give up, she called on the only magick she'd yet to try."

The next card is the one I've been waiting for, and Trello

turns it over with an unsteady hand.

The Magician looms before us both, his blue eyes wild as he points his wand to the heavens, his other hand toward the ground. As above, so below. The card of magick and manifestation, of personal power, of co-creation.

A new vision appears in my mind, and suddenly I'm standing inside a dark cave, watching a witch perform a ritual before a stone altar.

It's the Fool's Grave, I realize. The witch kneeling before the altar is my mother.

And I stand behind her, watching through Trello's eyes, through her memories.

Are you sure you want to do this? The younger Trello asks, but my mother won't be dissuaded.

It's the Winter Solstice, my mother replies. *I* must *call upon him tonight.*

I watch in awe as she lays a series of elemental and other offerings on the altar, the meaning of each item clear in my mind—A black candle, lit to honor the longest night of the year, and a gold one, to welcome the return of the sun. The skull of a deer and pinecones for fertility. Sugar cookies, meant as a gift and a sweet enticement. A chalice full of rich, red wine—another enticement. And a freshly clipped bunch of holly branches dotted with bright red berries, reminding me of the holly I brought back from the dream realm.

There's only one place she could've gathered fresh holly —only one place where it thrives on campus.

The Void.

Kirin's warning, spoken in hushed tones on my first day at the Academy, rings fresh in my mind.

It's said that there are places in this world so deep, so dark, so... compelling... when you peer down into them, they literally beckon you to jump...

Altar offerings complete, my mother retrieves her silver athame and slices her palm, filling a small bowl with her blood. She then adds a pinch of tobacco, a whole stick of cinnamon, and two crystals—moonstone and red jasper.

The final ingredient is the Magician card.

She drops it into the bowl, pressing it to the bottom and swirling it around until the blood covers it completely.

Then, whispering a prayer I can't hear, she lights a match and touches it to the liquid.

It ignites immediately, silver and white flames dancing along the surface, and she raises her palms skyward, still whispering her spell.

"She called upon the Magician in an attempt to manifest her own greatest creation," Trello says now. "You, Starla."

I watch as the flames grow brighter, tears spilling down my cheeks.

"She wanted you to be kind and compassionate," Trello says. "A healer. She wanted you to be blessed with her talents for divination, as well as your father's gifts for herbalism and plant magick. She also asked for the blessings of all four elemental deities, so that you might have a life filled with magick of every kind."

"The Princesses," I whisper.

"A gift from your mother." Trello's voice is soft and

kind, but then it shifts, a coldness seeping back into her tone that sends a chill racing down my spine. "What she didn't tell me was that she'd already seen your true destiny —that you'd be chosen as the Star Arcana."

"Is that what the Magician did? Gave her the Star as a daughter?"

"No. *That* was fate. The Magician's role was in helping your mother bring you into this world. She was not meant to have a child, but she willed it anyway, breaking the natural order. She called upon him during her Winter Solstice ritual, and he was all too eager to answer her pleas."

The memory shifts to a dorm room, my mother imploring Trello to understand. She explains what she saw during her ritual—that the Magician promised her a pregnancy, promised that her child would become everything she'd dreamed of and more.

"But he did not offer such promises without strings," Trello says now. "My Goddess, Starla, if you could've known your mother back then. She'd never met an obstacle she couldn't overcome, a desire she could not achieve. And there he was, this dark energy that none of us understood, that no witch in our circles had ever called upon, holding her greatest dream in the palm of his hand, glowing like a tiny star, just barely out of reach. All she had to do to claim it was agree to his terms."

"What happened?" I ask.

"Oh, she accepted without question. In her mind, she'd already held you in her arms, already looked upon your face. She'd spent her life falling in love with you. By the time he stated his terms, you were already hers. There was no way she'd turn him down."

Again, I see my mother, frantically trying to explain all of this to Trello. To justify it, despite Trello's obvious concerns.

"And the terms?" I ask.

"She had to grant him permanent access to her magick. To allow him to siphon it at will."

"Goddess," I breathe. "So all this time, he used her magick to gain his strength? To build his armies?"

"That's exactly what he did, for as long as he had access. But that's not all." Trello lets out a deep sigh, shaking her head. "When the time came—some future moment of his choosing—your mother would be required to relinquish the blood of the World."

The phrase strikes a chord inside me, and once again I remember Kirin's words, this time from a passage he read from one of the lore books.

It is said that he who is in possession of these objects, along with the blood of the world and an arcane spell of indeterminate origins...

"The blood of the World," I say, horrified. "My mother's blood, passed to me. *My* blood. Once he has that, along with the Arcana objects and some old spell, he can take control of magick forever."

"It would be months before she began to understand the magnitude of what she'd done," Trello says. "But by then, you'd already been born. And as predicted, she was in love with you. Both of your parents were. But she was also losing her mind, channeling prophecies day and night, searching always for a way to break her oath, even knowing that she couldn't. Everything that would come to pass— your lives in Tres Búhos, the decades-long murders of witches and mages, your enrollment at the Academy, the rise of the Dark Arcana, the trouble arriving on our very doorstep—she foresaw. She knew there would be no altering your fate, and ultimately, *that* is what drove her to the brink."

"But... I don't understand. If you were her friend—and from everything I've seen, I believe she trusted you—why did you drive my parents out of the Academy?"

Trello turns over another card—the Six of Swords. In it, a young couple sits with six swords at the front of a small boat, a cloaked man standing at the back, ferrying them to safer shores.

"An escape," I say, the message coming through. "They had to leave. It... It was her choice?"

"I was the only one who knew of her deal with the Dark Magician. Not even your father knew—he believed your mother had finally crafted an effective fertility spell, nothing more. Once again, soon after your birth, her need for secrecy drove her to my door. She insisted that we create an elaborate ruse. It needed to be so convincing, she said, that even your father would believe it."

The memory filters through, and I listen as my mother convinces Trello to begin spreading rumors to undermine her reputation, to convince other faculty members and advisors to break ties, to discredit my mother's research, and to ultimately banish my parents from the Academy and magickal community altogether.

Give us a convincing reason to turn our backs on magick forever, Anna, my mother implores. She holds me in her arms, a baby no more than a few weeks old, pink and wrinkly in my white blanket. *Her life depends on it. We have to protect her, no matter what. Promise me! Promise me you'll do whatever it takes, tonight and always…*

"Your mother believed—she *wanted* to believe—that if it looked like she and your father were breaking ties with magick, they might have a chance at cutting off the Magician's connection to her, and more importantly, a chance at hiding you. At pretending you were a natural child born of natural means, raised in a life of normalcy where the Magician couldn't reach you."

"But… but I *am* natural." I blink away the vision, meeting Trello's eyes again. "I'm a natural-born witch, daughter of Connor and Melissa Milan."

"A witch—of course. Born to Melissa Milan—yes. But Connor…" Her eyes soften, filling with a sympathy that makes my blood run cold.

"Wait. You're telling me he's not my real father?" I ask. And then—dark, cold, horrifying—another realization dawns. "Holy shit. Is my dad… Is the Magician… Is he?"

"No, of course not. Your *dad* is Connor Milan, the man who raised you. The man you've *always* called Dad."

I let out a sigh of relief, but Trello shakes her head, the pity in her eyes intensifying. "But biologically speaking…

Well, biologically speaking, I suppose the only way to describe it…"

She spreads the rest of the cards across the table, revealing every one of them, the minors and majors of the Tarot, all the suits, all the symbols and imagery that make our magick possible.

"Your biological father is Magick itself, Starla."

"That's… not possible," Doc says, startling me after remaining silent for so long. He reaches for my hand across the table, squeezing tightly.

"So much about her seems impossible," Trello tells him. Then, turning back to me, "Yet here you are. You can heal yourself. You're a Spirit-blessed emanation of the Major Arcana, further blessed by the four princesses of the Tarot. You can dreamcast, dream share, dream retrieve. You've already formed the type of bond with your familiar that most witches spend decades developing. You located the Arcana objects. Is it really so hard to believe?"

I blink away fresh tears, my brain threatening to shut down. This is crazy. This is bananas. This is so far out of the realm of comprehension, I'm starting to think I'm still stuck in the dream realm—like I never even came back from that trip with Baz and Kirin.

Hell, maybe they're not real either. Maybe none of this is real.

Maybe my entire life is no more than some other witch's dream, and if and when she decides to wake up, I'll just… stop existing. *Poof!*

"Everything the Magician wants," Trello says, "everything he's chased, across the boundaries of time and space, for millennia—*you* already have the power to command. *You* can unite the Arcana objects and reclaim magick for the witches and mages who seek to honor it. *You* have the power to unite the Light Arcana in the battle against the coming darkness. And when the rest of the world wants to give up, to lay down their arms and walk away from this fight, *you* have the power to inspire hope. To give us all a reason to keep living. To keep loving. To keep fighting, no matter what the cost."

Fire burns inside my chest, magick singing through my veins. But it's all too much to process, too much to carry.

"I don't *want* that power," I say. "I don't want any of it." I rub the pentacle tattoo on my wrist, willing my magick to fade, willing myself to wake up out of this witch's nightmare and return to my mundane life in Tres Búhos. "I would trade every *ounce* of magick inside me if it meant I could have my parents back. If it meant I'd be stuck in some dusty-ass desert town working at a tiny little tea shop for the rest of my life. If it meant I didn't have to face the Magician or this dark destiny or... or any of it."

"Search your heart," she says softly. "I think you'll find that's not exactly true."

I open my mouth to tell her I don't *need* to search my heart, but Goddess, she's right. I hate her for it, but she's absolutely right. As much as I'd give anything to have my parents back, losing them is what set me on this path. It brought magick into my life. It brought love and friendship into my life. It brought a deep sense of purpose, a fate I could no more outrun than my mother could outrun hers.

I squeeze Doc's hand and nod, letting out a deep breath of acceptance.

Magick. Fate. Destiny. Hope. All of it endlessly shifting, but always bringing me right back here, right back where I belong.

"Thank you," I finally say, a phrase I hadn't thought I was capable of offering the woman seated across from me. "Thank you for telling me about my mother. About all of this."

"It is your story, Starla. Your legacy. It was always meant for you to hear."

At this, the candles finally flicker out, the last of the spell releasing us from its hold. Trello sweeps her Tarot deck into a neat stack, save for a lone card that flutters to the floor beside me.

I crouch down to retrieve it. It's Trump eleven, the Justice card, featuring a stern-looking woman dressed in chainmail and a rich burgundy cape, holding a sword in one hand and a scale in the other. Perched at her side on a rocky bench, a brown-and-white owl looks on, a darker version of my Jareth.

The moment my fingers touch the card, I *know*.

"It's you!" I gasp, clutching the card and getting to my feet.

Trello rises from her chair and nods once, then extends her arms, whispering an ancient incantation I haven't the knowledge to translate. All around her, red and silver runes glow in the air, swirling on an invisible current. When they finally fade, she's standing before us with the sword and the scale, the cape draped elegantly over her shoulders.

It's only a moment, and then the magick fades, revealing regular Anna Trello once again.

Doc blinks up at her, his mouth open wide, his hand pressed against his heart. "But how… All this time…"

"You're the Justice Arcana," I say, a surge of anger keeping me on my feet. "*Justice*! Yet you lied to us, you kept us in the dark about your knowledge about the Magician and my destiny. You made a bargain with the Dark Hierophant, risking the lives of your own students and faculty. You… you… *Goddess*, I don't even know where to begin!"

All the goodwill she fostered tonight evaporates in the wake of this new treachery. I'm so mad I'm practically shaking with it, but Trello stands firm, her eyes holding a formidable challenge.

"Sometimes," she says, "in the name of justice, we must carry out unjust deeds. I chose to honor my promise to protect you, at whatever the cost."

"That sounds an awful lot like the ends justify the means, and it absolutely doesn't make it right, no matter *what* you have to tell yourself when you look in the mirror."

"There is no justifying the murder and persecution of innocents, Starla. There is no making it right. There is only choice." She holds her hands up in balance, imitating the scale she held just moments ago. "You choose to act through your own free will, or you choose to let the river of fate carry you where it may. In choosing to act, you don't always have the luxury of acting justly for all of the people all of the time. You simply make the best decision you can with the information available to you. Again and again and again. After that, all that's left is hope."

Hope. There it is. The dreaded h-word again. A gift as well as a burden—one I'm not sure I have the strength to carry.

I drop back into my chair, my head so heavy I can barely hold it up.

"I'm one person," I say. "One witch. It doesn't matter what you promised—I'm not worth the lives of all those students you risked. Their magick. Their essence."

"Yet in protecting you," she says, "in bringing you to this Academy, in uniting you with your fellow Arcana brothers, in opening your mind to the gifts your mother intended for you, we are protecting countless more lives. We are protecting the future of magick as we know it."

"I thought Justice was supposed to be blind," I say.

"A blind Justice is an ignorant Justice, and a liar to boot. We can no more walk into this blindly than we can tell our hearts who to love, no matter how inconvenient those truths might be." At this, she shoots Doc a pointed glare, then turns back to me. "Search your heart," she says again. "Your truth is already there, waiting to be heard and honored. And no matter what you decide, as well as what you believe, I will stand by your side through all of it. *That* is a promise."

At this, Anna Trello bids her farewell and heads out into the dark night alone.

No one moves from the living room.

And here in the kitchen, the warm air laced with the scent of candle wax and mugwort and magick, I take a deep breath, look into Doc's eyes, and make a promise of my own.

"The Winter Solstice is in two days," I say. "Time to summon my maker."

THIRTY-THREE

STEVIE

The match blazes to life before my eyes, filling the air with the scent of sulfur.

"Are you sure you want to do this?" Doc asks, the question calling me back to Trello's memory of my mother, of a similar scene unfolding on a similar night nearly a quarter-century ago.

It's the Winter Solstice. What I *want* is for us to cook up a big, ridiculous meal of roasted turkey and creamed spinach and butternut squash casserole and twelve different kinds of potatoes and mulled wine and more desserts than we can possibly shove into our mouths. What I *want* is to put on my favorite winter holiday playlist and decorate the Yule tree. What I *want* is to drink hot chocolate chai lattes in front of a crackling fire and exchange gifts with my friends and the men I love.

But tonight's not about what I want. It's about what needs to be done.

It's about meeting the Magician face-to-face and offering him the deal of a lifetime.

Upon his acceptance—then, and only then, will we have our true Yuletide celebration.

Because then, and only then, will we be free to rebuild our lives.

The match flickers, the flame burning toward my thumb. Doc's gaze grows more intense, his energy a white wall of fear and uncertainty.

He's the only one here with me tonight, sitting across from me on my bedroom floor, the moon glowing bright outside. Every few minutes, Jareth peers into the window, flapping his great wings. But Doc and Jareth and the moon are all the company I have.

I wanted *all* my brothers to be here for this, but in the days following Trello's visit, whenever I tried to tell Ani about my plans, my body went haywire. First, it was a coughing fit. Then a sore throat and hoarseness. After that, an attack of sneezing and yawning.

It was a message, loud and clear. I hate that it's come to this, but Ani can't be trusted. Not anymore.

So, while my gingersnap sleeps obliviously in his guest room downstairs and Baz and Kirin keep watch outside his door, Doc and I are tucked away in here, trying to save what's left of the world, one dark spell at a time.

Between us on the floor, a flat wooden tabletop serves as a makeshift altar, laden with all the offerings of the season —everything I could scavenge from the property and the house itself. In addition to the sugar cookies, wine, and black and gold candles emulating my mother's setup, there's a vulture's skull, a snakeskin, two black feathers, and—in place of the holly I couldn't find—dried evergreen needles and juniper berries.

I've also set up the bowl with my blood, the moonstone and red jasper, the herbs, and the Magician card.

Beneath it rests the Journey Through the Void of Mist and Spirit, a book we believe my mother retrieved from the dream realm. It's the only thing we have that connects both worlds—something that can get me a little closer, and help me find my way back.

There's only one thing left to do.

"I love you, Cassius Devane," I whisper. "And yes, I'm sure I want to do this."

Gazing down at my reflection in the bowl of blood, I speak the incantation.

Dreams of darkness, dreams of light
Hear me on this longest night
With trust and magick at the helm
Grant me passage through the realms

Blood of the World, blood of the Star
I call on the One, both near and afar
Connected by magick, connected by fate
Accept what I offer and unlock the gate

Then, just before the flame fizzles out, I drop the match into the bowl, setting my tiny world on fire.

THIRTY-FOUR

STEVIE

"You came alone? That is both surprising and unwise." The Dark Magician steps out from behind the stone altar inside the Fool's Grave, his black-feathered cape rustling, crazy eyes glowing blue in the darkness.

Everything about him screams *unhinged*, but I'm not afraid of him here. I'm not even here at all—not really. The spell Doc and I created allows me to project my consciousness into the Magician's awareness inside the dream realm without risking death or entrapment.

As long as I don't lose the moon-blessed athame I'm carrying, I'll be able to call myself back to my body—back to Doc—whenever I'm ready.

Meeting the Magician's creepy blue gaze, I lean against the wall of the cave and sigh. "Is this the part where you say, 'I brought you into this world—I can just as easily take you out?'"

"I do not wish to take you out of this world or any other, Starla. I am not in the habit of destroying my creations."

"Especially when you need something from them." I pull the athame from my pocket and slice my palm, letting the blood well up just enough to catch his attention before closing my fingers around the wound, willing it to heal again.

His face pales a bit, the only sign that my actions are affecting him.

"It doesn't have to be a fight," he says, eyes fixated on my blood-stained fist. He takes a few steps closer, holding out a hand, as if I might actually take it. "Not between us. You could join us, stand with us in power rather than cower in defeat."

"Hard pass, Vader. I'm the Star, remember? *Sooo* not Dark-Side material."

"Then why have you come? I'm neither hopeful nor foolish enough to believe you're here to fulfill your mother's broken oath."

"You mean to sacrifice myself on the altar of your noble cause? No, not exactly."

"I didn't think so. You're too much like her. Stubborn. Obstinate." A raspy chuckle escapes his lips. "I do miss her, though. The new World… He just doesn't have the same passion. Sometimes I regret what I did to your parents." He strokes his dingy white beard, feigning contemplation. "This is one of those times. But don't worry—the feeling always passes."

I grip the athame tightly, anger simmering in my blood.

"I wouldn't have resorted to such drastic measures in the canyons," he says innocently. "Certainly not in front of their teenaged daughter. But your mother kept trying to outwit me at every turn, cutting me off from her magick, hiding away in a mundane, humdrum life. If only she'd been a witch of her word."

He's fucking with me. He *has* to be fucking with me. There's no way he murdered my parents. That was a dark mage. That was...

Fuck. That was a dark mage.

Of *course* it was him. If not in body, in spirit.

"I see you're having some trouble accepting the reality of your situation," he says, faux sympathy dripping from his tone. "Let it be a lesson about the consequences of breaking a sacred blood oath. An oath that still requires fulfillment, I'll remind you. Her irresponsibility does not absolve you of that."

I take a step toward him, still gripping the athame. "You're stuck here in the dream realm, old man. Your power is limited. You're basically impotent."

He lets out another soft chuckle, his eyes still sparkling. "Well, that's not *entirely* true, is it?"

With a quickness I don't see coming, he grabs my arm, his thumb brushing the pentacle and serial number tattooed on my wrist.

"You're dangerous, witch-girl," he hisses, his voice dark and ancient, the words yanking me back in time to a storm on El Búho Grande, to the day when my friend Luke was possessed by a dark mage and tried to kill me.

Luke died that day. I was framed for his murder.

"It was you," I gasp, the pieces falling into place. Luke hadn't climbed the Grande that day—he simply *appeared* there, plucked out of his old life and dropped into the cave beneath the owl's wing deep inside the rock face. He attacked me with magick, and in the end, his body was tortured and destroyed by mages, made to look as if I'd murdered him myself.

It was a cruel, violent act. One that landed me in prison, and ultimately, at the Academy.

"I needed a way to reach you," the Magician continues. "The time had come to fulfill the oath."

"You possessed and killed my friend. You sent me to prison."

"Technically speaking, *I* didn't possess him, but that's neither here nor there."

"You killed him!" I scream, my voice reverberating off the cave walls. But this crazy motherfucker is unfazed, offering no more than a shrug beneath his ratty feathered cape.

"At the time, it seemed the most prudent method. Granted, obtaining your cooperation has proven a bit more difficult than I anticipated, but I'm confident we'll get there. You see, Starla..."

He's rambling now, going on about the nature of magick and manifestation and my all-important role in his big plans to fuck the entire planet in the ass without lube, but my mind is still stuck on the part about Luke. About *all* the witches and mages who've been accused of crimes they didn't commit—magickal crimes perpetuated by dark mages loyal to the madman who brought me into this world.

"People were poisoned," I say, cutting him off. "Innocent witches and mages. They were burned alive, tortured, raped... Their own family members were convicted of the crimes."

He grins and presses a hand to his heart, clearly pleased with himself. "Quite impressive when you list it out like that."

"You were behind all of it," I say, disgust turning my words into ash.

"I can't take all the credit. I had lots of people willing to help. Not right away, of course. But eventually."

"Those *aren't* people. They're dark mages, and they don't deserve to breathe the same air as the rest of us."

"I see." He steps closer, crowding into my space, his sour breath making my eyes water. "Those dark mages? The ones you say don't deserve to breathe? They were willing to *die* for the cause they believed in. Can you say the same of your Arcana brothers? Of yourself? All the people and things and causes you claim to value... How far are you willing to go to stand up for them, Starla Milan, Blood of the World, newborn witch who barely understands so much as one *iota* of the power coursing through her veins? How far?"

I take a step back, sucking in a breath of cool air, clearing my head. I didn't conjure myself here to listen to his propaganda. I came with an offer, and it's time to put the metaphorical cards on the table.

"I'll tell you exactly how far I'm willing to go." I slice my palm again, dripping blood on his precious altar. "Those all-powerful Arcana objects you probably jerk off to every night? I've got three of them. And despite the fact that having them in your possession will make you infinitely more powerful than you already are, I'm willing to hand them over."

His eyes narrow curiously, his energy pulsing with greed and desire. "Freely?"

"For a price, of course." Holding my bloody fist over the altar, I make my case. "I'll give you the objects, and in return, you'll allow earth-bound witches and mages to live out our lives in peace, without any interference or manipulation from you and your kind. Do whatever you want in your own realms, round up all the Dark Arcana assholes you can find, guzzle a case of Vodka and burn your homes to the ground for all I care. But whatever you do, leave us the *fuck* alone."

"Do you even realize what you're asking?"

"Only that you take your toys and go fuck off in your own damn sandbox."

"You're talking about my legacy, Starla. My father *died* for that magick."

His father—the First Fool. A man who abandoned his family and sacrificed himself so that the elemental beings would grant magick to humans. It's him we have to thank for the magick that runs through our blood today.

And, in many ways, it's him we have to thank for the epic shitshow befalling our world, with witches and mages turning dark and the mundane authorities looking for any reason to lock us up or shoot us on sight.

"All the more reason for you to take the deal," I say firmly.

He glares at me, the black feathers trembling. Then, out of nowhere, he throws his head back and laughs until tears stream down his wrinkled face.

"Did I say something funny?"

When he finally regains his composure, he looks at me with his usual crazy eyes and says flatly, "No. Absolutely not."

"No, I'm not funny, or—"

"No *deal*. You're wasting my time, and I can't say I appreciate it."

My heart drops into my stomach. That was my only bargaining chip. I figured he'd accept the deal, and the guys and I could work out how to break it later, hopefully murdering him in the process.

But that half-baked plan only works if he goes along with the first part.

"You don't want the objects supposedly made from your father's own flesh, blood, and bones?" I press.

"Of course I want them, but your terms are far too limiting." He paces the small cave, his voice growing more fanatical with each step. "I need an army, Starla. A *magickal* army. There are not enough beings in my realm for that."

"So you're just going to keep stealing them from mine?"

"Well, they're not exactly volunteering, are they? That's the problem with your kind. Most of you are weakened by a deeply flawed desire to be quote-unquote *decent* human beings."

"Until you force them to go dark."

"Oh, no. Even when captured and tortured, most witches and mages stick to their principals until the very end. It's quite touching to see if you're one to be touched by such sentiments, which I am not. Besides, even if they *did* fight for me willingly, how could I ever really trust their loyalties? No, Starla. My methods are significantly more foolproof than that. In my operation, the only *good* witches and mages are the *soulless* witches and mages."

A vision flickers to life in my mind, similar to the one I saw the day I was bitten by a rattlesnake, filled with zombi-fied witches and mages with glowing yellow eyes, just like Luke's eyes when he was possessed by darkness.

Not possessed, I realize now. *Soulless*.

I gasp, unable to hide my disgust. But as much as I want to tell him to shove his magick methods up his ass and bounce myself the fuck out of this nightmare, I can't. Not yet. The Magician is so enamored by his own dick-swinging, he's actually giving me a glimpse at some solid intel. Intel we might be able to use to upend his entire operation.

Forcing a quiver of fear into my voice, I look at him with wide eyes and say, "So you're taking their souls and replacing them with… what?"

"Magick, of course." He beams at me, chomping on the

bait like a starving shark. "Oh, it's beautiful, Starla. Here, let me show you."

Without warning, he grabs my wrist again and presses his thumb into my tattoo, flooding my mind with a new vision. Witches and mages—hundreds and thousands of them—packed into jail cells and cages, begging for their lives. Then, those same witches and mages, shot dead in shallow mass graves, their souls imprisoned in the spiral-marked cave beyond the holly thicket, their broken bodies left for the coyotes, their bones left to rot.

Only in this vision they *don't* rot.

They rise. Pale gray skin reforms over the gnarly bones, knitting them back together. Blood drips from sharp teeth, eyes glowing yellow as they scamper over the lands of Arcana Academy, devouring everyone in their path, leaving a trail of blood and bones behind.

That's what I saw in my snake-bite vision. The nightmare that's haunted me ever since.

The nightmare that's clearly headed our way, sooner rather than later.

So many magickal practitioners have been rounded up. So many executed.

For this. Always for this.

The Magician's words echo, chilling me to the very core.

I need an army, Starla. A magickal *army. There are not enough beings in my realm for that...*

"Oh, but you haven't even seen the best part!" He digs harder into my flesh, making stars dance before my eyes. "It's one thing to perform this kind of magick on regular witches and mages. But driving the light out of the Light Arcana themselves? Now *that* is a feat. No execution required! Very convenient."

"You won't lay a hand on any one of us," I grind out, my eyes watering at the pain shooting up my arm.

He lets out a heavy sigh, *tsk-tsking* at me like I'm a stupid child.

And in an instant, it all makes sense.

My stomach bottoms out. My blood turns to ice. And as my knees buckle and I hit the ground hard, I let out a cry like a wounded dove, the Dark Magician's most terrible vision sliding unbidden into my mind.

Standing on a wooden dock, glancing across a cheerful, pastel-colored town perched on the edge of the sea, an Arcana mage with coppery red hair and eyes the color of melted caramels lifts a fiery wand to the sky.

"Ani, no!" I cry out. "Fight him! Fucking fight him!"

"Ani can't come to the phone right now," the Magician says, his mouth hot and wet at my ear.

The vision begins to fade, but not before I see its final moments.

Ani grins, his whole body glowing with power.

He points the Wand of Flame and Fury toward the city.

"Burn," he whispers.

And the world is consumed by witchfire.

I bolt to my feet, backing up against the wall and pressing the tip of my athame to my chest, blinking away the last of the terrible vision.

"You're welcome to return when you have a better

offer," the Magician says with a final mad grin. "I'll be waiting for you with bated breath."

"Wait for your death," I choke out. "That's the only offer you're getting from me."

Without another word, I shove the athame into my heart.

The spell instantly shatters, sucking my consciousness back into my body.

I pull in a deep breath and open my eyes, ignoring the vertigo as Doc comes back into view.

"Stevie!" He reaches for me, blowing out a sigh of relief. "Are you—"

"It's Ani," I say, struggling to get to my feet. "We need to tell Broome to sedate him. Now."

"What did you see? What's happening?"

"He's got the Wand, and he's turned dark." I close my eyes, holding on to Doc's arm as the room slowly stops spinning. "There's only one way to get him back, Doc. We need to get inside his head. And we need to *break* him."

THIRTY-FIVE

CASS

Nightmare's Lullaby roils in the bottle, black and horrifying, as hungry as a demon.

It has one job, and unlike the rest of us, this potion never fails.

Stevie, Kirin, Baz, and I stand at Ani's bedside, looking down at the mage we're so close to losing. In repose, he seems to be at peace, but that's just the effect of Professor Broome's clever sedative.

The rest is up to me.

But despite what I promised the woman I love, despite the fact that some part of me knows she's right about this, I just don't have the balls to go through with it.

"I can't do this, Stevie. Not even for you." I set the potion on the nightstand and close my eyes, unable to meet her gaze.

"It's not for me," she says gently, her hands warm on my arm. "It's for Ani."

SARAH PIPER

"You're asking me to invade his mind. To change it. To trap him in a nightmare so vivid, so real, so damaging, he's got no choice but to break his current binds and flee."

"I'm asking you to bring him back to us and save him from torture, whatever it takes. If we had another option..."

I finally open my eyes again, looking deep into hers, losing myself for a moment in their beauty. Their realness. Their depths.

Goddess, how did it come to this?

"Nine times out of ten, you're talking about a complete violation," I say, parroting back her words from our first class together. "Isn't that what you said about mental magicks?"

"Yes, and I stand by it. But Doc? This is the one time. The *one* time out of ten." She grips me tighter, her eyes imploring. "I don't know how much clearer I can be. The Dark Magician is stealing the souls of executed witches and mages, turning their bodies into a soulless army with all the power and none of the conscience. He's doing the same thing to the Light Arcana—that's his plan. That's how he turns them dark. So unless you want to condemn Ani to that fate and lose him forever, we need to hack into his mind, scramble everything up, and break him out of Judgment's hold."

"If what you're saying is true," Kirin says, "we don't even know if that'll work. Ani's soul—the very thing that makes him Ani—is gone. Even if we could break Judgment's influence and turn Ani back to our side, what then?"

"That is tomorrow's problem," she says confidently.

Then, turning back to me, "I know how you feel about this. What happened to Elizabeth—"

"My father," I blurt out suddenly, the mention of Elizabeth's name forcing the confession from my lips. "*He* was the dark mage who manipulated her. And he did it simply to prove that he was better than me. Better at mental magicks. Better at cruelty. Better at the sheer terror that would keep me enslaved to him for my entire life, whether or not I ever set foot in his house again. But I *did* set foot in his house. I had to, one more time." I pick up the bottle, giving it another gentle swirl. The black mist climbs up the inside, desperate to escape. "One more time, to deliver my final message. My final proof that *no*, he wasn't better at cruelty. Not by a long shot. And I gave Janelle the same punishment."

She blinks up at me, thoughts flitting behind her eyes at a mile-a-minute. That's only part of the story, though. Part of my long and complicated history with this particular potion, with this particular trick.

There's no need to reveal the rest.

Why did you do it?

Sorry, I know. You're always sorry…

"We can try to prove how much we love him," I say, still trying to sway her onto some other path, any one but this one. "But he—"

"We don't need to manipulate him with love, Doc." She moves her hand to my chest, her eyes hardening right along with her resolve. "We need to do it with fear. We need to make him believe in something so awe-inspiring, so terrifying, it overrides his circuits and gives him a complete reboot."

I glance down at the bottle in my hand, the black smoke calling to some dark, secret part of my soul.

Shame burns a hot path across my chest.

"You want me to judge you for what you did to your father and Janelle," she says, reading my energy, damn near reading my thoughts. "To punish you for something that any one of us might have done in the same position."

"Might have, might not have. But I *did* do it, Stevie. More than once."

Kirin and Baz remain silent.

"We call ourselves Light Arcana," she says. "And our enemies are the Dark. It's an easy way to draw clear lines in the sand, right? But the truth is, there are more shades of gray between us than we can count, and most days, we're all just fighting for what we believe is right, deep in our hearts. For the people we love. For the people we most want to protect. So no, I won't condemn you for this, Doc. Not for your father. Not for Janelle. And not, when the night is over, for Ani. Because he's *ours* to love and protect." She presses a hand to her heart, her voice breaking. "*Ours*. The family he chose. The family that chose him. The family that wants and loves him. The family that needs his light in our lives—not because of some stupid prophecy or magickal war, not because we share DNA, but simply because he belongs to us, now and always."

Tears spill down her cheeks, but Stevie's smiling, her love for Ani bolstering her, giving her hope.

I wish I could feel it too, but when I look down at Ani now, all I see is the Dark Sun, the mage who incinerated an entire town—*his* hometown—murdering thousands of innocent people.

Ani—*our* Ani, the one we chose, the one we love—he'll never recover from that.

And the worst part is, I saw it coming. That night beneath the Towers of Breath and Blade, when he conjured the witchfire against Janelle and Casey, I knew he'd mined the darkest parts of himself, unearthing wounds so deep, so long-buried, there was no way he was coming out of that unscathed.

I wanted to bring him back from it anyway. To hope that I was wrong, that he'd survive it. That he'd survive the dream potion, the realm, all of it.

But he didn't survive. A part of him died. A part of him *keeps* dying, over and over. And now, all that's left is Stevie's hope combined with the most desperate, deplorable measure I know. Worse than death. Worse than punishment. A mental torture for which there is no cure.

A torture from which—for all but the strongest who endure it—there will *never* be a full return.

Warmed by my hands, Nightmare's Lullaby churns inside the glass.

Everything inside me is screaming in protest, my very blood burning with agony, my hands trembling.

But Stevie's right. When it comes to protecting the ones we love, the lines will *always* blur, no matter how firmly we think we stand on one side or the other.

Love is the first principle. The truest. As such, it trumps all others.

Ani is my family. My Arcana brother. And I have to fight for him, even if it means risking his sanity and his life in the process.

Closing my eyes, I call upon the energy of the reversed Moon, and speak the words into the darkness.

> *Black rider, void of light*
> *I call upon the Mare of Night*
> *Unleash the darkness in his mind*
> *For evil sown is reaped in kind*

I unstopper the bottle, urging the black smoke from the glass, holding it before his lips. It slides between them effortlessly, emptying the bottle until the glass is clear once again.

In my mind's eye, I see the black smoke defiling Ani's mouth, his lungs, his blood, his very consciousness. My stomach churns, my mouth filling with the taste of salt and shame, but I press on, calling on even more magick, pushing the darkness deep inside him.

Then, kneeling at his side, I take his hands and close my eyes, bending all of my will toward altering his consciousness, planting seeds of terror that bloom into monsters, into demons, into every last human fear come to life. I feed him mental images of the devastation in his hometown, the smell of burning flesh, the conjured screams of a thousand children melting beneath his witchfire.

I feed him death, and he drinks it, slow and deep.

When I've exhausted the last of my dark imagination, when I've pushed him to the very edge of what the mind can take, I finally open my eyes. Ani's body seizes, then contorts, arching off the bed at such impossible angles it looks like the movie version of an exorcism. His eyes fly open, black as the night sky, endless, hopeless.

"What's happening?" Baz asks. "Is it working?"

"The poison has taken hold," I say. "His mind is trying to reconcile his known reality with the imagery I've just implanted. It's fracturing him, body and soul."

"It's the only way," Stevie whispers, but at this point, I'm not sure which one of us she's trying to convince.

Silently, we watch him writhe. We watch him suffer.

And then the screaming begins.

Choked whispers at first, quickly escalating into moans of pain, then screams of abject terror dredged up from the very basement of a man's worst nightmares.

Still, the Arcana brothers and I stand at his side, tears hot on my cheeks, praying for the sunrise.

"I'm sorry," I whisper. "I'm so, so sorry."

"You will be," comes the haunted reply.

Then, in a blur so fast my mind can't even process what's happening, Ani launches himself out of the bed, taking me down hard. In a nanosecond he's got me pinned to the floor, impossibly strong, his black eyes wild.

The others jump in, trying to pull him away, but Ani's too powerful. One swipe of his hand, and a searing-hot magickal force throws them across the room.

"That was a *terrible* idea, Cass." He grabs my head and slams it into the floor, his knees crushing my chest. "No wonder your brother offed himself. Goddess, my head fucking hurts. How's yours?"

He bashes my skull into the hardwood again, my vision blurring, my ears ringing. Dimly, I'm aware of Stevie crawling toward me, but Ani's one step ahead of us, shoving her back with another magickal blast.

Outside the window, Stevie's owl batters the glass with his wings, screeching and howling, clawing at the glass, just as the other professors are doing outside the bedroom door. Someone rams a shoulder into the wood, but it makes no difference.

Ani's got us all trapped inside some kind of impenetrable ward.

"They're a little busy right now," he calls back toward the door, his voice a sing-song falsetto. Then, turning back to me, he folds his arms across his chest and says, "You know, on second thought, I'm *not* going to bash your skull in just yet. Judgment and the Magician have plans for you, and if I kill you before they have the chance to carry out their dastardly deeds... Well, let's just say that pissing off *those* two cranky old bastards is an even worse idea than pissing *me* off. But you know what I *would* like to do..." He taps his lips, his smile cruel and broken. "Since we're all gathered here together, I'd like for you to share a little story with the class."

Through the swirl of pain and confusion in my mind, his words cut deep, sending a bolt of fear down my spine.

"What story, you ask?" He claps, bouncing up and down on my chest like a child. "I know, I know! How about the one where your poor little brother died. Surely we'd all love to hear that one."

"Stop," I whisper. "Please. I... I wasn't much more than a child myself..."

"Oh, is that what we're telling ourselves now? You were man enough to know how to make that potion, right?"

I close my eyes, blood pooling on the floor behind my ear, hot and sticky.

"Tell them," he commands, wrapping a hand around my throat, forcing me to meet his gaze again. He raises his other hand, and suddenly I see it—the object of his sick fascination. The source of his darkest power.

The Wand of Flame and Fury.

"Oh, this old thing?" He bats his lashes, forcing a coy grin. "Just a little something I picked up on my travels. Great fuel efficiency. Really burns it up." Still clutching my throat, he points the staff at Stevie, the tip glowing red. "Now. I'll only ask you one more time. Kindly tell the *woman* you profess to love what you did to the *brother* you professed to love. Confess your sins. Let her see what a monster you really are. Let *her* be the judge of your worthiness."

"Ani, stop," Stevie begs, reaching for us both. "This isn't you."

"This isn't who you *want* me to be, but that doesn't mean I'm not the real deal, baby."

From the other side of the room, Baz and Kirin let out low, barely-conscious moans.

"Stop," Kirin breathes. "Cass, fight…"

Ani rolls his eyes. "Honestly. The four of you are *literally* the most pathetic excuse for a rescue squad this side of the realm."

"Ani…" I reach for his face, my head spinning at the movement.

He swats me away like a fly and digs his knees harder into my chest, his eyes blazing with fresh rage.

"Tell her!" he screams, pointing the Wand at Stevie. "Or she will know the pain of Judgment, and her cries will follow you into the afterlife!"

I strain to look at her, finally catching her eyes, holding her gaze, whispering the last words I might ever get to say before I die.

"I love you, my beautiful Star. Always." And then, taking a deep breath that rips fresh pain into my chest, I make my confession, torn from my very soul by the man I once considered more of a brother than the one who actually shared my blood.

"Xavier…" I choke out. "My brother. Twenty years ago, he committed suicide. I found him in the garage after he'd shot off half his face. He was still alive. Barely, but still alive." Tears leak from my eyes, blurring everything before me into a smudge of blood and fire and darkness.

"*And?*" Ani says, his voice high and mocking.

"And I held him in my arms. His blood was everywhere… He was gasping for air. I held him and I cried and told him how sorry I was... I felt his very life force leave this earth, and I knew it was over. He was dead by his own hand."

"Tell her the rest," Ani pushes, bouncing again. "Saving the best part for last... Love it!"

"Please," I whisper, one final attempt. "Let them go, Ansel. Let them go."

"No way! We're just getting to the good part." He smacks my cheek. "Why? Why did poor little Xavier shoot his own brains out?"

I beg him with my eyes, with my heart, with my very soul. But there isn't a single shred of Ani left inside. He's no more than a red-headed shell, a monster masquerading as a man.

And I've fallen victim to the very nightmares I tried to set loose upon him.

"Because of me," I finally say, too tired to carry this burden for another twenty years. "My brother killed himself because I used my mental magick to drive him insane."

THIRTY-SIX

STEVIE

My heart shatters for him, the pain in his eyes so vast and endless, I fear I might lose him forever.

I push myself up on my hands and knees again, dragging myself to his side, determined to touch him no matter how hard Ani tries to retaliate.

This time, however, he actually lets me pass, standing up from Doc's chest and giving me a clear path. There's no kindness or compassion in the gesture, though. His smug, twisted grin is all the proof I need; the Ani I know and love is no longer with us. Not here. Not now.

I take Doc's face between my hands, careful not to move his head, ignoring the monster looming over us like a shadow.

"I'm… sorry…" Doc pants, his breath crackling and wet.

Tamping down my fear, I smile, focusing on the stormy gray of his eyes.

"I love you, Cassius Devane," I whisper. "Do you

understand? I claimed you, remember? I love you, and I'm not letting you go."

Doc offers a weak smile in return, blood oozing out from between his lips, pooling with the dark wetness rapidly spreading beneath his head. "You… you gave me everything, my Star. And for a little while, I let myself be happy."

"Shh, don't talk." I press a powder-soft kiss to his cheek, sending him every last ounce of healing energy I've got left, willing his body to weave itself back together.

"I never deserved you," he whispers, reaching for my face. His bloody hand tangles in my hair, and a little more light dims from his eyes.

"Stay with me." My smile falls, my pulse thudding in my ears. "Please stay."

"Your light is too bright," he says, his own smile fading in response. "Too… too pure."

"No. No, no, no. Doc! Cassius!"

He doesn't respond. His eyes turn glassy, his chest going still.

Goddess, no…

"Oh, for fuck's sake." Ani shoves me out of the way, then touches his Wand to Doc's chest. His shirt burns away, and on the tender flesh of his chest, the mark of Judgment flares bright.

XX.

"Hate to cause mass chaos and run," Ani says, "but Dr. Devane and I are a little late for our next appointment. Catch you at the next family dinner, kids! Try not to die before then."

"Ani, wait!" I cry. "We can—"

My words fade away as Ani swings the Wand in a wide arc. A blinding white flash explodes in the room, sending me sprawling on my back.

It's a long time before I can move again—so long I start to wonder if I'm paralyzed. If I'm dead. If Ani spelled me into some sort of eternal consciousness, trapped inside a broken body cursed to rot while I watch from inside, unable to move, unable to scream.

But then my hands and feet begin to tingle, the blood slowly working its way through my system again. When the spots of light finally fade from my vision and the heat of the explosion recedes, when the dust settles, when the house turns so silent I fear we've all fallen into the abyss, I finally manage to sit up and take stock.

Baz and Kirin are slumped against the wall on the other side of the room, slowly coming back to consciousness.

The other witches are still locked outside the bedroom door, still trying to force their way in, just like Jareth at the window.

But Doc and Ani are gone, no trace of either of them but the gleaming black pool of blood seeping across the hardwood.

Fear threatens to send me over the edge, but I take a deep breath, willing myself to stay calm, remembering one of Doc's first mental magicks lessons:

Fear itself isn't real. Danger may be real, but fear is just an emotional response to that perceived danger...

But fear is still one of our most primal emotions. It can blind us.

And—if we can quiet our thoughts long enough to allow for grace, for hope—that same fear can unite us.

Doc always said conquering fear begins with presence and awareness. But love is part of that too, more powerful than any other emotion, than any other weapon the Dark Arcana can wield.

Doc's voice isn't the only one in my head now, giving me hope and grace. I hear Kirin too, keeping me focused, helping me put together the puzzle pieces that might just save our lives.

The curse isn't that the light and the dark exist within us— that's just our nature. The curse is that we will always be drawn to both, and anything can happen—at any point—to flip the switch... Here's the most terrifying part... It's not that the Dark Magician wants the objects so he can control magick, or that Dark Judgment may be trying to raise the dead. It's that they represent what each of us has the potential to become. The very things that made them go dark exist in all Arcana witches and mages...

Lala's in my memory now, her kindness and wisdom a beacon in the darkness.

True love is a formidable force on its own. When it sees itself reflected in the heart of another, it will lay bare and burn down anything that stands in the way of that union. The process can be terrifying and painful, but it's wholly necessary. Only love has the power to dismantle our fears and set free the pure, limitless heart within.

The Magician... Even he has something to say.

They were willing to die for the cause they believed in. Can you say the same of your Arcana brothers? Of yourself? All the people and things and causes you claim to value... How far are you willing to go to stand up for them, Starla Milan...

The voices eddy and swirl, filling me with hope and knowledge, with courage and strength. But of all the voices in my head, it's the Magician's that inspires me now, igniting a fire in my chest that burns hotter than any witchfire.

I pull myself to my feet, my magick already working its healing energy, my rage pulling double duty.

"Kirin," I call out, my voice strong and clear. "Baz."

Across the room, my mages help each other to their feet, bruised and bloodied, but alive. Standing. Strong.

"They're alive, and I know where they are," I say, before they can even ask, recalling the visions the Dark Magician showed me at the Fool's Grave, the secrets he spilled in his eagerness to shine. I remember one of Mom's prophecies too, one Kirin and I were working on the day the news broke from California, all the pieces slowly clicking into place.

> *Cities kneel before the flames*
> *Thus begins the deadly game*
> *When hope is lost the Star shall fall*
> *As Death arrives to conquer all*
>
> *From the ashes, called to rise*
> *With blackened hearts and golden eyes*

Souls imprisoned in a tomb
Soldiers marching for our doom

"We can save them," I say. "Both of them. I know where we have to go."

Lala's voice returns to me, reciting another prophecy.

Thus her ache shall find no ease, so shall the daughter of The World surrender to the emptiness, to the void within and without. By her own hand, of her own volition, The Star shall fall. Henceforth she shall take her eternal breath in utter darkness.

"What are you talking about?" Baz finally makes it across the room, gathering me into his arms. Kirin comes to stand beside us, encircling us both in a powerful embrace.

Love. Strength. Fear. Hope. Courage. Passion. Rage. All of it is ours, to accept and to wield. To learn from. To nurture.

"Where do we have to go?" Kirin asks.

Out in the hallway, Carly and Professor Broome are still attacking the door, hitting it with every spell in their arsenal. The wood is just beginning to splinter, hope shining through the cracks.

I think back again to what the Dark Magician revealed. The witches and mages he corrupted… They're dead, their bodies reanimated by his dark magick, their souls imprisoned for all eternity, nowhere to call home.

But the Light Arcana? No execution required. That's what he said.

No execution required.

Which means that Ani—the *real* Ani—is still alive, physically whole and unbroken, but his soul is trapped with the others, imprisoned in the spiral-marked cave beyond the holly thicket.

I've seen that cave in my nightmares, the dream-realm replica of a place that surely exists in our world, hidden in the mists.

It's the place where Judgment calls the Unworthy to atone.

A place we were never meant to wander.

Again, Kirin's voice echoes through my memories.

It's said that there are places in this world so deep, so dark, so compelling, when you peer down into them, they literally beckon you to jump...

A sheer cliff that descends hundreds of feet—maybe thousands —into abject nothingness. Before they finally warded and fenced it off in the 1930s, dozens of students and teachers committed suicide there—people that were otherwise completely content...

I take a deep breath, and gaze deeply into the eyes of two of the men I love, knowing that in order to save the other two, in order to reunite Ani with his soul and drive out the darkness, in order to bring them back from the precipice of death and finish this fight, in order to honor our vows to save magick and protect all who wield it...

We have to go to the one place pretty much guaranteed to kill us all.

"We're going to the Void," I tell them. "And we're going to fight."

* * *

This story continues in the final book, Spells of Mist and Spirit!

Everything is on the line as Stevie and her mages take on their darkest enemies and face their greatest fears in the epic conclusion of the Tarot Academy series! Find out what happens in **Spells of Mist and Spirit!**

* * *

Are you a member of our private Facebook group, <u>Sarah Piper's Sassy Witches?</u> Pop in for sneak peeks, cover reveals, exclusive giveaways, book chats, and plenty of complete randomness! We've got a great community of readers and fans (and fellow Tarot lovers too!), and we'd love to see you there!

XOXO
Sarah

Paranormal romance fans, do you know I've got another sexy series ready to heat up your bookshelf? The Witch's Rebels is a complete supernatural reverse harem series featuring five smoldering-hot guys and the kickass witch they'd kill to protect. Read on for a taste of book one, Shadow Kissed!

SHADOW KISSED EXCERPT

Survival instinct was a powerful thing.

What horrors could we endure, could we accept, could we embrace in the name of staying alive?

Hunger. Brutality. Desperation.

Being alone.

I'd been alone for so long I'd almost forgotten what it was like to love, to trust, to look into the eyes of another person and feel a spark of something other than fear.

Then *they* came into my life.

Each one as damaged and flawed as I was, yet somehow finding a way through the cracks in my walls, slowly breaking down the bricks I'd so carefully built around my heart.

Despite their differences, they'd come together as my protectors and friends for reasons I still didn't fully understand. And after everything we'd been through, I had no doubts about who they were to me now. To each other.

Family.

I didn't know what the future held; I'd given up trying to predict it years ago. But I didn't need my Tarot cards or my mother's old crystal ball to know this:

For me, there was no future without them. Without my rebels.

"Gray?" His whisper floated to my ears.

After several heartbeats, I took a deep breath and opened my eyes.

I heard nothing, saw nothing, felt nothing but the demon imprisoned before me, pale and shattered, fading from this realm.

"Whatever you're thinking," he said, his head lolling forward, "don't."

Looking at him chained to the chair, bruises covering his face, blood pouring from the gashes in his chest, I strengthened my resolve.

His voice was faint, his body broken, his essence dimming. But the fire in his eyes blazed as bright as it had the day we'd met.

"Whatever horrible things you've heard about me, Cupcake, they're all true..."

"Please," he whispered, almost begging now. "I'm not worth..."

His words trailed off into a cough, blood spraying his lips.

I shook my head. He was wrong. He was *more* than worth it. Between the two of us, maybe only one would make it out of this room alive. If that were true, it had to be him; I couldn't live in a world where he didn't exist. Where any of them didn't exist.

This was my fate. My purpose. My gift.

There was no going back.

I held up my hands, indigo flames licking across my palms, surging bright in the darkness.

The demon shuddered as I reached for him, and I closed my eyes, sealing away the memory of his ocean-blue gaze, knowing it could very well be the last time I saw it.

* * *

2 Weeks Earlier…

Don't act like prey, and you won't become it. Don't act like prey…

Whispering my usual mantra, I locked up the van and pushed my rusty hand truck down St. Vincent Avenue, scanning the shadows for trouble.

It'd rained earlier, and mist still clung to the streets, rising into the dark autumn night like smoke. It made everything that much harder to see.

Fortunately it was my last delivery of the night, and I'd brought along my favorite traveling companions—a sharp stake in my waistband and a big-ass hunting knife in my boot. Still, danger had a way of sneaking up on a girl in Blackmoon Bay's warehouse district, which was why most people avoided it.

If I hadn't needed the money—and a boss who paid in cash and didn't ask questions about my past—I would've avoided it, too.

Alas…

Snuggling deeper into my leather jacket, I banked left at

the next alley and rolled to a stop in front of the unmarked service entrance to Black Ruby. My hand truck wobbled under the weight of its cargo—five refrigerated cases of O-positive and three AB-negative, fresh from a medical supplier in Vancouver.

Yeah, Waldrich's Imports dealt in some weird shit, but human cops didn't bother with the warehouse district, and the Fae Council that governed supernaturals didn't get involved with the Bay's black market. The only time they cared was when a supernatural killed a human, and some-times—depending on the human—not even then.

Thumbing through my packing slips, I hoped the vampires weren't too thirsty tonight. Half their order had gotten snagged by customs across the bay in Seattle.

I also hoped someone other than Darius Beaumont would sign for this. I could hold my own with most vamps, but Black Ruby's owner definitely struck me as the shoot-the-messenger type.

No matter how sexy he is...

Wrapping one hand discretely around my stake, I reached up to hit the buzzer, but a faint cry from the far end of the alley stopped me.

"Don't! Please!"

"Settle down, sweetheart," a man said, the menace in his voice a sick contrast to the terrified tremble in hers.

My heart rate spiked.

Abandoning my delivery, I scooted along the building's brick exterior, edging closer to the struggle. I spotted the girl first—she couldn't have been more than fifteen, sixteen at most, with lanky brown hair and the pale, haunted features of a blood slave.

But it wasn't a vampire that'd lured her out for a snack.

The greasy dude who'd cornered her was a hundred percent human—just another pervert in dirty jeans and a sweat-stained henley who clearly thought runaway kids were an easy mark.

"It'll all be over soon," he told her.

Yeah, sooner than you think…

Anger coiled in my belly, fizzing the edges of my vision. I couldn't decide who deserved more of my ire—the asshole threatening her now, or the parents who'd abandoned her in the first place.

Far as I was concerned, they were the same breed of evil.

"Well now. Must be my lucky night." The man barked out a wheezing laugh, and too late, I realized I'd been spotted. "Two for the price of one. Come on over here, Blondie. Don't be shy."

Shit. I'd hesitated too long, let my emotions get the best of me when I should've been working that knife out of my boot.

Fear leaked into my limbs, and for a brief instant, I felt my brain and body duking it out. *Fight or flight, fight or flight…*

No. I couldn't leave her. Not like that.

"Let her go," I said, brandishing my stake.

He yanked the kid against his chest, one meaty hand fisting her blue unicorn hoodie, the other curling around her throat. Fresh urine soaked her jeans.

"Drop your little stick and come over here," the man said, "or I'll break her neck."

My mind raced for an alternative, but there was no time. I couldn't risk going for the knife. Couldn't sneak up on him. And around here, screaming for help could attract a worse kind of attention.

Plan B it is.

"All right, big guy. You win." I dropped the stake and smiled, sidling toward him with all the confidence I could muster, which wasn't much, considering how hard I was shaking. "What are you doing with a scrawny little kid, anyway?"

He looked at the kid, then back at me, his lecherous gaze burning my skin. The stench of cigarettes and cheap booze lingered on his breath, like old fish and sour milk.

"I've got everything you need right here," I purred, choking back bile as I unzipped my jacket. "Unless you're not man enough to handle it?"

His gaze roamed my curves, eyes dark with lust.

"You're about to find out," he warned. "Ain't ya?"

He shoved the kid away, and in one swift move, he grabbed me and spun me around, pinning me face-first against the bricks.

He was a hell of a lot faster than I'd given him credit for.

"So you're an all talk, no action kind of bitch?" He wrenched my arms behind me, the intense pain making my eyes water. His sour breath was hot on the back of my neck, his hold impossibly strong, my knife impossibly out of reach. "That ends now."

A few blocks off, an ambulance screamed into the night, but it wasn't coming for us. The kid and I were on our own.

"Mmm. You got some ass on you, girl." He shoved a hand into the back pocket of my jeans and grabbed a handful of my flesh. "I like that in a woman."

Of course you do.

After all these years making illegal, late-night deliveries to the seediest supernatural haunts in town, this wasn't my first rodeo. The one-liners, the threats, the grabby hands... Human or monster, guys like this never managed to deviate from the standard dickhole playbook.

But this was the first guy who'd actually pinned me to a wall.

At least he'd ditched the kid. I tried to get her attention now, to urge her to take off, but she'd tucked herself behind a Dumpster, paralyzed with fear.

The man pressed his greasy lips to my ear. "No more bullshit, witch."

You don't know the half of it, asshole.

He didn't—that much was obvious. Just another dude with a tiny dick who tossed around the word "witch" like an insult.

My vision flickered again, rage boiling up inside, clawing at my insides like a caged animal searching for weak points.

It wanted out.

I took a deep breath, dialed it back down to a simmer.

God, I would've loved to light him up—spell his ass straight to oblivion. But I hadn't kept my mojo on lockdown for damn near a decade just to risk exposure for *this* prick.

So magic was out. I couldn't reach my knife. And my top-notch negotiating skills had obviously failed.

Fuck diplomacy.

I let my head slump forward in apparent defeat.

Then slammed it backward, right into his chin.

He grunted and staggered back, but before I could spin around or reach for my knife, he was on me again, fisting my hair and shoving my face against the wall.

"Nice try, little cunt. Now you eat brick."

"Don't!" the girl squeaked. "Just… just let us go."

"Aw, that's cute." He let out a satisfied moan like he'd just discovered the last piece of cake in the fridge. "You'll get your turn, baby."

Okay, she'd saved me from a serious case of brick-rash—not to mention a possible skull fracture—but now she was back on his radar. And I still couldn't get to the knife.

Time for plan B. Or was this C?

Fuck it.

"Hey. I've got some money," I said. "Let us go, and it's yours."

"Yeah?" He perked up at that. "How much we talkin'?"

"Like I said—some."

Lie. At the moment, I was loaded. Most of the $3,000 I'd already collected tonight was in the van, wrapped in a McDonald's bag and shoved under the seat. I also had $200 in a baggie inside my boot and another $800 in my bra, because I believed in diversifying my assets.

My commission depended on me getting the cash and van back to the docks without incident. I couldn't afford incidents. Rent was due tomorrow, and Sophie had already covered me last month.

But I couldn't—wouldn't—risk him hurting the kid.

"It's in my boot," I said. "Left one."

"We'll see about that, Blondie." He yanked me away from the wall and shoved me to the ground, wet pavement biting into the heels of my hands.

With a boot to my back, he pushed me flat on my stomach, then crouched down and grabbed my wrists, pinning them behind me with one of his meaty hands. With his free hand, he bent my leg back and yanked off my boot.

Bastard.

"I hope you feel good about your life choices," I grumbled.

Another wheezing laugh rattled through his chest, and he coughed. "Choice ain't got nothin' to do with it."

Whatever. I waited until he saw the baggie with the cash, let him get distracted and stupid over his small victory.

The instant he released my wrists and went for the money, I pushed up on all fours and slammed my other boot heel straight into his teeth.

The crunch of bone was pure music, but his howl of agony could've called the wolves.

I had just enough time to flip over and scamper to my feet before he rose up and charged, pile-driving me backward into the wall. The wind rushed out of my lungs on impact, but I couldn't give up. I had to keep fighting. Had to make sure he wouldn't hurt the girl.

I clawed at his face and shoved a knee into his groin, but *damn it*—I couldn't get enough leverage. His hands clamped around my throat, rage and fire in his eyes, blood pouring from his nose and mouth as he spit out broken teeth.

He cocked back an arm, but just before his fist connected, I went limp, dropping to the ground like a pile of rags.

The momentum of his swing threw him off balance, and I quickly ducked beneath his arms and darted behind him, crouching down and reaching for the sweet, solid handle of my knife.

"You can't win," he taunted as he turned to face me. Neither his injuries nor the newly acquired lisp diminished his confidence. "I'm bigger, stronger, and I ain't got no qualms about hurting little cunts like you."

Despite the tremble in my legs, I stood up straight, blade flashing in the moonlight.

"Whoa. Whoa!" Eyes wide, he raised his hands in surrender, slowly backing off. "Hand over the knife, sweetheart."

"Not happening."

"You're gonna hurt yourself, waving around a big weapon like that."

"Also not happening."

"Look. You need to calm the fuck down before—" A

coughing fit cut him short, and he leaned against the wall, one hand on his chest as he gasped for air.

I held the knife out in front of me, rock steady, finally getting my footing. Chancing a quick glance at the girl, I jerked my head toward the other end of the alley, willing her to bolt.

Her sudden, panicked gasp and a blur of movement beside me were all the warning I had before the dude slammed into me again, tackling me to the ground. My knife clattered away.

Straddling my chest, he cocked back an arm and offered a bloody, near-toothless smile. "Time to say goodnight, witch."

"Leave her alone!" No more than another flash in my peripheral vision, the kid leaped out from behind the Dumpster, flinging herself at our attacker.

She scratched and punched for all she was worth, eyes blazing and wild. I'd never seen anyone so fierce.

But he simply batted her away like she was nothing. A fly. A gnat. A piece of lint.

She hit the ground hard.

I gasped, heart hammering in my chest, shock radiating through my limbs. She *wasn't* a fly or a gnat. She was a fucking child in a unicorn hoodie, lost and scared and totally alone, and he'd thrown her down.

Just like that.

Still pinned in place, I couldn't even see where she'd landed.

But I would never forget that sound. Her head hitting

the pavement. The eerie silence that followed. Seconds later, another ambulance howled into the darkness, nowhere close enough to help.

"What did you do?" I screamed, no longer caring who or what might've heard me. "She's just a kid!"

I clawed at the man's chest, but I was pretty sure he'd already forgotten about me.

"No. No way. Fuck this bullshit." He jumped up to his feet, staggered back a few steps, then took off without another word.

Still trying to catch my breath, I crawled over next to the girl, adrenaline chasing away my pain. Blood pooled beneath her head, spreading out like a dark halo. Her breathing was shallow.

"Hey. I'm right here," I whispered. "It's okay, baby."

She was thin as a rail, her wet jeans and threadbare hoodie hanging off her shivering frame.

"Jesus, you're freezing." I shucked off my jacket and covered her body, careful not to move her. "He's gone now. He can't hurt you anymore."

I swept the matted hair from her forehead. Her skin was clammy, her eyes glassy and unfocused, but she was still conscious. Still there, blinking up at me and the dark, cloudy sky above.

"What's your name, sweet pea?" I asked.

Blink. Blink.

"Hon, can you tell me your name?"

She sucked in a breath. Fresh tears leaked from her eyes. That had to be a good sign, right?

"Um. Yeah," she whispered. "It's… Breanne?"

"Breanne?"

"Sometimes Bean."

"Bean. That's a great nickname." I tucked a lock of hair behind her ear, my fingers coming away sticky with blood. "Hang in there, Bean. I'm going for help."

"No! Don't leave me here. I—" She reached for me, arms trembling, skin white as the moon. "Grape jelly. Grape—"

Grape jelly grape, she'd said. And then her eyes went wide, and I watched the spark in her go out.

Just like that.

"Bean!" I pressed my fingers beneath her jaw, then checked her wrist, desperate to find a pulse.

But it was too late.

Here in the middle of vamp central, the sweet kid in the unicorn hoodie—the one who'd ultimately saved *my* life—was dead.

* * *

Ready for more? Dive into the sexy supernatural world of The Witch's Rebels! Order your copy of Shadow Kissed now!

Sarah Piper is a witchy, Tarot-card-slinging paranormal romance and urban fantasy author. Through her signature brew of dark magic, heart-pounding suspense, and steamy romance, Sarah promises a sexy, supernatural escape into a world where the magic is real, the monsters are sinfully hot, and the witches always get their magically-ever-afters.

Readers have dubbed her work "super sexy," "imaginative and original," "off-the-walls good," and "delightfully wicked in the best ways," a quote Sarah hopes will appear on her tombstone.

Originally from New York, Sarah now makes her home in northern Colorado with her husband (though that changes frequently) (the location, not the husband), where she spends her days sleeping like a vampire and her nights writing books, casting spells, gazing at the moon, playing with her ever-expanding collection of Tarot cards, binge-watching Supernatural (Team Dean!), and obsessing over the best way to brew a cup of tea.

You can find her online at SarahPiperBooks.com, on TikTok at @sarahpiperbooks, and in her Facebook readers group at Sarah Piper's Sassy Witches! If you're sassy, or if you need a little *more* sass in your life, or if you need more Dean Winchester gifs in your life (who doesn't?), come hang out!

Made in the USA
Middletown, DE
20 June 2024